The FIREHAWK Chronicles

ASTERYM WAR

A Sci-Fi Action Novel

Nathaniel A Rose

This book is a work of fiction. Names, characters, places and incidents are products of the authors' imagination or are used fictitiously. Any resemblance to actual events or locales or persons, living or dead, is entirely coincidental.

ISBN: 978-0-9855818-3-1

Second Edition: March 2014

An *Original* Publication by Brothers-In-Arms Publishing

Cover Art & Written By: Nathaniel A Rose

Edited By: Ingrun Mann

Special Thanks

Daniel A Rose
Cynthia A Neal
Suzanne Jones

And last but not least...

The men and women of the U.S. Army, 3-319th
Airborne Field Artillery Rergiment and the 82nd
Airborne Division

And

The men and women of the 7th Special Forces
Group (Airborne)

De Oppresso Liber

...In Loving Memory of Art & Sophie Maynard

Prologue: Hell on Earth

On The First Day,

In Fayetteville, North Carolina, Lieutenant Shane Hawk's wife Angel was in their home, baking Christmas cookies in the kitchen. She was clad in nothing but his unit's black physical fitness shirt which featured his team's logo along with the blue, black, and yellow lightning bolt patch of the 71st Special Forces Group on the left shoulder with black tab with yellow "Airborne" written in yellow lettering.

The shirt was too big for her slender, sun-kissed body. The sleeves loosely fell down to her elbows, and the bottom of the shirt hung a few inches below her waist. She wore little white booty socks on this lazy day for her. It was on days like this that a large shirt and socks were all she wanted to wear while her husband was at work and her children in school. Despite the cataclysmic events raging elsewhere, Angel was keeping her composure. A woman of remarkably steely character, she had decided to ignore what was going on in the world. What was the use of worrying about matters she could not control, Angel thought.

She stroked a finger through her long, straight dark hair which shone with streaks of light brown highlights from her roots to the tips. After heating the temperature to four hundred degrees, Angel took a pan of the cookies and placed it in the oven. She set the timer and walked over to the counter where the next batch was still stirring in the mixer. Angel opened a bag of chocolate chip tear-drop shapes and poured the entire bag into the spinning bowl.

She smiled as she remembered the last time she made cookies. Shane had been helping her, and smeared some gooey dough all over her hands. She had landed a playful elbow in his stomach and they had a good laugh over it. He had wrapped his arms around her belly, holding her tight to his body, and kissed her neck several times.

"Oh you are awful today," she remembered muttering as she closed her eyes and tilted her head to the other side. She remembered how soft his gentle kisses were against her skin, and how she loved every moment of his naughtiness.

Angel smiled and stopped mixing the dough, dazing off into this cherished memory when suddenly the lights blew out. In the living room, the soap operas switched over to the Emergency Broadcast Network. Initial reports were indicating an unusual electromagnetic storm in the Atlantic Ocean, a tinny electronic voice announced. But Angel never heard the broadcast over the loud mechanical whine of the mixer which she had just turned on again.

All of a sudden, the whole house began to shake violently and everything that was not bolted down rattled and broke, producing an ear-splitting racket. Dirty plates walked themselves across the kitchen counter and shattered on the hardwood floor. Picture frames slid down walls; one smashed through the top of a glass end table in the living room. Angel then heard the TV fall off of the entertainment center and crash to the floor. "What the hell?" Angel wondered as she abruptly snapped out of her romantic daze.

As the earthquake intensified, Angel screamed. Struggling to keep her balance, she tried to hold on to the kitchen counter top. Suddenly, the hardwood floor boards shook themselves loose. The center light on the ceiling broke and crashed onto the dining room table. Shortly afterwards, the entire house seemed to jump up from its foundation in one powerful shift of the Earth's crust.

Angel could no longer hold on to the countertop and lost her balance, landing on her rear end. Watching in horror, she noticed several small cracks forming like spider webs at the corners of the walls; the largest one split open the ceiling from the back door all the way into the living room. The ceiling partially collapsed along the crack, but fortunately did not break off onto the floor. Afraid, Angel, covered her head and curled up in the fetal position as plates fell from the kitchen countertop and broke against her body.

To her great relief, the shaking soon stopped and amazingly the power even came back on. Angel got up, dusted herself off, and wiped the tears from her eyes. When she left the kitchen, she could hear dogs barking and car alarms blaring throughout the neighborhood. A moment later the phone rang. Hurriedly, she picked up the receiver on the end table next to the couch, pressing the talk button with trembling hands. "Hello?"

"Mom!" her oldest daughter's voice inquired anxiously. "Are you ok?"

"I'm fine," Angel assured her, "Are you kids ok?"

"We're all fine, mom," her daughter replied. "Mrs. Patterson is bringing us home. We'll be there in a few minutes."

"All right sweetie, see you in a few minutes then."

Knees shaking, Angel hung up the phone and looked out the window at the geyser of water gushing from a broken fire hydrant. A column of black smoke billowed somewhere behind the roof tops across the street, making Angel think, "Oh please hurry." She also wondered if her husband was alright.

Angel had a love-hate relationship with Shane's career choice of the military. She loved the patriotism and was proud of his accomplishments, but hated that his job often took him away from home. The constant danger and possibility of never hearing and seeing him again weighed especially heavy on her. Such was the life of a military wife, Angel was told, arguably one of the toughest jobs in the world.

Right now, she wanted to call his unit and talk to him, but then decided against it. The last time she had tried that someone gave her the run-around for thirty minutes. Angel resolved that it was best to wait until Shane came home. Hopefully the children will be knocking on the front door soon, she fretted, almost nauseous with worry.

Angel carefully stepped over the broken television and went up the flight of stairs into her bedroom. To distract herself, she searched through a dresser drawer until she found her favorite pair of faded blue jeans, pulled them over her bare legs, and buttoned them up. Before she returned downstairs, Angel stopped in front of the door-length mirror to her bathroom. Despite her inner turmoil, she took the time to pose in her favorite jeans, admiring her beautiful, slender figure.

Everyone in Shane's company thought him a lucky man for marrying such a beautiful woman. And even though she had four kids prior to their marriage, no one who would have ever guessed that she had given birth that many times. She's a remarkable woman indeed, as when Madison was born, she suffered a near fatal heart attack. She was laid up in the hospital for nearly a year, and after only the first month, her then husband Bubba Earl walked into her hospital room with his new girlfriend – Angel's then nurse. He said to her in one heartless statement, "This is your replacement; I don't want to be alone when you die."

He walked out on Angel and the kids that night. Angel did die inside, but when she met Shane two years later, her morbid world turned right-side-up again. Shane helped her with the divorce, and even after a year-long agonizing battle with breast cancer, four years after they had married.

By the time Angel had straightened up the house as best she could and taken a quick shower, she heard the children's familiar footsteps on the porch. The cookies had cooled off and were waiting on the few undamaged plates on the kitchen island, covered by plastic wrap. Overjoyed to see them, Angel showered her daughters and son with hugs and kisses.

"Have you seen the news mom?" her oldest daughter Emily asked her breathlessly. At fourteen, she was the spitting image of her mother, and already quite mature. "It's nuts out there!"

But Angel didn't really believe her...didn't WANT to believe her. She only knew that her house was in tatters as broken shards still lay scattered all over the floors. She also had not dared to bother with the old, heavy television.

"Did the earthquake do all this?" Jonathan, her seven-year-old son, and runt of his siblings as he had not quite had his growth spurt yet, inquired as he marveled at the mess in the house. Suddenly, his eyes grew wide with alarm. "My volcano!" he screamed, and ran up the stairs to his bedroom where his science project lay smashed on the floor. Sad and angry, Jonathan did not say a word, although he secretly wanted to cry. He and Shane had worked on the volcano project for a whole weekend, and now it was broken into pieces.

Jonathan's sister Madison was the youngest at seven years of age, and the only one of the siblings with golden blonde hair. Confused after seeing the shattered clutter in the living room, she tiptoed over to the couch to retrieve her stuffed brown teddy bear lying under the end table with the phone. She picked it up with a smile and a grateful hug.

"Mom, what's going on?" Emily asked.

Angel looked at her daughter, "Emily, call your Aunt Francis, tell her we're coming over."

Like a typical teenager, Emily rolled her eyes and dialed the number. "Phone's dead mom," she shrugged.

"All right fine, everyone get in the truck, we're going over there." Angel determined as she grabbed her keys off the counter.

Emily rushed Madison into the truck, but Jon was still upstairs. "Jon! We're going to Aunt Francis's house! Come down and get in the truck!"

Jon eventually appeared at the top of the stairs.

"I'm not going," he pouted.

"Mom said we're leaving! Get in the driveway this minute!" Emily yelled up the stairs.

That's when the aftershock hit, forcing Emily to cling to the banister. She screamed in terror as she held onto the wooden railing for dear life. A frightened Jonathan hugged the wall, while Angel braced herself in the door frame between the kitchen and living room. After the rumbling settled, she could see columns of black smoke and flames rising in the neighborhood and the city beyond.

Angel looked around the house a final time, wondering if they would ever return. She also wondered if her husband would make it home this time. Grabbing a piece of paper and pen, Angel scribbled a quick note to Shane which she stuck on the refrigerator door next to one of Madison's crayon drawings. She briefly glanced at the crude sketch. It was composed of stick people with messy hair; their names scrawled beneath each figure.

Angel kissed the tips of her fingers and planted them on the figure of Shane and herself, holding stick hands together. She then grabbed her wallet and hastily left the house with Emily and Jonathan.

The truck was big enough to fit all of them and then some. It was an extended cab with an eight-foot bed, a twelve-inch lift, and eighteen-inch radial off-road tires. Dual exhaust ran from the engine to the top bed of the truck like an old semi-tractor trailer. It was a bit redneck, but Angel loved big trucks, and this one was hers—paid in full with Shane's deployment money.

She turned the key and the engine throttled to life. The deep throaty roar of the exhaust was unlike any of the new hover vehicles, which made little or no noise. Emily sat next to her in the front seat, while Jon and Madison whispered excitedly in the back.

Angel carefully pulled out of the broken driveway and proceeded to the entrance of the neighborhood. At the Reilly Road intersection, the light was out and there was no traffic. It was not until they reached the bridge over the All American Express Way that they started to notice the real carnage. Almost every building in sight was burning or had collapsed. Few trees had withstood the punishing tremors, and thick branches littered the roads.

They waited patiently at the traffic light leading to the on and off-ramps. A green and black sports car flew past them at high speed, traveling north towards the base. It clipped a slower moving semi-truck and veered out of control on the opposite side of the bridge. Its front right bumper crumbled against a guard rail, sending the light, compact sports car into a tumble at over one hundred miles an hour.

Green painted sheet metal and carbon fiber flung around in all directions as the vehicle crashed onto a waiting family sedan at the top of the ramp. The sports car smashed its roof, and hurled up into the air, spraying glass and debris across the road.

Angel and Emily watched in horror as the once green vehicle hurled across the hood of another car waiting at the exit ramp, and then rolled out into oncoming traffic. Two cars swerved, only to crash into each other. The lead vehicle then flipped over and turned on its side, while the trailing car crashed head on into the wreckage of the sports car that had caused the accident.

More cars and hover vehicles began to pile up behind the light. Terrified, the children in the truck covered their ears to blot out the sounds of shrieking metal. Angel, however, heard it all, and tears stung in her eyes as she listened to the tortured cries of trapped and dying men and women.

Unfortunately, another speeding car—this one driven by a woman talking on her cell phone—failed to pay attention to the wreck in front of her. Her hover vehicle slammed into the wreckage of twisted metal and bodies, ultimately launching into the air above the pileup.

Deathly pale, Angel watched as this vessel of destruction shot right at her family. As her heart pounded adrenaline into her veins, she pressed the accelerator to the floor. The truck's tires burned rubber onto the concrete road, and Angel sped off the on-ramp. A few seconds later, the hover-car crashed into the spot where their truck had stopped only moments earlier. It tumbled off the right side of the road, and exploded into a fireball against a grouping of trees.

Sweat running down her back, Angel barreled her car down the on-ramp and jerked into the far left lane, barely missing a classic sports car. Luckily, there was no other traffic. Wiping her forehead, she looked back in her rear view mirror and watched as a man climbed out of a car window at the top of the bridge. But then, out of nowhere, a large semi-truck transporting gasoline plowed into the side-turned vehicle with the driver only halfway out of the wreckage. The fuel truck skidded off to the right and broke through the bridge's guard rails. Its cylindrical tank filled with ten thousand gallons of fuel then tipped over onto the left hand side. The truck itself ripped away from the trailer, hanging off the bridge from its back right tire.

Half a mile down the freeway, a frantic Angel was startled by the resulting explosion. By now, the entirety of the bridge was engulfed in a virtual firestorm that shot high into the sky. Flames spewed onto the freeway below, engulfing passing cars that swerved and crashed soon after.

Tears streaming from their eyes, but too traumatized to speak, Angel and the children looked back at the destruction in awed terror. They couldn't believe it. They didn't want to. Angel held one arm to her chest as her heart would not stop beating rapidly—a heart palpitation. It was a problem she had since Maddy was born.

Taking a deep breath, Angel pulled herself together by ignoring the discomfort. She just wanted to get the children to her sister's house, and by the time they passed Cape Fear Valley Hospital, she knew they were half way there. Still, anxiety about the safety of her family, especially her husband, assaulted her mind. Angel hadn't heard from Shane since he had left for work that morning. There was also her ten-year-old son Jake who was not with them in the car. He had decided to spend the upcoming weekend with his biological father. Although Angel had succeeded in pushing recent world events to the very back of her mind, she knew she could no longer pretend that death would somehow spare them...

Exhausted and shivering, Angel and the children finally arrived at the house in Hope Mills, but did not receive a very warm welcome by Angel's heavy set sister. "What do you want?!" Francis snapped. Angel's mood shifted from drained to angry. If Francis had not been over 350 pounds at five feet three inches, Angel would have already put her in a place a long time ago, especially for her rudeness towards Shane and her children. Shane... Francis hated him with a passion, and for no particular reason. So on occasion, Shane would run circles around her, when asked what he was doing, he would callously exclaim he was in orbit. This made him end up on his rear end on more than one occasion. Another was when it came time for a family photo, where he asked the photographer if the satellite had a wide-field view lens. She just didn't like people, including herself.

After some more griping, Francis reluctantly allowed them to stay, but made sure to give her sister another earful. Too tired to argue, Angel and Emily collapsed on the couch, while Jonathan and Madison napped in a bedroom. But Angel could not sleep. All she could do was think of Shane. She did not dare consider the worst.

Chapter One: Wrath of Thyrion

Dark thunderhead clouds rolled in from the east over the Atlantic. Built-up, ionized particles, supercharged by the energy distortion hidden beneath the choppy ocean surface, fueled the rising mega storm. Powerful bolts of lightning relentlessly touched down onto the ocean's surface.

From the Wilmington beach shore, an elderly couple marveled at the absolute power and beauty of this unsettling weather phenomenon. Their nearby beach house was immaculate; years of hard work and delicate care had kept their vacation cottage in pristine condition. But as the two stood with their bare feet in the sand, they watched the waters retreat far out beyond their line of sight.

Together, they braced for the inevitable tsunami, knowing full well that their lives, their comfort, and their profound love for each other would soon come to an end. The massive tidal wave that was about to crash over them would destroy everything they had known until now. At first it was just a dark blue line on the horizon, but as their final moments approached, it had climbed to unimaginable heights. In the blink of an eye, the elderly couple, their beloved beach house, and everything else along the eastern seaboard vanished under a three-thousand-foot tidal wave.

Clouds had been traveling at nearly the same speed, but when the wave swallowed up the shoreline, the rising air pressure slowed them down. It was during that sudden halt that a flash—more powerful than any lightning bolt man had ever seen—surged out of the dark rolling clouds. As the blazing light dissipated, a humanoid figure, dressed in dark alien armor with a massive arm cannon mounted onto his right arm and an equally colossal shield to his left, shot out of the clouds above the massive tidal wave that had already swallowed up the North Carolina coastline. The gigantic alien was named Thyrion, and he let out a triumphant roar as he flew across the sky.

His face was featureless, but beneath the thick grey armor shone a transparent, gel-like layer that seemed to glow red with rage. Though he had no eyes to speak of, two white lights flashed through the heavy coatings of film that entrapped the liquid-based alien life form. They soon fixed on a large human city, inundated by the dwindling tidal wave, and yet still burning from the catastrophes that had rocked every foundation on the planet's surface.

Heading for the disaster area, Thyrion could sense an invisible cloud of terror rising up around him as the creatures that had built this particular metropolis were perishing like flies. Perversely aroused by this vast sea of misery, the alien dove towards several towering monoliths. Its body broke the sound barrier many times over before crashing not so gracefully into the tallest one, causing it to sway badly. Thyrion then let his massive legs sink into the sides of the concrete tower as windows shattered throughout the building. Amused, the alien could hear the bipedal creatures scream in wild panic as the skyscraper shook violently.

He enjoyed watching the terror he created. These simple beings, Thyrion decreed, were his new playthings. After he had ascertained that the structure would hold his colossal weight, the monster from space peered inside. The curious alien eyed a group of tiny human playthings cowering behind small, insignificant structures. He could smell their fear as well as the body waste that some of the earthlings expelled on themselves.

One of the humans peeked out from around the corner of a wall and aimed a small pointed device at the staring monster. A loud popping noise and flash followed, and the beast felt something impact the beak-like center mass underneath his crown-shaped helmet. Unfortunately, it did little more than annoy him.

Aggravated by the tiny flesh ling, Thyrion crashed his giant cannon arm through the building, snatching up the annoying earthling and his handheld noise maker in his metal-clawed, four-fingered talons. He could hear the other humans scream in terror as he opened his hand and observed the small, meaty man. Growling in anger, Thyrion felt sound waves rippling beneath his gel-like layers: something about Earth's inhabitants reminded him of his creators. That was the reason why Thyrion had brought his armies to Earth. It was the final stop before invading the Masters' home world. It would take all the water and resources on this disgusting planet to create enough energy to teleport his Asterym armies to the Masters' planet.

Suddenly, Thyrion apprehended something roaring through the sky unlike anything he had ever heard in his millions of years of existence since the Masters had captured and imprisoned him in his current state. He looked around and finally spotted a mechanical object flying over the city. Soon after, the back of the contraption opened and a team of five humans jumped from the plane. They fell rapidly, without anything breaking their fall. Watching intently, the alien noticed tiny flame bursts at the bottom of their legs which appeared to slow their descent. Eventually, the team of four landed unharmed on the salt-water-flooded streets below.

Lieutenant Shane Hawk jumped out of the C-260 transport aircraft above the alien after his four man team, and dove head first towards the invader. The two tiny thrusters at his ankles ignited and the diminutive human, clad in powered armor, rocketed towards the enormous extraterrestrial. Thyrion tossed the stout man still clutched in his talons towards a building across the street. The helpless being screamed as his body hit a concrete wall, and then fell unconscious below.

Itching for confrontation, Thyrion pointed his massive arm cannon at the aircraft. The cannon separated into two halves, with electrical currents flowing back and forth, until the center at the back of the weapon glowed intensely. Fully charged, it fired off a powerful blast of energy which obliterated the human plane with just one shot!

Barely a second later Lieutenant Hawk sped towards Thyrion's massive torso. Caught by surprise, the alien lost his grip on the building as the minuscule and seemingly insignificantly armored earthling slammed right into his well-protected chest. While both fell, Thyrion roared in shock.

But Lieutenant Shane hung onto the alien's mighty chest. Two forty-inch blades—vibrating thousands of times per second and nuclear charged by power cells in the back of the suit—sprang forth from his forearms. Thyrion reached for the soldier as they tumbled off the top of the building, surprised by the man's strength. The earthling grabbed on to his massive hand, preventing him from throwing the pint-sized human away.

With a jab of his free arm, Shane buried one of the forty-inch vibroblades into the alien's thick armored chest. The giant roared in pain as the blade pierced through its armor. Enraged, Thyrion swatted the human off his torso before crashing into the ocean-covered streets.

The impact shook the entire block. Shane performed a jet-assisted, acrobatic tumble, and caught the unconscious security guard in mid-air, just before he was about to hit the concrete ground. Slightly dizzy, Lieutenant Hawk landed on his feet, and slid backwards to a halt, still facing the terrible beast. He retracted his vibroblades and set the lifeless security guard against the side of a washed-out car. Pulling his rifle from its magnetic mount on his back, Shane aimed straight at the stumbling Thyrion. But the alien rolled over and scrambled to his feet.

Shane was five feet, eleven inches without armor, and stood six feet, five inches in armor. The alien loomed over him, being twice his height at fourteen feet. Undaunted, Shane took the initiative and charged forward. Glowering at his tiny attacker with some bemusement, the extraterrestrial raised his mighty arm cannon and fired.

Shane jumped to the side, while the energy blast boiled the ankle-deep water behind him and cut a giant hole into the concrete. He then fired a burst of electromagnetically accelerated sabot rounds from his M22A2 weapon. The

Mach 2 rounds instantly rippled along the alien's shield as Thyrion held it out to protect himself from the weapon's fire. Snarling ferociously, Thyrion lowered his shield and was about to fire the arm cannon again when he lost sight of his adversary. Confused thoughts of invisibility ran through the alien's mind until a Lilliputian fist rifled up against his faceplate. Just then, four other, similarly steel-clad humans surrounded him.

Two seemed shocked at the sight of the beast, but the last pair fired their weapons fearlessly. The rounds struck, inflicting more damage on the alien who flinched, spun around, and backhanded the closest human from behind with his shield. The man lost his weapon and was hurled through a window on the second floor of an office building half a block away.

Meanwhile, Shane continued to fire his rifle, and rounds rippled along the giant's tree trunk-sized legs. Thyrion cringed and knocked the troublesome assailant to the ground with a quick kick. In response, the other human fired a 40mm plasma grenade from a launcher that was mounted under the barrel of his M22A3 model rifle. The small grenade exploded against the beast's shield in a colorful display of fiery blue and green plasma.

Slightly injured, the extraterrestrial stumbled backwards and winced as the burning plasma ate into his thick, armored shield. He struck out at the annoyance, hurling the human ten feet off the ground. Before he landed on his back, Thyrion jumped up and slammed the pointed end of his shield into the earthling, severing him in half. But before he could savor this gruesome victory, Thyrion was stuck by more enemy needles and bullets in his legs and chest. He shouted in anger and dove into an alley.

Shane yelled as he saw his comrade's maimed remains in a cracked crater of concrete. "Stay alert," he ordered his remaining men, "that thing is around here somewhere!" Just then, Shane noticed his other teammate climbing through the shattered, second floor window. He was shaking off glass slivers when a sudden beam of energy blasted his chest. The blistering laser melted the soldier's armor and cooked his flesh. Then the grenades on his belt exploded, set off by the intense heat. There was nothing left once the smoke had cleared.

"Nooooo!" Shane screamed in terror and anger. He aimed his rifle, squeezed the trigger, and fired the remainder of his magazine at the alien. Some rounds hit, but most struck the building behind Thyrion as he flipped over and landed on one of the men, squashing him completely. Satisfied, the behemoth belched out an ear-piercing roar.

Shaking with fright, the last man on Shane's team dropped his weapon. He turned and started to run, but before his Battle Suit was able to reach its ninety miles per hour max running speed, the alien beam cannon had struck the fleeing human in the back, killing him outright.

In that moment, Shane's nerves turned to steel. He opened a hidden compartment on his right thigh and pulled out a full magazine, simultaneously pressing the magazine release lever on his rifle with his index finger. As the alien leapt straight for him, Lieutenant Hawk shoved the new magazine into his weapon, released the bolt, and slammed the first round from the top of the magazine into the chamber. Thyrion advanced, and Shane squeezed the trigger. The first three rounds blasted out of the barrel and struck the extraterrestrial in the forehead at point blank range.

Temporarily disoriented, Thyrion cringed after being hit. He felt his head throbbing violently, stumbled, and missed Shane who slid through the water between his massive legs, aiming his rifle straight up into the monster's inhuman pelvis. Shane fired, with bullets riddling the bottom of the monster's underside to the top of his back. The alien fell forward, taking the full force of every bullet impact, and landed face first against the side of the building he had originally terrorized.

By now Shane's rifle was empty again, and just as he was about to change magazines, the beast's shield swung outward and struck him in the chest. Shane was thrown against the side of a building and suddenly found himself sitting against a wall. He was dazed with his chest aching, but he felt alright. Shane watched the alien stand back up and was helpless as a massive hand grabbed his head, smashing the two radio antenna ears and the small combat camera.

Boiling with rage, Thyrion lifted Shane off the ground and flung him down the road, ripping his helmet off. Shane flew end over end and landed with his back on the watery pavement, next to a heavy tie-down chain that had spilt out of the back of an over-turned utility truck. Meanwhile, Thyrion crushed Shane's helmet in his mighty hand, and then dropped the puny bit of scrap metal onto the flooded street.

The furious alien then ignited boosters on his back and hovered a few feet above the street. With an angry roar, Thyrion dove towards the pesky human, determined to rid his new world of this persistent annoyance. Shane quickly rolled over, grabbed the long chain, and lassoed his adversary. With impossible luck, he caught him around the ankle and the chain tightened. Shocked and surprised, the extraterrestrial took off into the sky. Shane held onto the other end of the chain and felt his feet leave the ground as he was towed behind. Thyrion growled ferociously as his shoulder armor clipped a neon advertisement sign which crumbled to pieces, some of which hit Shane.

The unlikely pair now flew high above the city streets to a small industrial factory where a military contractor built Armadillo combat robots. Shane tugged on the chain and simultaneously fired the engines mounted on his lower legs. He sailed below the alien and with another quick burst from his rockets, Shane flew right up to his massive head. Slashing the alien's neck with the right forearm vibroblade, he watched red goo spilling from the soft, gel-like layer. Shane's momentum then carried him over the behemoth's head.

Moments later, he realized that the extraterrestrial paid no attention to flying anymore, and was instead clutching his neck wound with clawed hands. His eyes, as they were, were shut in pain, and Shane felt the air whizzing past him as they plummeted towards the ground. Lieutenant Hawk panicked, screaming "Ooooooh crap!"

Shane let go of the chain just before he and the otherworldly beast slammed into one of the many large factory buildings on the east side of Raleigh. Debris scattered everywhere as the large creature tumbled through roof beams, flattened machines, and other industrial equipment. Igniting his rockets again, Shane followed him, slowly floating through the gaping hole in the side of the building that Thyrion had just produced. He could hardly see, however, as the alien's path of destruction sent up a massive plume of brown smoke and dust.

Luckily, Shane landed nimbly on his feet as he made his way through the mangled factory. Many buildings in the complex assembled parts for the Armadillo combat robots, but Shane wasn't sure which section produced what. He was thinking wearily about the potential hazards surrounding him, especially when he noticed a stack of large crates. Signs with radiological warning placards were stamped all over the crates' fronts. "Handle with extreme caution," these stickers cautioned not so delicately. "This must be nuclear reactor components," Shane frowned nervously.

Suddenly, he heard the scrape of a heavy foot behind him. Instinctively, Shane deployed his vibroblades in anticipation of defending himself. But before he could face the threat, something slammed Shane hard in the back, while the vibroblade on his left forearm pierced the crate in front of him. Gritting his teeth in pain, he realized that the alien had kicked him from behind. Even worse, his blade was stuck. Shane quickly spun around and used his free hand to loosen it. When the blade finally came loose, he turned on his heel. The freed metal glowed white hot at the tip. The alien punched Shane square in the chest and he fell back against the crate. He shook off the blow and stood up. Impatient, the monster swiped at him again, but Shane dodged underneath his arm. The extraterrestrial moved closer and was practically toe to toe with him. Shane noticed his neck was still oozing alien liquid, but the cut in the gel layer was healing itself. Determined to finish off the irritating human once and for all, Thyrion stepped back and aimed his massive energy beam cannon straight at Shane's head.

He reacted before the alien could charge the weapon. Using the rockets in his feet to leap up in the air, Shane came down on the right side of the beast's head. The hot white tip of his vibroblade sliced a gash from Thyrion's featureless eyebrow to the lower, jawless part of his face and then straight through the faceplate. The extraterrestrial roared in panic as the ripples beneath his gel layers reverberated with tremendous sound waves. The residual radiation from Shane's blade hurt like nothing else before in Thyrion's long existence. The alien rolled over to his left side and thrashed about while Shane landed on the ground, the tip of his blade scorching the dirt-covered concrete floor.

After taking a deep breath, Shane readied himself for another attack, but the monster continued to roar and flail, clutching the right side of his head and stumbling to get on his feet. Hawk charged again, but Thyrion just glared and leapt off the ground. Shane stopped in his tracks as the extraterrestrial fired the boosters on his back and suddenly disappeared through the hole in the wall. He could hear the alien's deep, throaty roar grow fainter as he flew away.

Aliens—more technologically advanced than humans—were not undefeatable like so many science fiction stories presumed, Shane thought with relief. He shivered knowing that he had just gone toe to toe with one! Luck, training, and good fortune saved him, but Shane was just as angry as the alien had been. Thyrion had killed the other four members of his team—all of them good men and brave soldiers with families waiting anxiously for them at home. Shane was no different than his dead teammates, and he felt sick to his stomach knowing that his comrades would not be returning to their loved ones on this tragic day.

Shane had married a woman who already had four children before him; four wonderful children he loved as his own and who loved him in return. One of them was visiting his biological father on the east side of Raleigh for the weekend, and Shane was close enough to be able to find him. He knew his wife would want him to bring the boy home safe—if safety could still be found in this world of total chaos.

Shane quickly left the building through an emergency exit and looked back at the city where a large cloud of smoke caught his attention. Raleigh's largest building—the high-rise where he had knocked the alien off the roof—had collapsed. He wondered if anyone had still been inside. But his thoughts quickly shifted. First to his Chain Of Command—which he had no means to communicate with since his helmet was destroyed—and second to his wife's oldest son Jacob. Shane needed to get there fast if he was going to be a hero today.

He carefully made his way back into the downtown area. Petrified people who lived and worked in the city were streaming out of buildings, nervously surveying the damage from the tidal wave. Countless corpses had washed out of the bottom floors of numerous office blocks and were now floating around, face down. A group of men and women approached Shane cautiously.

"Hey soldier," one man confronted him loudly, "What's going on?"

Yes, Shane was a soldier—not a reporter, weatherman, or politician. He stopped the man with a wave of his hands, "I need you all to go to your homes or to the nearest shelter."

"But the shelter has been washed out! The flood hit it before they could close the doors!" cried a woman, drenched from head to toe.

"Please people, go home," Shane begged calmly. As he was walking away, he noticed a fat man in a dirty, torn-up, but brilliant red Santa

Claus suit ringing an old brass bell. Two Raleigh City Police robots approached the portly individual in the red suit and fake beard, urging the scammer to take himself elsewhere. Meanwhile, children and their parents carried away bags of stolen goods from unattended stores on the other side of the street. Shane heard someone say, "Stupid 'bots' priorities never were very spot on."

Hearing a peculiar noise, Shane looked up and saw thousands of pigeons and other non-migratory birds fleeing the city, heading west. Chirping and flapping their wings in a mad craze, the birds' racket sent shivers down Shane's spine, and drowned out the sounds of people below. Everyone around Shane looked up in curiosity as hundreds of thousands of birds left the city in a hurry, flying in a very crowded and disorderly formation. The congestion forced some of the animals into the sides of the buildings, breaking windows from high above. Shards of glass and hundreds of dead and bloody birds rained down on the streets below.

Some pelted the crowds of already jumpy humans, adding further chaos to the pandemonium. A hail of glass slivers cut flesh and spilled more blood. Shane raised his arms above his head, shielding himself from the torrent of sharp fragments.

But it wasn't just the birds. Thousands of rats literally poured out of the sewers, scurrying in the same direction as the birds: out of the city. Women of all ages screamed at the sight of the disgusting rodents fleeing their underground labyrinth for any available dry patch.

Shane looked both ways down the street. Something was terribly wrong here, he thought as he felt the ground tremble. Another earthquake? Suddenly the entire city shifted and dropped from underneath his feet as a blast louder than a 155mm Howitzer cannon thundered through the streets. Everyone not holding on to something fell to the ground, knocked off balance by the trembling shockwave.

Vehicles of all kinds—hover, wheeled, even trains carried on suspended magnetic rails in between roads and under skyways—crashed as the city violently shifted. Car alarms began to blare in a panicked cacophony, and water mains busted from underneath ocean-covered streets. A gas main ruptured several blocks away as people struggled to get their bearings.

Shane peered down Glenwood Avenue. A large movement among the mess of tall skyscrapers and suspended railways caught his attention. A towering building was breaking away from its foundation and tilted over the boulevard several blocks away. People began to cry for help as glass and loose debris struck the sidewalks around them. A few moments later, the falling structure cut those faint screams short.

The top of the high-rise slammed into an equally tall edifice across the street. A sixty-foot antenna then broke away from the second building and plunged nearly one thousand feet into a thoroughfare below. The antenna pierced the center of a large Greyhound hover bus and pushed the vehicle into the flooded subway underneath the thoroughfare. Shortly afterwards both buildings collapsed, spreading a huge cloud of grey concrete dust through Raleigh and into the air.

Shane looked around and noticed dust plumes rising along the city's eastern edge. He also felt the ground beneath his feet trembling again. The situation continued to worsen as more glass shattered and shot down from windows high above. Shane caught a glimpse of a business woman treading through the water-filled boulevard in panic, just before a large sheet of glass cut her body in half. He watched in horror as her remains covered a dry patch of walkway—a red glittery mess of splinters and flesh. There was also her blood which added more red to the already crimson street water around them.

For the first time in his dedicated military career, Shane feared for his own life and began to run west down Hillsborough Street. Throngs of people were frenetic with fear and chaos reigned all around. He looked up just in time to see a huge chunk of concrete slam into the intersection in front of him.

He stopped and covered his mouth and nose with his elbow as the dust from collapsing buildings engulfed the area with a thick cloud. Shane carefully stepped over the debris and chunks of wall that were scattered about, and then jumped onto the trunk of a car. The engine, driver, and front passenger seats had been flattened by a huge slab of concrete and twisted metal rebar. Shane leapt off the concrete block and ran as fast as he could.

Throngs of people fled in the same direction, but struggled as they waded through knee-deep ocean water. They were trying to get out of the city as fast as possible, especially since the quaking ground was rocking the skyscrapers around them again. Gaping chasms appeared in the roads, forming crazy zigzag patterns. Buildings behind the fleeing crowds crumbled or fell over.

Shane looked back and saw an explosion blow out the base of a parking garage on the corner of Brooks Avenue and Hillsborough Street. A massive distortion of energy burst through its ground floors and cut across the intersection into the corner of another high-rise behind him. He coughed violently as the tall structures dissolved into smithereens.

Meanwhile, the energy spurt expanded across several blocks and then shot skyward. Soon after, its remnant waves reached Raleigh's historic Long-View Center and from there spread out in a multitude of directions. Instead of collapsing or falling, the building sunk into an ever-growing white orb of energy, and was gradually eaten away by heat rays surrounding the base of the tower. Within moments, the white energy expanded upward, swallowing the building whole. It was gone, vanished into thin air. In its stead, a towering mound of black, twisted alien steel as tall as a skyscraper with caverns that reminded Shane of an anthill remained. "What the f---!?" he swore to himself.

Seconds later, two more buildings behind Shane disintegrated. Inside them, people had been standing close to the open windows, only to drop out of the frames and onto the waterlogged street below. They landed with dull thuds that sent shivers down Shane's spine.

Then a storefront broke away from its foundation, raining concrete fragments, dust, and debris on him. The faint scream of terror in a man's voice suddenly got louder, but was quickly drowned out by the sound of flesh smacking against water and concrete. Shane barely caught a glimpse of the red smear the man left on the street which was almost immediately swallowed up by the flood waters.

Shane's Battle Suit and military training enabled him to plod faster through the knee-deep water than ordinary people, but even he could not shake the feeling of death chasing him relentlessly. As he approached Interstate 440, Shane finally cleared the zone of destruction with buildings still buckling behind him. Many weren't as fortunate. They perished in clouds of debris and a hail of concrete and steel.

He had gotten away just in time. An entire city block to the north collapsed in an instant. The sounds of cracking concrete and twisting metal echoing throughout Raleigh hurt Shane's ears as he shoved his way through throngs of people and large chunks of rubble blocking thoroughfares. A few hundred feet away, around a slight bend to the right, he could already see the intersection leading to the Interstate 40 junction. He needed to take it back east to get where he wanted to go, Shane calculated.

A businessman and woman, holding hands and running together ahead of him, stepped on a manhole cover. Just as they did, the lid blew up in a massive fireball as a gas line ruptured and exploded. "Whooooooaaaaaaaaaa!" Shane hollered. Although shaken, he did not take the time to dwell on the poor couple's unfortunate demise. Adrenaline was pumping through his system, keeping his mind focused on his family.

He darted to the other side of the road and covered his face from the searing inferno blasting high into the air above him. Racing past the conflagration emanating from the manhole, Shane glanced over his shoulder just long enough to see more structures vanish where he had stood only moments before. But there was something that frightened him even more: in the background, through the smoke and haze, loomed the menacing alien monolith.

Shane finally made it to the junction. He could see that engineering ingenuity had prevented the interstate from succumbing to the long, drawn-out earthquake, but it was still swaying badly from its support pillars. Shane heard concrete and steel supports groaning and creaking as they were twisted by the tremors. Taking a deep breath, he collected his energy for an all-out sprint across the freeway. But halfway across the intersection, the asphalt suddenly lurched upwards dramatically, and then slammed back down onto its supports. Shane stumbled as the pavement began to crack all around him, but managed to stay on his feet and run. "Oh, this is not good!" he yelled in panic.

He had made it three hundred meters down the road, when he was thrown a dozen feet forward as the expressway bent again in a giant wave of broken cement and steel mesh. The entire stretch of interstate screamed in an ear-piercing symphony of splitting concrete and tangled metal as it broke away from its supports. Shane scrambled to his feet and ran to the southern edge of the road, hopping over the median to the other side. The pavement began to break apart completely as vehicles and people on foot stumbled and careened. Halting in his tracks, Shane looked over the crash barrier at the ninety foot drop below. He leapt off the side and fell, but landed softly in the mud because of his leg thrusters. Seconds later, the interstate above rocked dangerously from side to side.

"Oh, hell no...," Shane mumbled to himself, running as fast through the thick mud as his Battle Suit would propel him. Soon after, the overpass crumbled into billions of pieces, and those unfortunate enough to be on it expired along with it, their screams drowned out by the death tolls of the dissolving infrastructure.

Shane tried to speed up as highway fragments
rained down around him. He cleared the disaster zone in less than a minute and looked back at the blooming cloud of destruction. Ninety percent of the city was consumed by dust rising into the sky now. Shane could barely make out a few remaining buildings and the alien tower looming ominously through the haze. He did not want to see who or what inhabited that strange spire and quickly headed

eastward. His step-son and family were, as always, on Shane's mind, but he couldn't shake the thought of all the people trapped in the destruction of the bridge. Where was help? Why was he alone in trying to save the city? Lastly, he couldn't help but anxiously wonder, *"Were his wife and step-children suffering the same fate as these poor souls?"*

Several miles east of Raleigh, in a small elementary school's baseball field, Shane spotted an 82nd Combat Air Brigade B-33 Fanjet loading a wounded soldier onto its back ramp. Excited and relieved, he raced over to the aircraft, but was immediately stopped by two men pointing M22A3 rifles at him. Shane halted in his tracks, arms raised above his head. "I'm Lieutenant Shane Hawk of Alpha Company 3-71," he panted, out of breath.

"Lieutenant Hawk?" a familiar voice answered. Shane thought for a moment, trying to match a face to the man's voice. The soldier approached with his weapon lowered. "That you Hawk?"

"Almazan?" Shane recalled, overjoyed.

"Hey man, how are you doing? Can you believe this?" Almazan looked around at the devastation: smoke billowing up from countless fires, buildings still collapsing in the distance, and screams of people tearing through the air.

"It's unbelievable." Shane wiped the sweat from his brow.

Almazan asked his old friend, "You're still in the 71st right? Where's the rest of your team?"

"They're gone. They died fighting some sort of giant alien warrior." Shane's shoulders drooped, but he quickly regained his composure, and looked his trusted comrade in the eye.

"No kidding, an alien, huh?" Almazan's eyes widened, his face filled with amazement.

"Where you guys heading to?" Shane inquired as he looked into the back of the fanjet. Inside were ten men. One was laid out on a stretcher, another sported a blood-soaked bandage around his head, and a third had a splint tied to his left leg. He also noticed two civilians inside; one of whom was Almazan's wife, Amanda.

She was beautiful despite the smoke residue and dirt on her skin. Her brunette hair was a mess from the prop-wash of the fanjets. Shane waved to her and she managed a tired smile.

"We're heading back to Bragg. My squad took a beating and we're heading back to refit. We got room for one more; need a lift?" Almazan pointed his thumb at the back of the fanjet.

"Yeah sure, but can you ask the pilot to make a quick detour over Cary?" Shane begged.

"Yeah, why? Looking for someone?" Almazan's brow furrowed.

"My step-son Jake."

"Sure, hop in." Almazan followed Shane into the back of the fanjet. "Hey Chief, we need to do a fly-by over Cary."

"Roger Sergeant, no problem," the pilot replied.

They stood on the edge of the ramp as the aircraft took off from the baseball field. Once airborne, the plane began to bank towards the north. Sergeant Almazan tapped Lieutenant Hawk on his arm, "Hey, how are Angel and the kids anyway? You never came to our Thanksgiving feast this year."

"They're good. At least before all this happened. I need to get back there to check on them."

Almazan raised an eyebrow. "How did this happen anyway? I mean, what the hell is going on?"

Shane looked away from the charred homes beneath them, "I have no idea," he sighed.

"Sergeant, we're passing over Cary now," the pilot announced over the radio. Almazan pointed down at more blazing neighborhoods.

"This is it."

Shane's heart missed a beat as he looked upon a singed no man's land razed by fire and earthquakes. Although he recognized the hopelessness of the situation, Shane wanted to have the pilot touch down so that he could scour the rubble for his step-son. Unfortunately, he couldn't detect any movement whatsoever. Soon after, Shane spotted the area where Jacob and his father had lived. It was completely gone. A yawning cleft in the earth's surface had opened up where their house had once stood and filled with sea water. Shane looked away in anguish. "Let's go home," he muttered, heartbroken.

"It could have been a lot worse," Almazan told him. "If that fissure didn't open up from north to south, the entire state all the way to Tennessee would've been swept away by the tidal wave." But Shane, fighting back tears, could barely look at his old friend. "I'm sorry, man," Almazan consoled him. "Chief, take us home." The pilot nodded, banking the plane back to the south.

As the sun was setting to the west behind cloud layers of ash, a B-33 fanjet carrying Captain Jesse Dyson landed in a field outside the Special Forces compound at Fort Bragg. A team of elite soldiers greeted the fifty-year-old captain and drove him in a military truck to the headquarters building of the 43rd Group's Special Forces compound.

The base was a disaster zone. Buildings which had stood for almost two centuries were damaged but still standing, while many of the newer ones had totally collapsed, killing scores of people. As for the eastern edge of the base on the other side of Bragg Boulevard, it had been swallowed up by the Atlantic Ocean.

Meanwhile, stern Captain Dyson was taken to see two-star General Madden. General Madden—as intimidating as he could be with his short cropped grey hair and harsh demeanor—was glad to see his godson among the survivors. "Good to see you're still alive Captain," the general's blue eyes marched across his desk to the younger man standing at attention in black civilian clothing.

"Thank you sir."

"Enough of the garbage," the general interjected quickly. "On to business. The bible calls this day Armageddon. I call it just another day on the job!" he exclaimed with a little laugh.

"Yes sir." Dyson agreed unenthusiastically.

"A head count earlier this afternoon left this entire base operating at a mere twenty percent. That includes the XVIII Airborne Corps, 82nd, 43rd, and 71st Groups and our guys," he droned on, reading from several data sheets. "Command structures in those divisions are virtually nonexistent, and we're all that's left. And, we're under threat from what some people are calling monsters or aliens. You believe that? Aliens!" the general looked up at him.

"Aliens? Seriously sir?" Dyson's voice was full of sarcasm. "That's what I said!" the general retorted exuberantly and jumped up from his chair. He pointed to an area map on the wall as his chair rolled up against a corner. "Downtown, some of the boys from the eighty deuce are combating some of these so called "Aliens"." He pointed to a location ten miles away from the base, near the Fayetteville Regional Airport. "There's a lieutenant out there from 71st Group inbound on a B-33 with some of our boys. They're going to insert by air and that lieutenant from the "Seventy-Worst" will lead the survivors back here. I want you to take a team of our guys out there and support them. Grab two Magnum Battle Suits and two Valkyries for support as well as four of my best soldiers to give them a hand."

"Yes sir." Dyson was ready for combat; he hadn't seen any action since he had deployed to Korea almost a year ago, after which his recruiting duties had taken him to Berlin. Still, the thought of searching for "alien" or "demonic" creatures wandering across the Earth had Dyson's blood boiling. What he really wanted was a command of his own group or division. He had been passed over for promotion several times by colonels and generals who didn't like him. Generally sour about the military leadership, he was comfortable with General Madden whom he had known all his life.

"We're still waiting for more soldiers to report, but communications are down everywhere and the destruction is making travel difficult. If you see any survivors or those in need, you are not to stop and render aid. Continue with your objectives," General Madden ordered with a grimace etched across his face. "Find and locate the 82nd rescue team and RTB. Your secondary objective is to gather enemy strengths and numbers en route to your primary."

"Understood sir."

"Get your gear from supply and hit up the armory for your weapons. Dismissed." Dyson readied to exit the general's office. "And Jesse...," Dyson turned and looked at his godfather. "Send 'em back to whatever hell they came from!" Dyson nodded with gritty determination and walked out, closing the door behind him.

"Lieutenant Hawk, incoming message from Command, sir," the pilot announced over the headset inside the aircraft.

Shane picked up the earpiece hanging from a support frame, "Go for Lieutenant Hawk."

"Lieutenant, you have new orders. You and your men will insert by air to a local neighborhood in Hope Mills. The 82nd Airborne Corps's 3-319th Airborne Field Artillery Regiment is there evacuating the civilians. You are to lead them back to base. You will be joined by Captain Jesse Dyson and his fire support team," the voice told him. Shane didn't recognize whose it was, but he knew not to question orders on a secure communication frequency. "How do you copy?"

"Roger, insert by air to Hope Mills neighborhood, rendezvous with 82nd platoon and meet up with Captain Dyson. Escort civilians from combat zone and return to base."

"Good copy Lieutenant, command out." Almazan looked at his friend, "You think?"

Hawk shook his head, "With all this going on? Yeah, she's probably there."

"Lieutenant! ETA ten minutes!" the pilot shouted.

"All right Almazan, I need you and your men for this op, get ready to jump." Hawk looked at each of Almazan's teammates. They were all wearing the right gear, and looked like they could jump right into the thick of combat which—of course—they were about to do. Shane readied to speak when the soldier with the injured leg grabbed his arm and offered him his helmet. Shane tucked it under his arm and snapped the man a picture-perfect salute.

"All right team; prepare to jump on my mark!" Hawk yelled over the roar of the twin fan jets. Almazan pressed a button at the rear of the aircraft and the tailgate opened. It was dark outside, but they could see fires burning all around Fort Bragg and Fayetteville.

Almazan took a moment to console his wife. Shane couldn't hear them speak, but he did see her eyes water and they kissed.

"One minute!" he shouted as the pilot turned on the jump light indicators. Hawk stared intently at the glowing red switch as Almazan jumped in line behind him. It seemed like minutes passed before the indicator light switched to yellow.

"Thirty seconds!" he yelled. Shane jammed the borrowed helmet onto his head and cleared the seals. All of a sudden the plane started to vibrate and shake fiercely. Hawk and his teammates had to hold onto the airframe to keep themselves from sliding out the end of the tailgate.

Shane looked at the city some fifteen hundred feet below. He could see tracer fire arching into the sky which reminded him of the Korean War he had fought in not a year ago. Then the green indicator button flashed.

"Follow me!" he yelled once and was the first to jump out of the back of the aircraft. As he fell through the sky, Shane passed through a billowing cloud of black smoke, which temporarily blinded him and made breathing difficult. After he had cleared the dark haze, Shane slapped a knob on his right hip that deployed a parachute out of the back of his armor.

He swiftly checked his canopy for damage and found none. Shane also made sure that he wasn't going to bump into any fellow jumpers. After ruling out any airborne threats, Shane scanned the terrain below and could see that he was going to land in someone's front yard, nearly two blocks away from the 82nd's signal flare.

Approaching ground, Shane pulled down hard on his toggles. The parachute caught a lot of air and slowed him down as he set down softly. Hawk rolled over on his right side, skimmed his surroundings for any hostile threats, and concluded that there were none. He then punched the same button on his side again, releasing the parachute from the armor on his back.

Detaching his M22A2 assault rifle from his right shoulder, Shane snuck through a number of front and backyards and hopped several fences. On one occasion, he almost landed on a home owner's little Chihuahua. Half scared to death, it yipped and barked at him.

Unperturbed by the miniature canine, Shane clambered the next fence. He paused in the shadows of a house to confirm that there was no visible danger, and suddenly noticed Almazan climbing off a roof across the street. Relieved to see his teammate, Hawk crossed the empty lane to check on him.

"They're on the next street over. Let's move," Shane whispered. Together, they rushed through another open back yard, jumped yet another hedge, and reached the corner of a house. In front of it, they spotted 82nd soldiers loading up big HMTVs with civilians.

Hover Military Transport Vehicle, or HMTV, is simply a 2 ton cargo truck with six large pods instead of wheels which allowed the vehicle to hover. The cargo bed of the truck could be modified to carry troops or cargo.

"Friendlies!" Hawk hollered out to two soldiers standing watch. At first they aimed their weapons, but lowered them quickly as they identified the two Special Forces soldiers.

Hawk and Almazan felt safe enough now to approach the guards standing watch. "Who's in charge here Private?" Hawk asked a young kid in uniform.

"Staff Sergeant McMeen, sir." The kid snapped to attention.

Hawk instructed Almazan, "Take charge of the load-up. I'm going to go find this guy and then I'll go see if I can find Angel and the kids."

"Go for it bro," Almazan assured him, "I got this here."

Half an hour later, an armored hover truck with Captain Dyson in the front passenger seat, four soldiers, a driver, and gunners in both the forward and rear cargo bed corner turrets, sped out of the main gate along All American Drive. Two eleven-foot-tall Magnum Battle Suits painted in digital black, grey, and cream colored camouflage—each carrying a single, eight-foot-long, three hundred pound rail gun mounted over their right shoulders—sprinted behind the hover vehicle.

Above them soared two winged, light blue and grey, digitally camouflaged Battle Suits called Valkyries. Both of the Valkyries also held rail guns in their hands. They weren't quite as tall as the ground-based Battle Suits, for the Magnums had the fliers seriously outgunned. The Valkyries, however, possessed the capability to fly, and were much, much faster, and more agile. Together, and working as a team, the Battle Suit-Valkyrie squad surrounding the hover truck was as effective a military unit as any commander could wish for.

As night fell, the sky was still ablaze with fires. Further off in the distance, the eerie glow of a distorted energy line could be seen against the clouds, though the line itself was not visible from the ground. Cars were scattered all over the freeway—some already burnt-out, others still on fire. A few had been left unscathed, but all were abandoned, while more lay wrecked after having crashed into trees, a guard rail, a bridge support, or another car. Bodies were just as numerous.

Everything appeared damaged, destroyed or dead, and nothing or nobody else was traveling on the freeway. Dyson's driver cautiously maneuvered the gun truck around each obstacle in their path. The two Magnums kept up with the vehicle, even though the driver sped in excess of over forty miles an hour whenever he was able to travel in a straight line.

Eventually, they reached the 401 Bypass and went under the bridge. A little further, to the right, Dyson and his men could see the entire Cross Creek Mall engulfed in an inferno. The unarmored gunners suffered past the intense heat and broke a sweat despite the cold winter air pounding their cheeks as the vehicle drove on.

But it wasn't until a few minutes later that the soldiers began to fathom the full horrors of the Cataclysm. All American Freeway had turned into Owen drive, and after a few hundred meters, the team came upon the ruins of Cape Fear Valley Hospital. Half of it had collapsed, forcing thousands of people outside into the main courtyard as emergency workers tried to save the most critically injured. Blood, sweat, and tears marked the throngs of survivors. Torn clothes and shattered dreams sat and waited for the first available medical worker. Army, Air Force, and NARC medical teams tended to those the civilians were unable to assist.

Captain Dyson knew not to stop and help. He and his rescue team could get stuck in a situation that would likely take up too much of their time. Some people looked at the passing soldiers, hoping they would help. Others sat there stony-faced and unflinching. They knew these particular soldiers weren't a medical team: they were the defenders of what was left of North Carolina.

They drove on through a street that was littered with garbage and debris, but relatively clear of scorched vehicles. Fires still raged in almost every building; only a church had been spared and now provided shelter for hundreds, if not thousands of people. Cars and trucks of all shapes and sizes were parked in the parking lot and on the street. It was strangely quiet, though, as the soldiers drove by.

They came to a second set of stop lights after the church, found their waypoint, and turned right on Southern Street. Once they rounded the corner, Dyson and his men were confronted by a horde of child-sized, grey-skinned, skinny creatures.

They looked nearly identical: elongated faces like a lizard, razor sharp beaks, and slanted yellow eyes. The alien beings sported small, three-fingered hands with razor-sharp claws. Their forearms and lower legs were larger than their upper arms and thighs, while the creatures' chests appeared huge compared to their tiny waists. Trashing everything around them, including junk, the strange animals seemed to be running amok. A cluster of them dragged a struggling human being out of a home—a young female with short, red hair.

They all turned to face the truck with the two behemoth Magnums behind it. Obviously flustered, the startled aliens snarled and flared their beaks at the soldiers before charging the gun truck. Some ran, others flapped their bat-like wings and assaulted them. At first, the top gunner hesitated at the sight of the ugly creatures, but then he unloaded his mounted M3A9 .50 Caliber Rail Gun. Brass shell casings and links pinged noisily all over the top of the hover truck as he sprayed the horde with burst after burst of rounds.

The extraterrestrials unlucky enough to stand in the gunner's sights were torn apart piece by piece and limb for limb as the fifty caliber rounds simply ripped them to shreds. Pitilessly, the muzzle flash of the weapon threw hundreds of rounds about, cutting down the demonic gang.

A group of beaked creatures rushing out of an alley to join the fight were immediately obliterated by Captain Dyson as he fired his laser weapon out of the passenger door of the truck. The two rear gunners covered the left and right flanks as well as the back of the vehicle, blasting away any extraterrestrial that tried to pursue them. Meanwhile, the two Valkyrie pilots swooped down out of the black sky above them, raining electromagnetically accelerated rounds on those beasts that had slipped through the crossfire and were threatening to climb onto the truck.

Dozens of alien beings were gunned down; several were unfortunate enough to be overrun as the driver slammed at full speed into their frail bodies with the large, armored front grill of the vehicle. The few extraterrestrials that had somehow gotten away soon faced two Magnum Battle Suits positioned on both sidewalks at the end of Southern and Owen. The warriors reached back as their infamous artillery cannons swiveled over their right shoulders. They took aim, and pulled the triggers. Jet boosters mounted on the cannons drew power from the nuclear engine on the back of the Battle Suit, and heavy stabilizers dropped to the ground from each leg. The boosters and stabilizers helped prevent the Battle Suit from being knocked over by the immense recoil of the cannon. The Battle Suit on the right fired a split second before the other one.

A shockwave of air blasted out of the barrels of the eight-foot-long cannons as the Magnums each discharged one heavy, five pound Glasser slug at Mach 3 speed. Sonic booms accompanied the slugs, deafening those creatures who had managed to survive the passing hover truck.

Dyson was just about to shoot one creature as its head disappeared from its shoulders. Regrettably, the unfortunate woman being held captive by the aliens freed herself at the wrong moment and also vaporized into pink mist from the waist up as the cannon slugs annihilated everything in their path. The beasts near the truck suffered the same fate as the Magnums fired a second volley. The sound wave hit a split second later as it rushed to keep up with the rounds. The two successive sonic booms dazed even Captain Dyson for a moment, but he shook it off.

Minutes after the engagement, there was nothing left. Everything in the slugs' path was flattened or had simply disintegrated. With a range of ten miles, the slugs had torn up the road, including fences, mailboxes, street lamps, parked cars, and anything else unfortunate enough to be in their way.

After the encounter, a tired Dyson and his teammates drove on without speaking a word. Meanwhile, the Valkyrie pilots swooped down and quickly finished off the remaining creatures as the beasts fled the sonic booms of the thundering cannons. The Magnums slung their weapons over their shoulders and disengaged the boosters, retracted the leg stabilizers, and raced down the street to catch up with the gun truck.

Dyson's team proceeded a mile and a half further to a grocery store and small shopping complex. It had been virtually left unscathed by fire and tremors, but there were people inside raiding the stocks of food and other goods. In the parking lot, two policemen fired shotguns at an odd looking being that resembled a scorpion balanced on two strong legs. The two cops launched several rounds into the copper-colored, armored hide of the humanoid scorpion crossbreed until it fell over dead. Unfortunately, just before its demise, the monstrosity had lashed out with its spine-like tail and stung one of the policemen. The officer fell over dead; his heart punctured by the creature's spine. His colleague, rushing to his partner's aid, let out an anguished scream. He cradled the dead man's head, rocking back and forth and crying pitifully.

Suddenly, the dead cop came back to life, and sank his teeth into his fellow officer's neck. The latter screamed and tried to pull away, but the zombie had bitten through his jugular and he was gone within seconds. Dyson jumped out of the truck after the driver had stopped the vehicle behind an overturned delivery van, determined to eliminate the zombie with his assault rifle. Hearing the truck door open, the undead policeman rose to challenge him, only to have his head explode as Dyson pulled the trigger. His legs shaking, the captain climbed back into the truck, stunned at what he had just witnessed.

After Dyson signaled his men to continue, the gun truck and the Magnums crossed an intersection, rumbling over downed power lines and destroyed stop lights. An old McDonald's restaurant was completely enveloped in flames as they passed by.

They drove on a little further, and then made a right onto a narrow cul-de-sac that had another side street intersecting on the left. To their horror, many of the homes in this particular neighborhood had been flattened as if something large had plowed right through them. Small fires burned weakly among the rubble, while houses on the other side of the block were still fully ablaze. Smoke lingered over the road, limiting the team's line of sight to a few meters.

Dyson checked the GPS tracker installed in the cab of the hover truck. Because communication systems all over the globe were barely functioning, the GPS ran sluggishly as it fed their information directly to the satellites in orbit. Without an antennae booster, tracking friendly unit positions was a painstaking endeavor now. Luckily, Dyson knew they were close; he recalled the snaking street from maps in General Madden's office.

They arrived at another T-shaped intersection, and one of the Valkyrie pilots radioed in to Dyson, "Delta 4-1, this is Sierra-Echo-017, I got a visual on the eighty-deuce boys, and they're not five hundred feet from your position. Make a left and then take the first right. There are two Hover Military Transport Vehicles and three MHMMV-44 combat gun trucks parked in the street there. Call-sign of contact is Hardcore-Eight, over?"

"Roger Sierra-Echo-017," Dyson then changed the frequency on the radio mounted on the center of the truck. "Hardcore-Eight, this is Delta 4-1, over."

"Delta 4-1, this is Hardcore-Eight Romeo, read you loud and clear, over." Someone came back over the channel. "Hardcore-Eight Romeo, I have a gun truck, two Magnums, and two Valkyries approaching your position from the east to render support. Do not engage to the east, over."

"Roger that Delta 4-1, I copy friendlies coming in from the east. Over."

"That's a good copy, Delta 4-1 out." Confident that the army unit wouldn't open fire on them, Dyson pointed to the left as the driver applied more power to the hover truck's twin engines, quickening their pace. As soon as they rounded the right turn, they could see the back end of another gun truck pulling rear security and two HMTVs loading up survivors and wounded soldiers. Dyson counted nine or ten troops helping about twenty civilians onto the HMTVs.

While his driver parked the truck, leaving the engine running, Dyson climbed out of the vehicle. "Monitor the radio," he ordered, and rudely tossed the hand-mike to the irritated driver.

Circling the front of the truck with his weapon ready, Dyson approached a rather tall, hefty sergeant dressed in the standard urban white, grey, and black Digital Combat Utility Uniform of the 82nd Airborne Corps. He was helping an elderly woman onto the back of the lead HMTV. The sergeant was of Scottish heritage, and looked as though he hadn't shaved today—or yesterday for that matter. His armor vest had seen recent combat. Dyson noticed three large slashes across the chest plate which dug a few millimeters deep into the armor. Whatever creature had raked its claws across the sergeant's protective covering had been very strong. The man turned to the captain and rendered a salute. He didn't muster the words for the proper greeting, but at this point, who would care? "Good to see you made it here safely sir."

Dyson returned his salute and the sergeant relaxed. "Glad to see you're all still here, Sergeant." Dyson looked into the back of the HMTV and saw half a dozen more wounded survivors. "What's the situation here?" he asked.

"Lieutenant Hawk is currently at the house behind us. His family in there is the last to be evacuated, but I think his wife's sister is giving him problems. We don't have much time left. There's a huge alien robot in the area. We were able to fend it off twice, but not before it grabbed a civilian and one of our men and ran off with them. One of the survivors hiding in the ruins of his home saw the monster tearing them apart."

"What kind of robot?" Dyson was interested.

"I dunno sir, it wasn't man-made. Definitely alien. It stands nearly four stories tall and is very tough. We barely even damaged it the last time it came through here."

"What's your name soldier?" Dyson asked. "Staff Sergeant Douglas McMeen, sir."

"Thank you Sergeant, get the rest of these survivors mounted up, we're out of here in five mikes."

Dyson then walked through the yard of the home the sergeant had mentioned. As soon as he stepped on the porch, he heard a woman screaming in anger and a door slamming. Dyson looked inside, and saw two children trying to get their shoes on and another looking for them. The oldest kid was also searching for a dog's leash and asked her mother if she knew where it was. The dark-haired woman looked tired and pale, obviously exhausted by today's events. A man suddenly appeared from the kitchen. He was in uniform, wearing the Battle Suit specific to the 71st Special Forces Group. A standard issue M22A2 assault rifle was mounted into a socket across his back.

Lieutenant Hawk didn't even notice the captain standing in the doorway. "Angel, if she doesn't want to go, then we can't force her. Let her stay here. We need to get you and the kids to safety," Shane urged.

"Lieutenant, what's going on here, what's the hold-up?" Dyson approached him.

"It's like leading a horse to water, sir. My wife's sister refuses to leave." He pointed down the hallway to the left. Dyson peered down the hall, and saw a little girl come out of a room on the right. Despite her young age, she gave him a stern look of disapproval and went straight to her mother.

"Mom, mom!" she yelled impatiently until Angel gave her the attention she wanted. "I can't find my shoes, and what about the bunnies?"

But Angel, too drained to worry about footwear and pets, just scooped her up in her arms. "Let's go kids! We're leaving!" she snapped, clearly frustrated.

The fate of nine dogs, three cats, two rabbits, and other household critters that his sister-in-law collected was apparently still open to some debate, but Shane had reached the end of his tether. "There's no time," he told Madison firmly. "The pets are staying here with your aunt, and she will look after them." Reluctantly, the children followed their mother and the lieutenant outside.

Shortly afterwards, Dyson knocked on the door to the sister's room which was locked. "Ma'am, we need you to come with us, it's not safe here."

"Get out of here!" snarled a loud and angry voice.

"Ma'am, don't make me come in there and get you," Dyson warned.

"I said piss off!" she thundered defiantly after flinging something against the wall.

The captain realized that he would have to convince her the hard way. He took a step backward to give the door a hard kick. The flimsy lock broke immediately as the frame splintered, and the door swung wide open on broken hinges. A large, three-hundred-fifty pound woman sat propped up against the wall, holding the lifeless body of a man in her arms. A large weapon had ripped open the corpse's chest, revealing flesh and bone underneath. Dirty dishes and clothes were scattered about the room, while a cheap, little television set had fallen off the armoire and broken on the floor. By then Dyson knew that his chances of evacuating the bulky civilian were slim to none.

In addition to angry, the woman was also panic-stricken. Rocking her husband's body back and forth, she caressed his black, oily hair, and talked to him as if he was still among the living. A large hole in the ceiling indicated to Dyson that whatever killed this man had attacked from above. "She will never come willingly," he concluded scornfully, "and even if I could convince her, there is not enough room on the HMTV for her and the rest of the refugees. I don't even think the added strength of a Battle Suit could lift her onto the back of *a truck!*"

Resigned to leave her to her own devices, the captain walked out the front door and across the yard to the HMTV where Lieutenant Hawk was loading his family into the back. "Almost done here sir," Shane reported. Angel and the two youngest children were already seated, while Shane assisted the oldest one.

When they were all buckled up on either the bed of the truck or the troop seats, Lieutenant Hawk pulled the rifle from over his shoulder, and was about to say something to Captain Dyson. But before any words could leave his mouth, a sudden crash destroyed the house next to Angel's sister's home. Then, something right out of a science fiction movie appeared from the dust.

It was a terrifying machine: huge, armored, and ready for action. The giant apparatus stood on four enormous legs, but could crawl like a spider. Each extremity sported three, long claws for toes and fingers, with one massive, non-articulating claw on the back of each leg for balance or grip. The creature had a large head with a single, bulbous eye, and a long mechanical neck resembling like a human spinal cord. A bulging torso and prehensile tail that measured the length of its head, neck, and body gave the Cyclops an additional air of invincibility. For at the end of the tail swung a large, menacing spike that looked as though it could pierce through anything.

Utterly stupefied, Shane still had the presence of mind to fire off round after round of electro-magnetically accelerated, steel alloy sabot bullets from his M22A2 rifle. The projectiles launched out of the barrel of his weapon at speeds near Mach 2. Although his thoughts were racing, Shane's aim was steady and each shot struck the machine's head—unfortunately, to little avail. The rifle seemed to barely put a dent into the alien mechanism's outer shell.

Split seconds later, the other soldiers started firing while running for cover. Both airborne Valkyrie pilots shot their rail guns into the chest of the creature, while hundreds of additional rounds slammed into its body, only grazing the thick alien armor with holes that oozed black, oily blood.

Then the gunners fixed their weapons on the monstrous target. Two plasma bolts and a stream of slugs from a rail gun finally tore up the beastly machine. It reared up in protest, but dropped to its knees only moments later. Although the behemoth was still very much alive, each round punctured its armored plate further, eventually resulting in a gush of liquid, red goop. As furious rounds continued to pepper its outer layers, the machine fixed its sight on the first human who had attacked it. But Shane—aware that this alien apparition was by no means indestructible—was not intimidated and fired again. It was a perfectly aimed shot that punctured the being's sole eye. The eye bubbled up and let out a stream of yellow ooze before it exploded from its socket in a gooey mess. Momentarily paralyzed by pain and anger, the machine let out a demonic and deafening growl. Then it charged blindly at Shane, roaring in stride.

Shane continued to fire as did everyone with a weapon, but started to sweat as the creature threatened to plow over him and the truck with all its precious cargo inside. Luckily, the extraterrestrial stumbled and at last toppled over on its left. Chunks of metal twisted and screeched, and a thick, red liquid burst from its head and onto the lawn. The two Magnums kept their huge, eight-foot-long cannons aimed at the creature even as it lay dead—just in case it wasn't after all.

At the same time, those without ear protection were deafened by the breaking of the sound barrier. The sonic boom had shattered all of the neighborhood's intact windows, and the children in the back of the HMTV were beside themselves with fear. Madison, the youngest one, held onto her mother and her teddy for dear life, traumatized by the terrible events. She was crying and clutching her ears; no one could hear a thing.

Relatively unfazed, Dyson tapped Shane on the shoulder, "Can we leave now?!" he asked rhetorically.

"Yes sir!" Shane replied enthusiastically as the soldiers loaded up the vehicles to return to the main headquarters on Ft. Bragg.

Tired, but overjoyed that his family was still alive, Lieutenant Hawk sat in the back of the HMTV with Angel and her children. She snuggled up next to him with her youngest daughter in her lap, and rested her head on his padded shoulder. Shane reached into a small storage foot locker and pulled out a handful of ear plugs. He gave one set to each survivor, aware that they would not do them any good now. "Here kids, these should help if the Magnums have to use their boom guns again," Shane soothed as the vehicle began to move.

On the ten mile road trip back to base, the convoy ran into occasional trouble. Dyson's men spotted some aliens, but the creatures mostly ran off into the night instead of attacking the heavily armed party. As Hawk and his teammates passed the hospital, they came upon an entirely different scene: the whole building had collapsed by now, and the people that had been waiting outside in the afternoon lay dead and buried under the rubble. Fires still engulfed whole areas, and in a dreadful scene recalling visions of hell, aliens of different sizes and types feasted on the bodies of the deceased. Dyson ordered the team to keep moving, and engage only if necessary. Everyone gasped in horror as they passed the dreadful carnage.

Further up the road, gunners opened fire on a throng of beastly creatures, slaughtering most of them. Tracers ripped into the night, targeting everything that did not look human.

Homes and businesses burned all over Fayetteville. Everywhere Dyson and his men turned, they saw flames raging unchecked and alien creatures running amok—largely unchallenged. When they entered the base through Fort Bragg's All American gate, Dyson's gun truck and the two Magnums broke from the convoy and took the Gruber Road exit.

The HMTVs and the two 82nd gun trucks decided on an alternative route, and after driving through the base for a few minutes, they came to a halt in front of one of a dozen buildings still standing. Here they felt safest, since the 82nd boys had already built up a defendable perimeter. It was the Headquarters of the 82nd Airborne Corps. Most of the division, however, was on leave or presumed missing or dead as units had made hundreds of futile attempts to contact their men. Many had left the base to tend to their families, their fate unknown. Others had simply abandoned their posts, never to return. After all, it was the end of the world.

Chapter Two: Chaos Convoy

On The Second Day,

The following morning, soldiers, friends, families, and survivors stood in line for an early morning military breakfast. Lieutenant Hawk made sure his wife Angel and their children received what they needed before letting anyone else go up to the buffet counters. It seemed a bit selfish, but no one was complaining. Soldiers' needs were paramount, but all insisted that the children eat first.

Shane waited until everyone else was fed before taking a plate. Unfortunately, there was no hot food left by that time; it had all gone cold and fresh fruit and other nutritious snacks had disappeared as well. One of the supply sergeants broke open a case of Meal, Ready-to-Eat, or MREs, and distributed them among those that had selflessly waited for everyone else to finish. There was still plenty of coffee, orange juice, and water though, and Lieutenant Hawk had more than his fair share of coffee—at least until the sugar ran out.

Throughout the meal, Valkyrie Battle Suits screamed overhead, gliding towards the firing ranges. To the dismay of the overtired survivors, the unsettling sounds of battle and alien howling could still be heard from miles away. There was also the depressing color of the sky. Instead of sunshine, Shane's children saw nothing but the sickening grey of ash mixed in with black, oily smoke on the horizon—a result of the fires that had burned the city of Fayetteville to the ground overnight.

Lieutenant Hawk sat together with his family, but no one said a word. Except for Madison, who demanded more of the runny scrambled eggs. Angel found it hard to explain to her daughter that they had to be careful how much they ate now. If they had too much today, she told her youngest, there wouldn't be anything left for tomorrow. Madison didn't much care though; she wanted more runny eggs. In the end, her sister Emily, who found them quite disgusting, scraped the rest of hers onto Madison's tray. The little girl finished them happily, but announced that they would've tasted better with a bit of ranch dressing on top.

The smell of bad food couldn't mask the smell of smoke and dust, but there was something else in the air that crinkled human noses. Many soldiers and civilians had walked up to the top of a hill on the east side of the compound. More and more people were joining them, curious to see what was holding their interest. Lieutenant Hawk told Angel he would take a look as well. As he reached the incline, Shane froze: ocean waves were gently lapping a new shore. Baffled, he gazed out over the water that consumed half the base and far beyond his line of sight. As for the unpleasant smell: it was the foul odor of thousands of dead bodies washing up against the slope near the old track and field sections of Towle Stadium.

Feeling nauseous, but afraid to take a deep breath, Shane's senses were assaulted by the combined stink of salt water and rotten corpses. He was not alone. Many others on the hill, who had observed the sight after finishing their morning meals, backed away to vomit. Yesterday, there had been fifty miles of land between here and the coast, Shane thought, frightened. Some crumbled buildings and trees still protruded from the ocean's surface, while most base homes were in the process of being washed away into the sea. Heaps of debris and bodies drifted with the tide as it rushed in and back out again. Fayetteville was beachfront property now, and half of the old city was under water. All along the eastern seaboard, miles of beautiful coast line had been reclaimed by the ocean—from the southeastern corner of Georgia up into Canada.

To make matters worse, earthquakes and aftershocks had continued through the night, keeping everyone awake and on edge. The last one had only been an hour ago. Shane thought that the tremors were lightening up, but it surely was not quite over yet.

Tidal waves had wiped the United States Marine Corps base in Jackson, North Carolina off the map, with thousands of Marines perishing in the tsunami. Seymour Johnson Air Force Base lay devastated after another alien spire had destroyed the entire installation. The Naval Academy at Annapolis was also obliterated; floods had swept it out to sea.

According to Valkyrie patrols using standard, short-range radio frequencies and generating news reports, Washington D.C. was gone, so were Boston, Philadelphia, New York City; large sections of New Jersey, Connecticut, Rhode Island, Delaware, Maryland as well as Atlanta and Columbia in South Carolina were either completely or partially washed away. Radio broadcasts spoke of unprecedented damage along the eastern seaboard. At the moment, even the president's whereabouts were unknown.

After listening to the alarming news bulletins, Shane watched three gun trucks with four Magnums roll into the perimeter and park between the hill and the sports field. Everyone was wearing armor, uniforms, and carried standard issue weapons. One of them, Captain Jesse Dyson, who looked as though he hadn't slept a wink the night before, walked up to Lieutenant Hawk. Hawk saluted. "Lieutenant, the Special Forces compound on the south side of the base was attacked last night before we returned. We're the only ones to survive. I know you've taken command since this all began and you're the highest ranking officer amongst those here in the 82nd. I know that you've been taking orders from the SF compound as well, but now you and I are the only officers here. Last night, General Madden was killed in his office by something that slipped right through our security."

Dyson looked around warily and noticed soldiers relaxing while on guard duty. With the Magnums patrolling the perimeter, the men felt less anxious and huddled together in little groups, whispering about their fears to anyone who would listen.

"We received a communication roughly an hour ago about a large North American Regional Command task force moving from Fort Benning to Detroit." He continued, "We're going to meet up with them and proceed north from I-77 to Detroit via the Ohio Turn-Pike."

"I know the route well sir," Hawk said. "I used to drive it when traveling back and forth to Michigan to see my family. I can lead the way sir. But why Detroit?"

"Because it's the only city that we're still getting communications from. This means there are survivors. And if there are survivors, then there's still something of a city left." Hawk nodded, wondering if Detroit had already been destroyed in the meantime.

"Good," Dyson was pleased. "There's a motor pool across the street with enough vehicles to move everyone here. I've been sending Valkyrie patrols out looking for survivors since 0300 hours this morning. They've flown as far as Raleigh and Greensboro and as far west as Charlotte, but none of them have come back with any good news. The major cities are either ghost towns or completely destroyed, and the surrounding areas are nothing more than swampland reclaimed by the ocean. Last reports from the west indicate that the Yellowstone caldera has erupted. There's a massive ash cloud heading this way."

"When do you want to leave sir?" Hawk asked.

"As soon as possible. The ash falling from the sky will play havoc on engines and equipment along the way. So the sooner we get moving, the farther along we'll be before we start having some major mechanical issues," Dyson explained.

"Have any of your scouts reported on what's between here and Winston-Salem?" Hawk wanted to know.

"Swampland," the captain replied with a sigh. "It's like the entire state has turned into nothing but swampland again. We're going to rendezvous with Lieutenant General May's NARC convoy at Winston-Salem. From there we will proceed north to Detroit and pick up any survivors along the way."

"Roger that sir." The plan sounded promising to Hawk.

"Get your men together Lieutenant," Dyson ordered. "We leave in one hour."

"Yes sir," Hawk snapped to attention. Then he walked down the hill and made his way between the parked trucks to Angel and the children.

Sergeant Almazan, having seen Hawk talking to the captain, approached them. He was aware that something was going to happen, and was curious to find out what. Hawk looked at both Angel and Almazan. "Get the men together, Sergeant, head over to the motor pool and gather as many vehicles as possible. We're leaving. We're gonna rendezvous with the NARC forces in Winston-Salem and head to Detroit from there."

"Why Detroit? I hate snow," Almazan grinned.

"Apparently there are survivors, and Captain Dyson seems to think the city might still be intact."

Angel frowned; North Carolina was her home and she did not want to leave. But she also knew in her heart of hearts that she had no choice. There was nothing left for her here. Her oldest boy, Jacob, was missing with his father and there was no telling where they were. The least she could do was remove her other children from harm's way.

Angel and everyone else had been disturbingly depressed since yesterday. The world they knew appeared to be coming to an end, and like many others looking for loved ones, Angel despaired for her eldest son's life. To find him, she had tried to make it into the Raleigh area the previous afternoon, but was stopped short when Shane arrived at her sister's house to see them to safety.

While Angel agonized, Dyson's team managed to pull together four more gun trucks and four HMTV hover transports. Hover pods hummed gently in place of wheels as the trucks were loaded up with passengers, weapons, ammunition, and supplies. Hawk, Almazan, his wife Amanda, Angel, and the kids all gathered in a MHMMV-44T modified troop Combat Gun Truck. It was a few feet longer, and, instead of the normal seating for five in the MHMMV-44 variant, could hold an additional six troops comfortably.

After a convoy brief with the Tactical Commanders (TCs) of the vehicles, Captain Dyson gave the order to move out. The TCs were on the right side passenger seats; they monitored the radio and plotted detours on route, using the String of Pearls Satellite System with A.D.A.M. Drivers also attended the briefing to familiarize themselves with the itinerary and to get an idea of the dangers lying ahead.

Lieutenant Hawk briefed everyone in attendance, "All right, check it out men. We're getting out of here, all of us. We're going to meet up with a large NARC convoy out of Atlanta." He unrolled a road map of the United States and spread it out on the hood of his MHMMV-44T Combat Gun Truck. Almazan helped hold the map down. "Our route takes us just south of the Raleigh-Durham area. From there we'll head west along I-40 towards Winston-Salem. Once there, we'll wait for the Atlanta convoy to meet up with us. When we get on 52 North, we'll proceed up to Mount Airy and merge onto I-74. That'll eventually join I-77. I-77 will take us up through Virginia and West Virginia. We'll stop at two locations along the way." Shane pointed at two different towns on the map, "The first will be Wytheville, Virginia, the second Charleston, West Virginia." He paused.

"Then, once we reach Ohio, we'll stop in either Canton, Akron, Sandusky or Toledo off Interstate 80/90. We'll continue on the Ohio Turnpike until we reach either I-280 or I-75 North to Detroit," he added.

He was interrupted by Almazan, "Don't forget to stop and pay the tolls along the way," he chuckled. Everyone in the group snickered as well. Almazan was always good at breaking the ice.

"And finally, once we're done there, it's a straight shot into Detroit," Hawk finished.

"Sir, what's the estimated distance and travel time," a small wiry fellow, a specialist by the name of Downes asked.

"Normally? When the world hasn't gone to hell? Fourteen or fifteen hours. I do know it's twelve hours to the Michigan and Ohio borders and the city of Toledo. It's a six hundred and ninety-nine mile drive. Add another thirty or forty miles on top of that to get to Detroit."

Hawk looked around for more questions. "What if we run into any problems, sir?" another young soldier, who stood taller than the rest and was slightly more built than Downes, asked.

"Good question Specialist Lock. If we encounter any hostiles, and I mean hostiles that aren't human, you have permission to shoot first, ask questions later. If we come across groups of survivors, we'll pick them up if they so choose," Hawk explained the Rules Of Engagement.

Almazan continued, "The ash and snow mix will play havoc on our equipment and engines, so each time you stop, it's your job to clean them out as best you can." A big man of Scottish descent raised a large hand up in the back.

Almazan looked at him, "Yes Sergeant McMeen?"

"Oiy, do we have a plan of action 'gainst anythin' bigger than say, a skyscraper?" he asked.

His Scottish accent wasn't hard to understand, but Downes looked utterly dumbfounded. He turned to Lock, "What did "Shrek" say?"

Lock frowned, but then chuckled as "Shrek's" big hand smacked Downes on the back of the head. "If we run into any say, oh I dunno, dragons? Shoot everything you have into it." Hawk emphasized.

Almazan raised an eyebrow, smiling, "You got something against dragons now?"

Hawk grinned back, "Only if they think I'm on the menu! Now, if there's nothing else, get to your vehicles. We roll out in two minutes."

The group of TCs and drivers hurried back to their trucks and helped the last few passengers inside. Hawk and Almazan climbed into theirs, and the latter stepped on the throttle. The nuclear powered engine gave torque to the axle and the vehicle glided forward. Leaving the safety of the compound, the trek took Longstreet eastward. They made a left on Reilly, then a right on Butner, and followed that road out of the base. Turning left on Bragg Boulevard, the convoy proceeded towards Sanford about thirty miles north.

It didn't take long before they were passing now familiar scenes of destruction, but the trek made it to Sanford unopposed. The town was deserted, except for a few bodies still lying about the streets. They had either been the victims of a mob, buried under rubble, or worse. The expedition continued through charred city blocks, some of which were still burning, and picked up a few exhausted and traumatized survivors. The team also engaged and killed two or three alien critters about every mile or so along their route.

An hour north of Sanford, they came upon a pack of grey skinned extraterrestrials with bat-like wings that were threatening a group of refugees from Raleigh. The frightened humans were armed with broomsticks and shovels, but one portly man carried a katana sword. The convoy stopped and Hawk dashed towards the group, firing off a few rounds into the air. The mere noise of the gunshots scared the aliens and they dispersed running or flapping.

Then the man with the sword approached him. Hawk could hardly believe his eyes as he recognized the individual: it was Angel's deadbeat ex-husband Bubba Earl. Although he had never met him before, Shane recognized the ridiculous mullet hair, dark, greasy beard, and lardy body from pictures Angel had shown him. One of the laziest men he'd ever heard of, Bubba Earl made Shane's temper flare as he stopped in front of him. In fact, Hawk wanted to shoot him right then and there. In his opinion, any man who lied, cheated, and stole from his own family for fourteen years didn't deserve to live. This sorry excuse of a human being had never held a real job, and was entirely without ambition. With his pronounced mean streak, Bubba Earl enjoyed making other people—like his ex-wife—suffer with his complaints and endless arguing. Like her obese sister, Shane thought grimly, Bubba Earl had no love for Angel or anyone else for that matter, including his children.

His spirits were lifted when he noticed Jacob running out from the throng of people. He was ten years old—and despite his leech of a parent—a good kid. At his age, Jacob was of course unable to see the truth behind his father's motives. Meanwhile, Bubba Earl pointed the tip of his sword at the concrete and snarled, "It's about time you jarheads showed up. Give us some food and a ride out of here."

After hearing her ex-husband's voice, Angel felt a wave of nausea rise up in her throat. With her mind racing, she quickly opted not to let Bubba Earl know that she was alive. But Emily, her fourteen-year-old daughter, excitedly pointed at Jacob. "Look Mom! Jake's alive!" she blurted out, unfastening her safety belt.

Angel shook her head in terror, "Stay right where you are! Don't go out there," she commanded with clenched teeth. Taken aback, Emily paused and then sat back.

Memories of her unhappy first marriage flooded Angel's mind, making her wish that Shane would just shoot her ex-husband. She prayed fervently, "Just one false move and he will. *God please don't bring him with us!"*

Meanwhile, Hawk responded to the rude man's request with icy politeness, "How many of you are here…sir?"

Bubba Earl looked at his son, "I'm just asking you to take me and my boy."

"What about these other people?" Hawk retorted scornfully as Captain Dyson, Specialist Lock, and another kid, Specialist Bruzinski, approached them.

"I don't care about them baby-killer, just my son and I," he snorted.

Captain Dyson, who was known for his short fuse, foamed with outrage. "What did you call him?!" he yelled.

But Bubba Earl, always thirsting for a confrontation, grew even angrier and shouted, "You fools, my son and I are starving and we need to get out of here. I fought off some demon-like thing about twenty minutes ago and it ran off. We need to leave here now!"

Skeptical, Hawk and Dyson looked at Jacob who merely rolled his eyes at his father's assertions. It was obvious that Bubba Earl was lying. After battling aliens like the monster in Francis's neighborhood, they knew this little fat man could not have warded off an extraterrestrial with such a basic weapon.

An old woman from the survivors' group approached them. "Sir, this man is a murderer!" she exclaimed, pointing at Angel's former spouse. "He killed a policeman who was leading our group out of the city."

"Shut the hell up wench!" Bubba Earl exploded, his face turning bright red. Bubbling over with rage, he raised his sword.

"Drop your weapon now!" Dyson barked furiously, but the man grew even more hostile and angry. Jacob jumped to the side as his father took a step backwards, flailing his sword around. Intimidated, the woman shied away.

"Drop your weapon!" Hawk repeated sternly, but Bubba Earl still refused to comply. Instead, he raised the blade and looked at it, a weird grin spreading across his unappealing face.

"I'll put my sword down if you lower your weapon first," he challenged Shane. Lieutenant Hawk and Captain Dyson glanced at each other, both wearing an expression of "yeah right" on their faces.

"You're insane!" Jacob yelled and ducked for cover behind Hawk and Dyson who both switched their rifles from safe to semi. "You didn't even care to see if Mom, Jonathan, and my sisters were still alive! You just care about yourself!" he sobbed.

That's when the door to the gun truck opened and Angel climbed out. Jacob ran to his mother. "MOM!" he laughed, overjoyed to be reunited with her. She just grabbed him, tears running freely down her face, and gave him a huge hug.

Bubba Earl, now completely fed up after realizing who was standing in front of him, reared his sword to swing it at Hawk, roaring, "You coward! I'll kill you!" Just then he was struck in the back of the head by a broom stick. His eyes rolled back and he crashed chin first onto the concrete. The elderly lady, proud at having defused the situation, sighed with relief as the two soldiers lowered their weapons. After thanking them, she spat on the spread-eagled, unconscious murderer.

"Ma'am, go ahead and get on the back of one of those hover transports," Dyson pointed his thumb over his right shoulder. Although he was impressed by her assertiveness, the captain thought it paramount to keep moving. Together with the group of survivors, the woman hurried to the rear of the vehicle and climbed inside.

Hawk looked at Dyson, "As much as I'd hate to ask it sir, but do we take this clown with us or do we leave him for the dogs?"

"It's tempting to leave him, Lieutenant, but we are to bring the helpless to safety, regardless of their criminal behavior," Dyson replied, shrugging his shoulders. He then motioned Lock and Bruzinski to secure Bubba Earl's pathetic bulk.

Hawk took another look at him. "Angel isn't going to be too happy about this," he thought. Although all of her children were alive and well, the person she hated most in the world sat handcuffed in the back of a Military Police hover car. Personally, Hawk was disappointed too; he had always imagined that a fight with Angel's ex would have been more gratifying.

Heading back to his truck, Shane was glad to see Jacob receiving hugs and kisses from his siblings. "Thank God he is alive," Angel cheered, brimming over with joy. Hawk took off his helmet, and she hugged him exuberantly, planting a big kiss on his lips. "Thank you baby," Angel said softly and put her arms around him again, closing her eyes. Shane just stood there, savoring the moment.

"Who knows when we can enjoy some private time again," he thought wistfully. With his free hand he held her head against his chest and smiled.

The journey from Raleigh to Winston-Salem was slow and treacherous. The convoy lurched past large chunks of debris from downed bridges and buildings which cluttered the highway for long stretches. In a dense forest west of Greensboro, a slushy mixture of rain water, ash, and mud covered the road for miles. To make matters worse, giant flakes were still raining from the sky in a blizzard of cinders and rain. It was hard to tell whether it was night or day as dust clouds obscured the setting sun and sky. The clock on the dashboard read 17:23. In an hour, maybe less, Shane calculated, they wouldn't be able to see without the aid of night vision devices.

Staff Sergeant McMeen peered through the window of his MHMMV-44 Combat Gun Truck, the second vehicle in the convoy. He sat in the TC's seat, monitoring the radio and keeping lookout for… well, anything. Suddenly, he noticed in his rearview mirror that one of the sturdy trucks was swerving out of control. The erratic movement jolted the sergeant's attention, but his eyes widened in sheer terror as a giant, thirty-foot-tall creature with an enormous maw and long tail crashed out of the woods on three legs. The beast sprinted alongside the HMTV, but McMeen had the impression that the alien being was capable of much greater speeds.

His hands trembling, the sergeant ripped the microphone off the dashboard and shouted into the radio, "Heads up lads! We're under attack!" Hawk heard the announcement, immediately checked his rear-view mirror, and spotted the giant monster with its outsized head, massive arms, and razor sharp teeth slam its entire body into the side of one of the HMTVs. The Hover truck lifted up, its left side hover pods scraping against the ground, until the extraterrestrial let off to prepare for another strike.

The Hover truck had just settled back onto all four air jets when the behemoth sideswiped it again—this time with more force. The truck was first lifted onto its left side and then flipped over, landing on its roof. The unfortunate passengers in the back were thrown from the vehicle, their bodies rolling on the ground until they landed in a ditch. The truck eventually came to a screeching halt as sparks from the steel top sprayed both sides of the vehicle as well as the back end. The front windshield imploded when the cab slammed into the road. Shattered glass cut the driver and the TC to shreds.

Shocked, Dyson signaled the entire convoy to stop, while Hawk jumped out of his seat to assess the situation. Children and grown-ups alike were panicking. "What's going on Shane?!" Emily asked, shaking with fear. The question was repeated by everyone until they fell silent, awestruck by the sheer size of the beast.

"Vehicle down! Vehicle down!" a voice cried out over the radio. Almazan dismounted from the driver's side and aimed his M450C SAW II Squad Automatic Weapon at the monster.

"Get back in," his fellow passengers screamed.

"Ignacio get back in here now! Are you crazy!?" his wife Amanda yelled, and then looked on in disbelief as her husband sprayed the creature with a burst of sabot rounds.

Hawk opened the top of the turret hatch and swung the heavy M3A9 .50 Caliber Rail Gun around, aiming it squarely at the creature. He pulled back on the charging handle which released the rear bolt with a thud and clang. Shane charged the weapon a second time and another round loaded into the magnetized breach. He then pushed the charging handle forward and locked it in place.

In the meantime, Almazan fired a short, three round burst at the extraterrestrial, but missed when it turned and snatched a body out of the ditch, swallowing it in two gulps. Angel told her children to close their eyes as she noticed an arm stuck between the alien's massive teeth. While the monster chomped down on the fleshy bones, bullets bore into its hind end. The third passenger of the overturned HMTV had crawled out of the cab window, rolled into a sitting position, and began firing his own SAW II in short, controlled bursts. The alien's eyes fixed on him as it first heard and then saw its next meal crawling out onto the road.

Several shots rang out from behind the creature and struck it in the side along the rib cage. It flinched in pain, rearing around to locate its attackers. Scanning the convoy, the creature first squatted down and then leapt surprisingly high into the air. With a thundering crunch of concrete and a monstrous roar from its lungs, the ground shook as it landed. The unlucky driver suddenly found himself wedged between the monster's giant, clawed feet. It peered down at his "dinner," puffing forcefully, as men rushed to change firing positions. Undisturbed by the commotion, the beast arched its jaws and bit down on the driver, chomping down with relish and swallowing both halves of the poor man's body. The SAW II stopped chattering ...

Outwardly unperturbed, Hawk took a difficult aim at the back of the creature's head and opened fire with the devastating weapon mounted on his truck. Fifty caliber sabot rounds zipped out of the rail gun with blazing speed and accuracy, while tracers outlined the firing line just a hair high above the alien's skull. Almazan also launched another burst, striking the creature's massive center thigh.

Meanwhile, Staff Sergeant McMeen ordered his men out of the Combat Gun Truck to engage the terrifying creature. On his command, the soldiers opened fire with super-heated, magnesium-tipped lead rounds and shot them into the beast's rear end. Cringing, the monster backed away, stepping on a lifeless body that had been thrown from the doomed truck. The team could hear bones being pulverized under the alien's weight, along with the sound of squishing flesh.

Hawk aimed a bit lower and rippled .50 caliber sabot rounds up the giant's spine and into the back of its skull. A single burning tracer round ricocheted off its thick cranium and spiraled through the air until it disappeared into the clouds above.

Livid, the creature stepped forward, catching its balance and snaking its body towards the heavier weaponry on the attack vehicle. As it readied to charge the lead gun truck, Almazan resumed fire. Eighty rounds rippled off the behemoth's head, tearing skin from bone. Tracers lit up the falling darkness behind the monstrosity, while the sound of sonic booms reverberated through the air.

Then the rounds from the Magnums' powerful cannons ripped through the blizzard of ash like a spiraling tornado. Unfortunately, the five pound slugs missed as the creature leapt onto the roof of an HMTV, its sheer weight pressing the cab into the floor, shattering glass, equipment, and everything else inside. The driver and the TC still fired at the monster from both sides of the vehicle, but dashed to the rear as it tried snapping its giant jaws shut on the TC. Fortunately, it missed.

Undaunted, Hawk fired again, spraying rounds from the bottom of the alien's torso to the top of its ugly head. The .50 caliber rounds tore huge chunks of flesh off its body and severed one of its small arms. Projectiles blasted through the massive skull and exited out the back of its head. Fatally wounded, the extraterrestrial fell over, bouncing off the concrete with several loud thuds as the head and tail smacked onto the highway. Blood splattered and then poured from large bullet wounds, inflicted by the .50 caliber weapon. With its last breath, the creature sighed in an almost human manner, and then expired with a faint wheeze.

Lowering his rifle, Almazan walked right up to the dead alien, staring it in the face. Several other soldiers came up from behind and fired a few more bursts into the monster's carcass. After making sure that it was truly dead, they all reloaded their weapons. Almazan gave strict instructions to move equipment and the injured from the destroyed HMTV onto other vehicles.

Hawk dismounted the gun turret, closed the hatch, and climbed back into his seat. The children were all staring out of the truck's back window—petrified, crying, and scared. Angel tapped Shane on the shoulder, "Hun, is that..?" trembling, she stopped herself short of her own answer.

"Yeah, it was," he sighed. Seeing that the creature was certainly dead, the kids started to gawk at it.

Jacob yelled out, "Wow! A real live alien!" He could hardly believe what was happening. His brother and sisters, after swallowing their dismay, all pointed at the monster, amazed and excited that they were looking at a beast that resembled a dinosaur. Unfortunately, they could also see three severely injured passengers that had been thrown from the HMTV being carried away. They were still alive—a mere three out of twenty, Shane thought grimly.

In the meantime, a discussion had flared up among survivors whether the soldiers had really battled an extraterrestrial or just a wild, earthly creature. Hawk spoke up so that everyone could hear him. "No, it *was* an alien," he stressed. Suddenly, several hundred meters ahead of them, a new flock of otherworldly beings crashed through abandoned homes and trees. Of varying sizes, they moved in a herd and stood on four legs like any grazing animal on Earth. "Herbivores," Hawk thought to himself, "at least they shouldn't be a threat." Angel, Amanda, and the children looked out of the back of the vehicle in complete amazement.

Ten minutes later, Almazan returned. He opened the door to the driver's side and climbed back in. Handing a digital camera to Amanda, he was eager to show her pictures of the monster alien he had just taken. But his wife just slapped him on the back of the head. "Hey, what was that for?" Almazan put his hand on his head, hunching over to avoid another slap.

"Don't ever scare me like that again!" she yelled, visibly angry. After seven years of marriage, Almazan knew better than to argue with her. He also knew that the excuse "It's my job" wouldn't cut it with Amanda.

"Ok! Ok! Just don't hit me again!" he grinned.

Hawk climbed in to the driver's seat and closed the heavy, armored door. He sighed and, after taking a moment, looked over his shoulder at the kids, "So what are we going to call that thing?" Jonathan spoke up immediately, "Gigantisaurus?"

Madison gave him a smug, disgusted look. Obviously, she didn't like it.

"How about Reamer?" Jacob asked. "Why Reamer?" Shane was perplexed. "Well, because if you're not careful, it'll ream you a new one," he explained, almost doubling over laughing.

Almazan laughed too, but Angel looked at him sternly, "Jacob!" Jacob shrugged.

Shane joined the laughter, "Ok, Reamer it is."

It was completely dark now, and the convoy finally continued on the water-clogged road. While the adults whispered amongst themselves, the children kept a watchful eye out for more Reamers. The supposed sight of another Reamer turned out to be bushes or trees every time. Still, occasionally one of them would shout out "I seen one!" putting everyone on edge. Much calmer now, Amanda cycled through the pictures and shared them with Madison and Jon.

With the moon hidden behind thick dust clouds, visibility was limited to a few feet. Vehicles in the convoy closed in on each other until the taillights from the truck in front were just barely visible. The children were quiet by now, while Shane and Almazan discussed how things had turned out differently than they had ever thought possible. "So, no kidding, there I was," Almazan continued, "sitting in church, minding my own business—coloring. And the preacher comes up to me and says, "Do you need saving my child?" And I said "No, but if you have an orange crayon that would be great!""

If it hadn't been for the rumble of the twelve-cylinder, nuclear-powered engine, one could have heard a pin drop. All of a sudden Shane started laughing. It was like Almazan, he thought, to come up with something funny to say out of the blue. As he chuckled, Angel and Amanda joined in as well. But once the laughing faded, it became very quiet. No one even smiled. They were still on the road, and it was snowing ash outside. Fires continually glowed in the distance. People were still dying. And Almazan never attended church.

Shane was particularly withdrawn and spoke hardly a word after the Reamer attack. Deep in thought, he wondered how such an enormous alien creature could have even made it to Earth. Where were the extraterrestrials coming from? They obviously didn't land in space ships. Then he thought of the giant spire that had appeared out of nowhere in downtown Raleigh. Did these beings teleport to Earth? Was it possible that they teleported themselves as well as their planet's technology? Was the spire the teleportation device? Or was something else at work there? Shane didn't know the answers, although he wished he did. A sinking feeling in his gut told him the answers were all of the above.

Slugging along, the convoy turned onto the I-74 corridor junction and proceeded north from there. Off to the west, they could see fires burning from what was left of the city of Winston-Salem. In the blizzard of ash, Shane could hardly make out any buildings, but it was obvious that not many had remained on their foundations. The Bragg contingent was keeping a wary eye on the city when a two-hundred-story building imploded in a massive brume of dust and debris. It was a scary sight. "How many people had been in that building?" was the thought on everyone's mind.

Shane checked the display screen of the Blue Force Tracker II unit on his dashboard. There were no signs of friendlies within fifty miles of the city, but Hawk knew of a few, small farm fields to the north where they could camp out for the night while waiting for Lieutenant General May's NARC convoy to arrive from Atlanta.

About ten minutes north of Winston-Salem, the trek pulled off the highway and onto a tobacco field, breaking through a wooden fence in the process. Shane knew the owner would not mind. He was either dead or had taken refuge somewhere else. The road was only a dozen meters away as the soldiers set up makeshift shelters.

Lieutenant Hawk pulled out two fast-tents stowed in the vehicle's cargo hatch, and Angel and the children all gathered into one. Almazan and Amanda took the other, and almost everyone fell asleep rather quickly. Maddy lay nestled between Shane and her mother. She was still wide awake, although sad and tired. Worried about all those people who had lost their homes, the little girl wondered if they were alright. She tilted her head back and looked at her mother for reassurance. Angel placed a hand over Maddy's head and stroked her long blonde hair. It felt oily, "You need a bath Maddy."

But Maddy just stared at the top of the tent, ignoring her mother, "Mom, do you think Aunt Francis is ok?" Angel didn't know what to tell her daughter and just remained quiet. "Why didn't she want to come with us?" Maddy persisted as she rubbed sand from her drooping eyelids.

Angel sighed, "I dunno baby."

"I hope she's ok," Maddy mumbled, rolled over on her side, and closed her eyes.

Lost in thought, Angel still had Francis on her mind. After putting up for years with her sister's foul moods and off-putting rudeness, she didn't much care anymore if she was alive or dead. Angel had done everything humanly possible for her unhappy sibling: paid her bills, bought her alcohol and junk food, and fulfilled many other unreasonable demands. In return, Francis had never repaid her in kind or even shown an ounce of gratitude. In fact, she was grossly disrespectful towards the entire Hawk family. Just thinking about scenes of past arguments upset Angel. With the world possibly coming to an end, she no longer wanted to waste precious time on mean-spirited people like Francis.

While his wife mulled over family feuds, Shane had trouble sleeping and decided to get up. Angel looked at him, "What's wrong punkin?"

"Nothing. I'll be back in a little bit." He stepped outside with pen and paper and wrote down guard shifts for the forty plus 82nd and Group soldiers under his and Captain Dyson's command. After roughly an hour, as Shane discussed convoy ops and strategies with the captain, gunfire rang out from the perimeter.

Odd screeching from an alien creature and yells from his troops broke the silence of the quiet night. Hawk grabbed his weapon and sprinted to the edge of the camp without his helmet. He watched his men fire at several oddly colored, dog-like critters rushing about some bushes. Each had light grey skin with yellow and orange splotches as well as brown spots along their spines. Their massive musculature resembled that of an oversized bulldog, except that each paw sported a long, razor-sharp talon. The beasts' skulls were covered with plated bone and eight tentacles concealed a beak-like mouth, which Shane only saw when one of them raised its head and bellowed a clarion-like call signaling the hunt.

In no time, one of creature leapt up and dug its claws and two massive talons into the chest of a 82nd soldier. Defending himself with his plasma cannon, the man screamed as the alien wrapped its tentacles around his helmet. Then, with one wrench of its neck, the monster ripped the man's head off his shoulders. Jerking and chewing, it eventually spit it out along with the helmet, both tumbling off into the tall tobacco weeds.

Furious, Hawk aimed his rifle and fired a burst of rounds into the beast's chest. The creature squealed and then fell over dead after one of Shane's well-placed rounds punctured a lung and blew out the bottom of its heart. The alien's talons were still digging into the headless body as it stumbled. They tore large wounds into the corpse, spraying crimson blood into the air.

Staff Sergeant McMeen darted out from his tent, clad in just a black t-shirt and shorts and without his armor. He stopped short after running a few meters, and pointed his M22A3 rifle at one of the critters approaching fast through the field. McMeen opened fire on full automatic, letting the rounds rip through the attacker's body like a hot knife through butter. Fatally injured, it skidded across the blood-soaked grass to its final resting place.

Meanwhile, several squads targeted the four remaining creatures with relentless suppressing fire. One already lay dead as another slashed open the armored vest of one of the 82nd soldiers. The vest now hung from Private Bruzinski's shoulders, but he was able to push a tri-barreled shotgun through the alien's tentacles and right into its beak. Bruzinski pulled the trigger. The tri-barrel blast splattered fragments of skull and brain matter all over its back as the extraterrestrial dropped to the ground.

Agitated, the remaining creatures regrouped, and with a flurry of tentacle gestures, fled the battlefield. Hawk stood next to Bruzinski, who was taking off his useless vest. "These small ones seem much more intelligent than the big one." Bruzinski looked to his lieutenant, "Bastard got my vest sir, tore the damn thing to shreds." He held it up to show Lieutenant Hawk the damage.

"You'll have to find another one Bee. I don't think we have any extras in my truck."

"Roger sir." Bruzinski nodded and walked off, tossing his shredded armor into a campfire.

Some of the soldiers still on the field fired laser beams and tracer rounds into the blackness of night, targeting creatures creeping to the edge of the eastern wood line. They stopped shooting once the aliens had disappeared from the motion trackers built into their helmets. One was spotted, and a volley of laser beams cut across the field. No one could tell though, if they had managed to exterminate it from one hundred and ninety meters away.

Dyson stepped out of his tent and walked around the camp. He found Lieutenant Hawk looking out across the field to the wood line, ever vigilant. "What was that?" he asked, yawning.

"Smaller alien critters, sir," Hawk paused. "Nasty things and these seem smarter." Hawk provided a detailed description of the new adversaries and their behavior.

"They fled?" Dyson asked him.

"Yes sir."

Dyson already had trouble believing in the giant Reamer, but now smaller, more vicious beasts? What was the world coming to? Of course, he didn't doubt Hawk's account, especially after his men were dragging the alien carcasses to the middle of the field.

"Why are my soldiers lugging those things out to the middle of the field? Are they nuts?" Dyson was getting upset.

"I ordered them to, sir. No one knows for sure how keen the aliens' sense of smell is. Whether it's dull or not is still beyond us, but if it's acute then I don't want those other ones to come sniffing for the meat of their dead. Or worse, one of the bigger ones detecting another meal and finding it in our camp." Hawk crossed his arms as one of the teams dropped the last dead beast at the center of the field and then sprinted like track athletes to the safety of the perimeter.

Dyson put some thought into his next command. "Double the perimeter guard tonight," he ordered grimly. "If any more than four of them things come out of those woods, I want the whole camp up. If anything bigger appears, looking for an appetizer, I want the Magnums on standby and ready to send it back to whatever hell it came from."

"Yes Sir!" Hawk understood the order, but resented Dyson's tone of voice. "Standby" meant a long watch for the men in the cramped confines of the Battle Suits, and Hawk did not relish passing on that directive. The Magnum pilots hadn't had a breath of fresh air, since this nightmare had begun.

Hawk stared off into the night, just barely able to see the tree line one hundred and ninety meters away. Dyson returned to his shelter. Acting on a hunch, Shane retrieved his helmet and camera from his tent. He switched the helmet's visor view from normal to night vision mode and suddenly made out movement in the tree line.

Concerned, Shane motioned two other soldiers, and together they crept to the spot where the men had dropped the cadavers of the dead aliens just half an hour earlier. Hawk took pictures of each one, and quickly scanned the tree line, but discovered no targets. When he was finished, Shane and the two soldiers strode quickly back to camp.

Looking back one final time, he paused. Good, Shane thought with satisfaction, they had instilled the fear of man into the first group of aliens. As long as they kept up their guard, the creatures would probably not attack again—or so he hoped.

Back at his tent, Shane noticed that his entire family had huddled up under a blanket. "It's ok guys, it's safe now," he assured them.

"What was it?" Emily poked her head out.

"Here," he showed her the images of the dead extraterrestrials. Madison sat up as well and looked at the camera screen.

"Gotta name them," he told her and she gasped, ducking back under the cover of the comforter.

"Squiddies," Madison squeaked.

Shane looked back at the camera screen, smiling, "Squiddies it is!"

Chapter Three: The Road of No Return

On The Third Day,

Late the next morning some people still stirred in their sleep while others were waking up. Overnight ash and snow had fallen heavily and blanketed the farm field with the North Carolina soldiers and survivors.

Lieutenant Hawk crawled out of his tent, fully dressed in his standard digital utility uniform and combat tactical vest and gear. He had also taken his Firehawk Battle Suit, securing it in the hidden compartments of the gun truck. Wary of another ambush by aliens, he then scanned the tree line with a set of binoculars. When he didn't see any movement, Shane put them back in the truck and grabbed a case of MREs, handing them out to his family. The children each snatched a package, while he and Angel shared one.

"I gotta admit," Shane munched, "I've always hated Jambalaya." Angel ignored him and stole his crackers and peanut butter packs. She smiled for the first time in two days. "Oh that's messed up," Shane joked as he tried to reach for them. When his wife hid them, hands behind her back, he laughed and tickled her sides. Angel giggled and squirmed, trying not to drop the packages.

"Ahhh! Quit!" she laughed harder. The kids looked on as though their parents had gone crazy.

Shortly afterwards, Shane stopped tickling and also gave up smiling. But not for long! When he peeked inside the MRE package, his eyes got wide with excitement as he pulled out a package of "chocolaty goodness"—Army slang for candy-coated chocolate disks.

As soon as Angel spotted the bright orange package, she tried to grab them with her free hand, but Shane held up his arm, away from her reach. She glared at him in mock outrage. "Awww, fine," Shane gave in, handed her the candy, and pouted.

Angel smiled, opened the package of chocolate candies, and offered him one. Shane opened his mouth and she graciously placed one piece on his tongue. He pressed his lips together and licked the tip of her finger with the tip of his tongue. "Oh gross!" she pulled her finger away and wiped it on his shoulder. Shane smiled and chewed the candy.

An hour after they finished their morning breakfast Shane and Almazan were sharing a cigarette next to the gun truck. Suddenly someone yelled across the perimeter, "Incoming!" Hawk and Almazan picked up their weapons and ran to the eastern camp edge. Like a pack of wolves, sixteen Squiddies were about to dash across the field. Group and 82nd troops immediately started firing on the Squiddies as they rushed towards them. Four Squiddies went down after taking a barrage of gunfire from the men on the line.

Hawk, McMeen, Bruzinski, and Almazan took up positions behind an MHMMV-44 and launched bursts of rounds at one of the approaching aliens. Almazan's bullets struck the creature in the head and it dropped dead in the field. McMeen and Bruzinski's shots struck and brought down another.

Two Squiddies broke the perimeter and jumped on two 43rd Group soldiers. Their buddies retaliated by blasting the two beasts with laser beams and plasma bolts. The plasma balls exploded, knocking down the critters, and lighting them afire. Flames quickly engulfed the first creature, but also landed on the soldier, setting his uniform ablaze. As the critter fell over and died, the soldier screamed. The plasma fire was burning his flesh, but he extinguished it by rolling in the ash-mixed snow.

Sadly, the other soldier wasn't so fortunate. The laser beams that had singed the Squiddie only infuriated it further, and it gouged giant wounds into the man with its talons, ripping out his intestines and other vital organs with its front claws. The young soldier screamed in agony and finally choked on his own blood.

Alarmed, Captain Dyson ran out of his tent and jumped on the hood of one of the Combat

Gun Trucks. One of the Squiddies followed him, digging its talons into the hood. The Squiddie then struck out with its tentacles and snatched Dyson's laser pistol out of his hand. The captain watched horrified as the alien creature placed the pistol in its beak and crushed it with one powerful chomp. Dyson grabbed his other laser gun, jammed the barrel down the critter's throat, and pulled the trigger. Fatally wounded, it released his arm, slipped off the truck, and crashed onto the blanket of ash with a heavy thud.

Losing no time, Dyson climbed into the truck's turret with the RC-40 Rocket Cannon. He swung the weapon around and obliterated a Squiddie charging towards the tents with a rocket. The impact of the explosion catapulted the body off the ground, while shrapnel blew giant holes into the beast's corpse.

With the humans distracted, six other Squiddies were sneaking up behind the encampment. They were using the main pack to distract the humans so that the elders could flank their positions. Roaring triumphantly, they roared through the camp, feeling success within their facial tentacles.

They had rejoiced too soon. Followed by a terrible thunder, two of the six vaporized in the blink of an eye. A third exploded into pink mist and flesh confetti as another powerful explosion rocked the air. Three Magnum Battle Suits held their ground facing the road, MARG-3 Cannons drawn, while loading the next volley of powerful Glasser rounds. Fearing for their lives, the elder Squiddies banked off to the right, away from the terrible, armor-clad humans with their loud, thundering boom sticks. But the Magnums chased them relentlessly and the remaining Squiddies soon evaporated as well.

More than half of the aliens lay dead by now, while the remaining ones were so afraid of the lethal missiles that they darted back to the tree line. Four more succumbed to weapons fire or were reduced to a cloud of goop by the Magnums' cannons.

With the attack over, the men reverently buried the dead soldier. He was just a twenty-year-old kid straight out of the Q-Course. The chaplain's assistant said a prayer for him, but departed swiftly for his tent, overcome by grief. Hardly anyone uttered a word for the next few minutes.

The following half of the day passed in either silence or subdued whispers until the Squiddies returned for a final assault. This time, they attacked in full force, en masse through the tree line. But the soldiers were ready and blasted their weapons as the aliens popped their heads out of trees and bushes. Snipers slaughtered two from a distance; two more were brought down before they made it even halfway across the field. A plasma grenade exploded and killed the fifth. As the rest of the Squiddies approached mid-field, ten claymores went off in two lines of five explosions, destroying the majority of the beasts. Staff Sergeant McMeen dropped the triggers of the M28A3 Claymore II Mines in his hands and roared obscenities at the dead aliens, "Aye! Eat dat you wee beasties!"

One very courageous 82nd soldier, Specialist Lock, went toe to talon with the last Squiddie that broke the line. The critter leapt at the young specialist, but was caught by surprise when the human ducked and rolled underneath before it hit the ground. Lock then jumped up and landed squarely on the Squiddie's back. The twenty-three-year-old Texas native held on tightly as the beast jerked and bucked to throw off its adversary.

Quick-thinking, Lock reached for his vibro knife and thrust the blade into the extraterrestrial's neck. The Squiddie lurched forward and Lock lost his grip. He fell off and rolled to the ground, knife still in hand. Flinching at the pain in its neck, the alien reared up to snap its beak down on Lock's head. But Lock darted towards the Squiddie just then, jamming his blade through its jaw and into the bottom of its brain. Writhing in pain, the critter staggered forward, its large, right rear talon digging deep into Lock's thigh. He screamed in pain as his attacker toppled over and twitched in its death throes.

"Bastard!" Lock yelled out as pain shot up his leg. The Squiddie had stopped moving and Lock backed away, clutching his wounded thigh and stumbling to his feet. Bruzinski, Downes, and McMeen rushed over to help him. After placing a tourniquet two inches above the wound, McMeen carried him to the medic's tent. "Hang on lad, you're gonna be okay," McMeen reassured his brave soldier.

Inside the tent, Bruzinski and Downes carefully placed him on a field stretcher and then left to find the medic. McMeen stayed with the injured Lock, praising him, "Good job out there kid, but don't ever do that again."

Lock proclaimed proudly, "I killed it Sergeant."

"I know and you almost got yerself killed in the process. Don't e'er do dat again. That's an order," McMeen pointed a finger at him.

"Roger Sergeant, it won't happen again."

"Good, now whe'e's that damn medic?" McMeen looked to the entrance of the tent. "Be right back." After he had left, Lock leaned his head back on a pillow. He smiled, brimming with confidence because he had personally exterminated an alien creature.

Twilight came quickly. Hopeful that the Squiddie threat had been dealt with for now, some of the soldiers felt a little more relaxed and sat around small campfires, weapons at hand. Most, however, were still on edge and regularly scanned the perimeter, ready to deal with whatever lurked in the woods. Medics tended to the wounded, and Captain Dyson paid Specialist Lock a visit. Staff Sergeant McMeen was with the captain, and together they presented the injured specialist with a Purple Heart medal.

"Congratulations Specialist, your bravery and courage in dealing with the Squiddie threat was outstanding. How's the leg?" Dyson asked him as if he pretended to care.

"Good sir, nanobots are doin' their duty, should be healed up in another few minutes," Lock replied. He had regained his color, and appeared ready for another fight.

"Good to hear," Dyson mumbled perfunctorily and walked out.

Staff Sergeant McMeen waited for Dyson to be out of earshot until he spoke up. "That guy didn't give two hoots about what you did today," he griped, "I had a spat with that cake eatin' clown for an hour before he finally agreed to award you with those."

Lock shook his head, "What a jerk, stupid officers…," he sat back on his cot. "Wait, what do you mean by "those"?"

"'Ere," McMeen tossed Lock a Velcro patch. "Better get used to wearing stripes Corporal.

We need leadership in the field now." Lock was speechless. He had long hoped for a promotion to corporal. Although the specialist rank was the same pay grade, a corporal carried out extra duties that came with a Junior Non-Commissioned Officer.

Lock welcomed the additional responsibility and affirmed happily, "Doesn't come with extra pay, but I'll take it."

McMeen turned to walk out, but then paused and said, "I hate officers too; thankfully there are only two of them here."

"I dunno...that Hawk guy seems to be an all right fella." Lock remembered Lieutenant Hawk engaging in battles with the Reamer and pulling his weight during numerous rescue missions in Fayetteville. Just then the medic came in to examine his leg and to undo the bandage wrapped around his thigh. The wound was healing nicely with a stitch and a dose of nanobots, but the skin was still flush with burst capillaries.

Nanobots are microscopic machines that resembled spiders and each one was about the size of a red blood cell. Their purpose was to quickly repair tissue and blood vessel damage. They served a variety of other purposes too. They could be programmed to repair organ, bone, and even lung damage. However, they could not be used to repair mutated cells such as cancer.

"Looks like you're healing up just fine Specialist," the young, eighteen-year-old female medic assured him as she faced him with a smile. "It's Corporal now," Lock grinned from ear to ear. She caught herself blushing and quickly turned to some boxes of medical supplies on a small field table. As the nurse fidgeted with compresses and gauze, Lock shot McMeen a meaningful look.

The sergeant rolled his eyes and shook his head laughing, "Oiy, troopers these days…" Before McMeen left, he told the nurse, "Take care o' him sweets; I think his head is hurting." Lock could hear his heavy footsteps crunching through the ash before receding slowly.

Meanwhile the nurse took another look at her patient who had turned beet red while he interlocked his fingers behind his head. Playfully, she walked over to him and sat on the side of the cot. "Where does it hurt?" she asked in a serious tone and placed her fingers on his temples, mock-examining him. By now, Lock was beaming, yet still afraid to meet her gaze. The cute medic was less shy, smiled gingerly at him, and eventually removed her patrol cap to Lock's great delight. She pressed her lips against his temple and kissed away the pain. Lock smiled, and then pointed a finger on his cheek. So she kissed his cheek. Then he pointed at his lips and she kissed his lips. He then pointed at his heart and she kissed his chest. He then pointed between his legs, and moments later, his eyes rolled into the back of his head.

As night fell, Lieutenant Hawk patrolled the perimeter. Snow was falling a little heavier than the evening before, and he could barely make out the heap of dead Squiddie carcasses in the center of the field. Men sat around small campfires, but mostly kept to themselves. After taking a deep breath, Hawk realized just how cold it really was. He was shaking, despite wearing polypros under his uniform.

As he passed the medical tent, Shane heard a slight commotion inside. It didn't take a rocket scientist to figure out what was going on in there. Normally, he would have barged in and taken the two to task, but circumstances were far from normal now. Billions were dead and many more were dying. The military was in shambles, and nobody knew if a system of government was still in place. He therefore let the incident go unpunished. Instead, Shane continued his walk around the camp, concluding that it could be the last time for either of them...or any of them.

Suddenly, something caught his attention on the eastern side of the tree line. At first, Shane froze in place and didn't move a muscle, but then he started to gasp, shaking nervously. The cold only added to the problem. He slowly turned his head and through the blizzard of ash barely made out something large—really large—moving around the center of the field near the carcasses.

Concerned about his family, Shane overcame his fear, and quietly, carefully, placing one step in front of the other, moved from tent to tent, campfire to campfire, ordering every man, woman, and child not to make a sound and to put out the lights and fires.

He crept back into his shelter and told Angel to keep the kids as quiet as she could. Maddy was restless though, bored of being cooped up inside all day. "What is it?" Angel inquired with a whisper.

"Another alien," Shane whispered back. "A Squiddie?" Madison asked loudly. Emily and Jacob shushed her, while Jonathan's eyes widened and his lips tightened.

Shane grabbed his helmet, opened the tent flap, and activated his visor's night vision. The visor dipped everything into a world of green, but he could see much better and clearer now than with mere eyesight. On the other hand, Shane's precision view only made matters worse: no longer hidden in the dark, he observed a large, armored alien towering in the middle of the field.

This one wasn't like the alien creatures he had dealt with in the last couple of days, although he had seen it before. Twice the size of a human in a Firehawk Battle Suit, the extraterrestrial carried a large shield on one arm, while a huge, particle beam cannon was mounted to the forearm of the other.

Shane did not move as he watched the monster clamp down on a Squiddie carcass, picking it up with its giant, clawed hand. "**What are these doing here?!**" it growled before tossing it to the side.

Shane couldn't figure out how the alien had learned to speak English, but he watched in awe as it sifted through the other corpses. Throughout the camp no one dared to stir as they listened to the monster's nocturnal rumblings, unable to tell how far away or what it was. They followed their lieutenant's order, and didn't move a muscle or make a sound.

Angel sensed that something very dangerous was lurking out there, and held onto Madison in her lap. Maddy didn't want to be held though and squirmed in her mother's embrace. Afraid and frustrated, Angel tightened her arms around her daughter, hoping that she would stop wiggling. But her grip was too tight and Maddy blurted out, "Mommy, your arms are hurting me!"

The other children in the tent froze, Angel froze, and Madison stopped fidgeting. They all looked at the tent's canvas roof, straining to see if anything alien was approaching. But there was nothing but an eerie, creepy silence that petrified them. Shane had heard Madison as well and so did half the camp. If they could, surely that monster did too.

Apprehensive with fright, Shane saw the colossus snap its head in the direction of the faint noise. By now, Shane wasn't quivering—he was trembling and sweating profusely. The extraterrestrial's head arched back as it readied its beam cannon and stomped towards the camp. No one dared to breathe.

The monster was so heavy that the ground trembled with every thud. The small tent encampment had fallen deathly quiet as the alien stared at the strange objects surrounding it, searching for the source of the noise. Meanwhile, Shane took a second to guess the strange being's height, measuring it from the ground to the top of the head. Excluding the horn-like metal plates, it stood over fourteen feet tall. Gigantic in build, the beast must have weighed more than a ton.

But reality soon caught up with Shane as the colossus spotted the tent with Shane's family inside. Lowering its head, the alien snaked its featureless face towards the canvas. Shane began to raise his rifle, slowly and carefully moving the selector switch from safe to semi to burst to full auto. Each click of his weapon scared him, certain that the behemoth would hear it. Then he calmly aimed his rifle at the giant's head, every nerve in his body tensing up.

Meanwhile, Angel and her children trembled pale faced as they heard the alien's metal armor rattle only a few inches away from the tent roof. Tears ran down Madison and Angel's cheeks as they shuddered, huddled up against each other. Jake and Jon sat buried with their heads between their knees, while Emily remained upright and cross-legged, looking around at the others, wondering if she was more scared than they were or if they were more scared than she was.

After a moment, which seemed like an eternity, the monster swung its head into the air, stretching its neck to full length. Shane noted a long scar running from its cheek through the beast's eye to the eyebrow. After drawing itself up to its full height, the alien let out an unsatisfied growl which was followed by a thrice repeated, ear-piercing bark. During the last bark, the boosters on its back sprang to life. The enormous extraterrestrial, its mighty and ungodly roar finally ebbing, suddenly jumped hundreds of meters into the air and with one mighty burst from its boosters, disappeared into the clouds with tremendous speed. Moments later, snow and ash swirled around in fierce gusts. The canvas of Hawk's tent flapped violently in the wind rush, and Angel and her children covered their heads.

Moments later, the tent door flipped open and Angel and the kids jumped up, gasping. But it was only Shane who gingerly stepped inside and took off his helmet. Bone tired, he first knelt beside his wife and then looked at Maddy and the other children. "Is everyone all right?"

Angel nodded absentmindedly. Her nerves couldn't take any more tonight and she just sniffled and sobbed. The children let out sighs of relief, while Shane simply sat back, hugging his wife. "What was that thing Shane?" Angel still trembled.

"Another alien, a powerful one. It was the first one I encountered and fought with. It was the exact same one," he explained with a sigh.

"What was it doing?" Emily shivered.

"I don't know. It was looking for something, but I don't know what."

It was the morning of December 24, and nobody was celebrating. Instead, many of the soldiers and survivors clustered around the chaplain's assistant. Shane wasn't particularly religious, but he joined his family in prayer. Sergeant Levi Baal spoke softly, praying for God's protection for all of them and asking for forgiveness for their sins.

Afterwards, he recited a passage from the biblical book of Revelation 16:17 to 16:21, "Then the seventh angel poured out his bowl upon the air, and a loud voice came out of the temple of the throne, saying "It is done." And there were flashes of lightning and sounds and peals of thunder; and there was a great earthquake, such as there had not been since man came to be upon the Earth, so great an earthquake was it, and so mighty."

He continued, "The great city was split into three parts, and the cities of the nations fell. Babylon the great was remembered before God, to give her the cup of the wine of His fierce wrath." His voice rising dramatically, the sergeant intoned, "And every island fled away, and the mountains were not found. And huge hailstones, about one hundred pounds each, came down upon from heaven upon men; and men blasphemed God because of the plague of the hail, because its plague was extremely severe." Shane ignored the rest of the passage, agonizing instead how they would survive this nightmare.

After prayers concluded, most of the survivors started to cook meat over a large campfire. They had gutted the Squiddie carcasses and were looking forward to the meal. There were some, however, who remained wary of what was being cooked. They refused to eat the alien meat, while their compatriots cheerfully demanded seconds. The latter group claimed that with a little Tabasco sauce from MRE packs, their dinner was just like a chewy chicken.

Night came again and there was still no communication with Lieutenant General May's convoy out of Atlanta. Shane sat alone in his truck, monitoring the radio and the Blue Force Tracker 2.

Frowning, he pushed a button on the display screen in front of him. The device was a satellite tracking unit designed to locate and pinpoint the exact locations of friendly forces in a fifty-mile radius from whatever vehicle was accessing the system. He detected the blue icons from his convoy and green icons from another NARC unit some five miles north of them. "They have to be the other NARC forces we're supposed to rendezvous with," Hawk thought anxiously.

Shane scrambled out of the truck and took a brisk walk to Captain Dyson's tent. Inside, he found the good captain reading Tolstoy's, "War and Peace" as if it was just any other winter evening. "Sir, I'm tracking a NARC convoy just north of our position," Hawk reported excitedly.

Dyson looked up from his book, "Good, Lieutenant, pack everything up, we're leaving."

Within thirty minutes, the Bragg contingent was ready to move again. Everyone was inside their vehicles, engines churning. On the radio, Dyson called out to the NARC forces heading towards them as his trek rolled out from their campsite.

A female voice came in over the radio, "Devil Six, this is Alpha One, glad to see you guys finally made it. We were about to presume you were lost."

"That's a negative Alpha One; we ran into some trouble along the way and lost some of our elements. I lost some good men along the way," Dyson replied.

"I'm sorry to hear that Devil Six, what's the total headcount of your convoy, over?" she asked.

"One hundred three, Alpha One, forty-nine military, forty-nine civilians. Five injured, over."

"Roger, I copy forty-nine military, forty-nine civilians, five injured, over." she repeated.

"Roger Alpha One, good copy. Be at your location in ten mikes, Devil Six out." The radio fell silent.

Twelve minutes later, the convoy passed a series of road flares until they came within a few feet of a robot sentry standing guard outside the perimeter of the Atlanta National Guard forces. The robot was one of the large, thirty-foot-tall Armadillo Combat Robots. Fog lamps mounted on its shoulders lit up every flake of ash and snow falling from the sky. It was as blinding as the sun.

Almazan stopped his vehicle between two gun trucks parked on both sides of the highway. Four NARC soldiers and one officer stood talking between the two MHMMV-44s defending the small checkpoint. The short officer approached the driver side door and Almazan lowered the heavy, reinforced window.

The officer was a three-star general. In fact, it was Lieutenant General Michael May himself. He was forty-four years old, stood at five foot three inches, and was stocky for his size. He climbed onto the support step of the vehicle, holding onto the edge of the window. "Good to see you guys made it. I'm Lieutenant General May, pull your convoy inside the perimeter and park it," he ordered.

"Yes sir," Lieutenant Hawk acknowledged, and moved the truck over.

Shane and Almazan counted three NARC APC-56 Armored Personnel Carriers, eight MHMMV-44s, and MHMMV-44T Combat Gun Trucks forming the Atlanta Guard's camp boundary. They also noticed thirteen Magnum and eighteen Valkyrie Battle Suits, along with fifteen hover buses in the middle of the perimeter.

Almazan parked alongside one of the buses, and the rest of the convoy followed suit. They felt safe now. Almazan turned the engine off, while Hawk shut off all equipment except for the radio, which he left on just in case they received the call to roll out.

Tired, Almazan turned and looked in the back of the truck. All of the children slumbered in their seats, leaning against each other. None of them moved. Angel was nodding off fast;

Amanda had already passed out. Hawk smiled under his helmet, comforted by knowing that they were among friends now. At a loss for words after the tumultuous events of the last few days, Almazan and Hawk just looked at each other. Shane finally told the sergeant, "Get some sleep, we got a long day ahead of us tomorrow."

Almazan didn't waste any time, for he was exhausted as well. He leaned back in his seat and was fast asleep in no time. Hawk stayed awake for a little while longer and eventually dozed off with his head against the corner of the door. He hadn't gotten any rest during the last couple of nights and was amazed that anyone did.

Christmas morning came and went. Lieutenant Hawk found himself standing at attention in front of soldiers and a few civilians in the middle of the highway. Lieutenant General May was next to him and about to speak.

"In these trying times, there has been a lack of good leadership," the general started. "Lieutenant Hawk has demonstrated his outstanding leadership abilities time and again by ensuring the survival of our brothers and sisters from Fort Bragg, North Carolina. He has valiantly faced death and mustered the courage and the will to save his fellow comrades and those civilians we have all sworn to serve and protect. For his achievements, Lieutenant Hawk deserves more than a simple medal," he continued. "I hope that his example will be imitated by many of you, and that those who learn from him will lead our people on this desperate journey of survival for years and years to come. I hereby promote Second Lieutenant Shane Hawk to the rank of First Lieutenant," he finished. "Congratulations First Lieutenant Hawk!" May patted Shane on the shoulder and started clapping. The other soldiers joined in, while Angel and the children cheered for Shane in the back of the crowd.

General May reached for Hawk's collar and replaced the magnetic butter bar rank patch of a Second Lieutenant with the black-colored bar of the First Lieutenant. Upon finishing, he snapped him a crisp and respectful salute which Shane returned. He then shook Lieutenant Hawk's hand and walked away from the crowd, followed by a few of his officers and guards.

Captain Dyson was the first to congratulate Shane. They shook hands and Dyson patted him on the back, joking, "You can thank me for this some other time." Hawk didn't reply, but just nodded as Captain Dyson walked off. Then his comrades from the 82nd and his family crowded around to congratulate him and shake his hand. Afterwards, everyone retreated into the safety of their vehicles. Angel and the children were the only ones left. The kids didn't say much, but Angel smiled, gave him a big hug, and whispered congratulations in his ear.

She also kissed his cheek and told him, "I love you."

"I love you too, baby," Shane responded.

Still frightened, the children were eager to return to the inside of the truck. They worried about Reamers and Squiddies coming out of the woods to eat everyone alive. "All right, let's get back in the truck then," Shane agreed. "We've got a long day ahead of us." While Emily and her siblings piled into the vehicle from both sides, Shane and Angel walked back leisurely, holding hands. "We'll be leading this whole convoy north," he informed her. "So at least we'll be up front again."

Chapter Four: Forever Unresting

On The Fifth Day,

The convoy approached North Carolina's Pilot Mountain. The Big Pinnacle, its tree-covered, dome-shaped peak, loomed like a signpost as the mile-long trek followed the highway north to the Virginia state line. Nobody knew they were being watched. Up on the summit, a single red eye glared down at the human procession trudging along the road through ash and snow. The alien, much like the one Lieutenant Hawk had battled in Raleigh, stood atop of the mountain, methodically scanning the passing vehicles filled with earthlings.

His name was Havok and he was a mechanical extraterrestrial whose helmet and armor were unlike Thyrion's. For example, a long particle beam cannon had been grafted onto his left elbow joint which was vastly different from the other aliens' weapons.

As Havok watched intently, Thyrion and three fellow monsters landed—not as gracefully as one would think—next to the mechanical beast. "**Report!**" Thyrion bellowed gruffly. "Lord Thyrion, the human convoy is slithering its way along that grey trail to the north. I've scouted the mountains ahead; there will be plenty of places to ambush them." "**Good work Havok. I**

want to know if the human that scarred me is among them," Thyrion growled and pounded his right arm on his massive shield.

Havok's single eye was designed for long range sniping and scouting. It could zoom in on various vehicles in the Bragg convoy, but also shift picture spectrums. As he scrutinized each truck, the eye flipped from night vision to colored, from thermal to x-ray, and back to color again.

"The one you seek is in the lead vehicle, along with four human females of different types and three additional males, one of them a warrior as well," Havok summarized. The scar on Thyrion's right eye seemed to intensify his glare as he swiftly focused in on the vanguard truck. He stared through its passenger window and inspected a young girl child. Thyrion noticed something peculiar about this small earthling: a strange but brilliant white aura surrounded Madison. Intrigued, he decided to bide his time. When the humans stopped to rest, Thyrion decided, he would move in to investigate.

It was a long drive, but eventually the survivors made it into the mountains of Virginia. Angel looked back over the plains of North Carolina as the convoy struggled up the winding mountain road. She shed a tear, knowing that all she loved and cherished was gone forever.

She would never see home again as she had once known it.

May's expedition slugged along as they followed the highway for another nine miles, stopping once at an abandoned convenience store to pick up food, supplies, and other necessities. It took three hours to reach the first large town, Hillsville, along I-77. Its name was painted over on every sign and replaced with "Hellsville" in red spray paint.

May ordered several units to search for survivors and tasked Lieutenant Hawk with checking on the only high school in town. It was three miles away to the east, hidden from the highway behind a series of jagged hills. Almazan drove along the ash and snow-covered road through a dense, wooded area until they spotted the school up on a slope. No vehicles remained in the parking lot, but all the buildings' windows had been smashed in, the football stadium bleachers destroyed. The goal posts were lying about uprooted, and scoreboard pieces littered the field.

Almazan pulled up to the entrance. The playground off to the left sported a set of swings, jungle gym, sandbox, and small yard for kickball. The chains on the swing sets swung gently in the cold breeze and the chains creaked. Almazan and Hawk both dismounted the vehicle. Eager to get out as well, Emily asked her step-father, "Shane, I want to go in too."

Shane looked at her mother, and when Angel didn't say a word, he gestured her to come with them. Happily, she unbuckled herself and opened the door of the truck. "The rest of you stay here," he told them sternly.

Meanwhile, Madison was eyeing the playground. "Mommy can I go play on the swings?" she pleaded with her mother sitting in front of her.

But Angel firmly shook her head, "Sorry punkin, we're not staying here for very long."

"But Mom?" Madison insisted. "Pweeeze?"

"No Maddy," Angel replied with a sigh while Madison pouted and crossed her arms over her belly.

Almazan, Hawk, and Emily walked up to the front of the school, pausing to wonder if anyone was still inside. Almazan pulled a door open, and as they entered, the swings in the playground stopped moving. Together, they wandered down a hallway. Paper, pencils, pens, and books were scattered about in a total mess. Lockers lining both sides of the hallway were also in disarray. Some had been broken open, others were locked up with some kid's stuff still inside.

All of a sudden, a strong gust of wind blew towards the building and jostled the truck. Angel, Amanda, and the children began to shiver when the school's front door began to swing open, moved by a seemingly invisible hand. Inside the hallways, pieces of paper fluttered around as the eerie wind rush blew through the corridors. Confused, Emily watched the front door slam shut, while Hawk and Almazan stared in disbelief as the papers settled back onto the floor, forming perfect piles. Almazan eventually shrugged, "Just the wind."

In the truck, Angel anxiously watched the school entrance, "I got a bad feeling about this place," she muttered.

By now Emily was very frightened, but Hawk continued down the hall. He opened the first classroom door on the right and looked inside. It was a biology lab with jars of preserved creatures on back shelves and dozens of broken microscopes on the center tables and the floor.

Meanwhile, Emily pulled a pink and blue backpack from one of the open wall lockers. It only contained a few pens and pencils, a small notebook, and a folded piece of paper. It was a love note from one classmate to another, and after she had finished reading it, Emily reverently folded it back up and put it back in the locker. She closed it, forcing back tears.

Emily then joined her step-father and noticed a biology book still on the counter along the wall. Interested, she moved past Shane and studied its contents for a moment. It was quite new, with only a few creases and dents on the hardback cover. She picked it up and stuffed it into the pink and blue backpack that she now carried. "Good idea Emily," Shane nodded with a smile.

In the meantime, Almazan had entered another classroom just off to the left side of the hallway. It was a little further away from Lieutenant Hawk and Emily, and he noted that all the schoolrooms down this particular corridor were offset from each other. He went inside and noticed math equations on the chalk board. Several geometry and algebra study books laid strewn about the floor, along with the usual mix of paper and other trash. But no one was inside, and he turned around as Hawk and Emily walked up to him.

"Anything?" Hawk asked.

"Nah, just an empty room," the sergeant reported.

Emily inquired, "Did you see any text books in there?"

Almazan noticed the slightly heavier pink and blue backpack, "Yeah, I think I saw an algebra and a geometry book in there. He really had not paid too much attention to the garbage on the floor.

"Cool!" Emily smiled and went inside. She searched around for a moment until she spotted both textbooks and placed them in her backpack. Almazan didn't understand why anyone would spend their time on math and gave Shane and Emily a quizzical look.

"Why do you want those?" he wondered as she came out of the classroom.

"Because," she replied primly, "school is still important, and the more we gather now, the more we'll have to work with to teach future generations." She smiled broadly.

Almazan nodded thoughtfully, the corners of his lips arched downward and his eyebrows raised. "Smart kid," he told the lieutenant. Hawk shrugged with a grin. "I hated high school," Almazan continued with a chuckle, "If we rebuild society we should leave school out."

But Emily stuck up her nose and walked away from him, "Hmmph! Jerk." Almazan just laughed, with Shane joining in. After the trio left the classroom the math equations on the chalkboard changed to some words, "DIE WITH US!"

The unlikely trio then searched three other classrooms in the same hallway. Emily found a textbook on American history spanning Christopher Columbus's discovery of the Americas in 1492 to the enacting of the North American Allegiance in 2057. As they neared the end of the corridor, they noticed that it branched off into a left and right. "Let's split up. Emily and I will go right; you take the left, Sergeant," Hawk suggested.

"Ok," Emily agreed.

"Too easy," Almazan nodded, "I got this."

Emily stopped the sergeant before he turned to the left. "Hey, if you find any other text books…"

He interrupted her, "I gotch'a, I'll pick 'em up for ya. I'm telling you, I got this!" He grinned and slapped his hands on his chest with a bravado that was only his. She stuck her tongue out at him, and then turned right with Hawk.

Soon after, Sergeant Almazan checked each classroom on both sides of the hall. He found two schoolbooks for Emily—one on English literature as well as an Introduction to Spanish. As he opened the door to the third classroom, a mysterious wind rushed at him, and he caught a glimpse of someone standing in front of the chalkboard. But when Almazan took a second look after the wind had died down, there was no one there. Instead, he noticed a single word up on the chalkboard where he thought he'd seen the shadowy figure. It was written in Spanish.

Almazan nervously thumbed through the Spanish textbook until he found the word which translated into "DEATH." Unsettled, he rummaged through the room some more. He couldn't hear himself think, because his heart was pounding rapidly in his chest. On each desk, stacks of books and loose paper piled high to the ceiling. He found it strange, but thought it even stranger when another word suddenly emerged on the slick, black surface of the chalkboard. Again, he couldn't make sense of it, because it was in Spanish. Even though Almazan was of Mexican heritage and had grown up in Texas, he couldn't read, write, or speak a lick of that language.

"Huh…," he mumbled and left the classroom. As Almazan turned the corner, the ghostly figure of the female in a white dress reappeared in front of the chalkboard. She swung her wraithlike head towards the door as he walked out.

Shane and Emily went into three other schoolrooms, and she discovered a text book on earth science to add to her collection. As they explored the hallway a bit further, it veered to the left. After rounding a corner, they arrived at a set of double doors. Blood and bits of flesh covered the windows in a ghoulish display of horror. Deathly pale, Emily backed away and vomited in a trash can. Shane, equally alarmed, shouted, "Emily, go back to the truck. I don't want you to see this." The teenager nodded weakly and immediately turned to leave.

She hurried down the corridor, nearly running into a wall locker. Further ahead, Emily could already see the entrance and the waiting truck. But as she bee lined for the doors, the hairs on the back of her neck suddenly stood up. Emily stopped in her tracks as sheets of loose paper floated towards her feet. Seconds later, a white vapor cloud drifted out of the first classroom at the end of the hall. Emily's eyes widened in sheer terror. Trembling violently, she wanted to run and scream, but couldn't utter a word or move her feet.

The vapor cloud slowly morphed into a ghostly white female with long, straight, platinum-colored hair and sunken white eyes without pupils. Wafting across the hallway, the ghost eventually paused and then turned its head to face the petrified Emily. Its eyes turned glowing white and then returned to their pale shade. Rotating freely in the air, the specter swirled in the direction of the double front doors. Moments later, it withdrew into its vaporized cloud form and slipped away through the narrow gap at the doors' bottom.

Emily still stood there frozen, but suddenly jumped up screaming as she felt a hand on her shoulder. "Hey kid," Almazan had come up behind her. "Whoa, don't be so jumpy, it's just me." But Emily just cried with relief. She had never been so happy to see another human being and hugged the sergeant tightly. "Hey what's the matter? Where's the Lieutenant?" Emily still could not say a word. She sobbed, holding him close, and he could feel her trembling.

Angel had closed her eyes and was leaning her head on the headrest of her seat. Suddenly Jacob shouted, "Oh my God! What is that?" and pointed at the school's front doors. His mother's eyes shot open and immediately fixed on the vapor cloud gathering at the entrance. Goosebumps rising on their arms, everyone watched nervously as the dense mist transformed into the shape of a female wearing a dress. The apparition hovered a few inches above the front steps and Angel watched it raise its ghostly arm, pointing behind the truck in warning. Her heart skipped a beat as she turned to look out the back window. Something was coming out of the woods on the other side of the road, about a hundred meters away from them. More beings followed. They were slimy, disfigured swamp creatures with black skin that crawled on worm-like strands of flesh. They marched towards the school with one purpose: to collect their souls.

Amanda looked back at the school and noticed that the ghostly female had disappeared. Meanwhile, Angel scrambled out of her seat buckles as the kids began to scream in panic. Ready to defend her loved ones, she crawled and pulled herself up into the turret of the gun truck, opened the top hatch, and swung the .50 caliber rail gun to the rear.

She had to search for a moment to find the safety which she then switched over to fire mode. Angel didn't have to cock the weapon, because Shane had left it loaded after the engagement with the Reamer. Carefully aiming down the sights of the gun, she squeezed the butterfly trigger with her thumbs. The weapon jerked and Angel struggled to control it as the first few rounds blasted out of the barrel, completely missing their mark. Trees exploded behind the ghastly creatures lurching towards the truck.

Shane was just about to exit the school building when he heard a creepy child's voice giggle along with the pitter-patter of bare feet. He turned to look, but no one was there. All of a sudden, tiny footprints in bright red blood painted themselves on the floor and toddled towards him. Terrified, Shane stepped back against the wall as the bloody prints headed straight for another set of double doors. At the same time, the child's voice wailed, "Follow me."

Horrified, Shane's heart pounded wildly in his chest as it had never done before, but he was too curious not to go along with the phantom. He gently pushed the doors open and stumbled into the school's gymnasium. The sight that assaulted him was so horrendous that the blood seemed to freeze in Shane's veins. He had to fight the urge to vomit, but thanked his helmet makers that he didn't have to smell the air.

In front of him, corpses of hundreds of children and several adults were laying sprawled in pools of their own blood. Mangled bodies with exposed bones and organs posed in horrifically agonizing positions. Flies swarmed around the dead, rats feasted on their flesh, and maggots squirmed from open wounds and orifices. The gymnasium floor was so soaked in blood that it also covered the walls and dripped from the ceiling rafters where additional maimed remains sat twisted against the steel supports.

Believing himself stuck in a living nightmare, Shane turned around and darted out of the gymnasium as fast as his feet would carry him. He could hear the voices of the hundreds of bodies rotting behind him, "Come back!" and, "Come play with us!"

He almost slipped, but regained his balance in the hallway. Shane suddenly noticed that the walls and floors were smeared and painted in gore. Satanic pentagrams, all pointing downwards, had been drawn on the walls in blood which also leaked from the ceiling. The loose papers scattering the hallways were soaked in it as well. As he dashed through the school, Shane tripped at the sight of one classroom submerged to the ceiling with red fluid. The door was closed, but blood seeped out of its cracks and seams. Through a door window, an eerily panicked face of someone in the process of drowning bumped into the glass pane. The often stern lieutenant gasped, shivers running down his spine. And then he ran again.

Almazan and Emily also came rushing out of the building. As soon the sergeant saw Angel in the turret, firing at creatures coming out of the woods, he handed the two textbooks over to Emily. He then bolted to the rear right side of the truck and pointed his rifle at the approaching monsters. They had made it to the road unscathed until Almazan fired his weapon. His shots blasted through the disfigured head of the first demon which fell on its back, bleeding all over the concrete.

At the same time, Angel focused the rail gun more steadily at another monstrosity limping towards them and pressed the butterfly trigger once again. Fifty caliber sabot rounds tore the disfigured fiend into pieces. As rounds impacted its body, limbs blew off and sprayed thick oily blood over the snow and ash.

Moments later, when Shane had almost reached the double door exit, a flood of thick red blood rushed after him, filling the halls behind him to the ceiling. Luckily, he made it to the outside and jumped down a few steps. The blood gushed out of the front doors as he ran straight for the truck. Despite his shock, Shane immediately noticed Angel and Almazan firing at creatures flanking the truck. He ran over to Almazan's side, raised his rifle, and shot off two rounds at a pair of atrocities limping together. He struck both of them in the head.

As the dead mutants collapsed onto the road, Angel blasted more rounds, but had a hard time getting the rest of the attackers into her sights. Suddenly and without warning, a blast of energy enveloped the road, covering the advancing hellions. Dumbfounded, Shane, Angel, and Almazan watched as the creatures dissolved in the energy stream. The large alien from the night on the tobacco field was swooping down on them, pulverizing the undead with its massive particle beam cannon. It then flew right over Hawk's truck, banked over the school, and finally let out another uncanny roar.

Shane tapped Almazan on the shoulder, "We're getting out of here!"

"You don't have to tell me twice!" the sergeant responded, spun on his heel, and ran to the driver's side door. Shane climbed in the passenger seat while Almazan started up the engine, threw the vehicle in drive, and slammed on the gas. The tires first spun in the ash and snow, but when he finally turned to the right the vehicle slid and swerved. He had to correct his direction as the truck rumbled back towards the road. As they sped off, Thyrion landed on the playground, crushing the play sets beneath his massive, clawed feet. He then flung his head back and lunged forward, weapon aimed.

Seconds later, the entire building exploded, torn apart by the massive energy blast.

Lieutenant Hawk was still trembling from the horrors he had just witnessed. His eyes were flush with tears and he felt sick to his stomach. All his years in military training and combat deployments had not prepared him for what he had experienced just now. Emily was quietly sobbing as her mother climbed down from the turret, closed the hatch above her, and slid back into her seat. Meanwhile, Almazan drove recklessly fast until Amanda put a hand on his quivering shoulder. "Baby slow down!" she begged him. "Slow down Ignacio!" He let off the gas slightly and followed the road back into town.

They were the last truck to return to the highway, and Lieutenant Hawk ordered Almazan to stop at Lieutenant General May's Command Armored Personnel Carrier (APC). Still shaken by recent events, Shane briefed his commander about the incredible carnage at the school. Afterwards, he appeared a bit more relaxed.

"Sergeant," Hawk began as he climbed into the TC's seat of his vehicle. "Move us up to the front of the convoy, we're rolling out now." Almazan didn't say a word, but swiftly complied with the order. He drove nearly three hundred meters to the front of the trek where they assumed the position of scout vehicle. There, they waited for a short time until Alpha One gave the order to proceed north over the radio. Almazan stepped on the gas and the entire convoy followed his truck up I-77.

Chapter Five: The Eighth

They continued up the road and within an hour arrived at a tunnel that had been badly damaged. The robots couldn't fit through it, forcing them to make their way up and over the mountain. It was a small detour that nevertheless had the rest of the trek waiting as the machines traversed the treacherous terrain.

A few hours later, soldiers and survivors came across another tunnel in Jefferson National Forest. Unfortunately, this one had totally collapsed, while the elevation above it was much steeper than the previous one. The convoy idled as the head brass gathered for a tense crisis action brief. Unfortunately, nobody could come up with a solution—at first. One sergeant thought it a good idea to have the robots and Battle Suits carry the other vehicles over the peak, but General May quickly dismissed that suggestion, still weighing different options.

Hawk analyzed the slope and tried to imagine the entire convoy heaving up the incline. The military vehicles could easily do it, he calculated, but the hover buses and HMTVs would experience serious problems. Then it came to him, "General, how about this. I know the CGTs and APCs can make it up the mountain side, so why not have the robots and Battle Suits carry the hover buses and HMTVs while the rest go on their own power? If the hover buses and HMTVs set their power to maximum, they should be able to lessen their weight."

May peered up the mountain. "What do you think Captain?" he asked Dyson.

"It might just work, but it'll be tough," the latter responded. "There's no other way Lieutenant?"

"No sir. Sorry," Hawk concluded.

"Might have to make several trips, but it could be done," the sergeant who had thought up the original plan chimed in.

"All right, let's do it," May agreed with a sigh.

They parted and returned to their vehicles. It took Hawk and the young sergeant half an hour to explain the plan to the drivers and pilots. Minutes later, the Magnums braved the climb. Shane watched them uproot trees on the mountain and toss them aside with relative ease. They disappeared after negotiating the pinnacle and descended on the other side while clearing a path for the rest of the trek. The whole process took about half an hour.

Hawk's Combat Gun Truck was the first to maneuver up the incline. Almazan gave the CGT all the power it had as it struggled on the slope. He had to muster his best driving skills to navigate over and through the holes the Magnums had left behind. As they neared the top, the Battle Suits had already returned to the south side of the mountain, marching back towards the convoy.

Meanwhile, Almazan hardly used any gas as he practically smothered the brake all the way down the opposite side of the slope. Several times he felt the vehicle slip under its own weight and was forced to hammer his foot on the brake pedal. It was tricky and extremely rough, and everyone let out a sigh of relief when they finally connected with the freeway again, scraping the front grill as the truck lurched back onto the level road.

It took May's expedition almost eight hours to complete the hazardous operation. To be sure, there had been a few close calls that nearly spelled disaster for some hover buses. Transporting the hover vehicles had proven the hardest and most time-consuming part of this latest adventure.

As night fell, the convoy lumbered into West Virginia, snaking up a road that was long and treacherous towards Charleston. Hawk told Almazan, "Sergeant, this corridor of highway bends and snakes through mountains and runs along the Kanawha River. It's fun to drive in a sports car, but keep in mind that we have a mile-long trek following us. Maintain maximum safe speed and keep an eye out for mud or rockslides."

"Roger that," Almazan sped up a little as the path in front of him began to wind around the base of a river framed by mountains. The interstate had collapsed in a few places with debris tumbling down the slopes, but there was still enough of it left for the convoy to traverse it safely. Soon they arrived at the first of three toll plazas which welcomed all travelers to the West Virginia turn pike. Buildings still stood undamaged, but no one was manning them and there was no electricity powering the plaza. Almazan stopped the truck just short of the first toll booth.

"Gates are locked," Hawk cursed.

"Do you need some change?" Almazan joked, jovial as ever. Hawk climbed out of the vehicle and put his helmet over his head. Carrying his rifle, he approached the toll booth to open the gate, but there was no power to operate the machine. "Alpha One this is Scout, over," he called over his helmet's internal radio.

"Go ahead Scout, what's the hold up?"

"The toll booth gates are locked, I'm going to need a Battle Suit up here to remove one."

"Roger that Scout, break," General May continued. "Sierra-Echo-1-1-7, approach the head of the convoy and assist scout element over?"

"Roger Alpha One, moving now, over," a voice returned.

"Alpha One out," he replied.

Moments later a lone Valkyrie Battle Suit—lifted off the back of a hovering cargo truck—

flew towards the front of the convoy. Lieutenant Hawk could hear its engines approaching and waved his hands in the air to signal the pilot. The seven-foot-tall Valkyrie landed a few meters in front of him. "Need assistance sir?" the pilot asked Hawk over the Battle Suit's external megaphone.

"Yeah, remove one of those gates, would ya?" he pointed.

"Roger." The Valkyrie immediately aimed his VMG-30 Rail Gun at the gate joint.

"Whoa big guy!" Hawk stopped him.

"Sir?" the pilot paused, lowering his weapon.

"Just use your hands, no need to attract any attention."

"Roger, sorry sir," the pilot replied and marched over to the gate. Placing the Valkyrie's hands beneath the thick iron gate, he rattled the heavy bar blocking their passage. It quickly came loose as the joint hinge snapped off with a slight bang. Job accomplished, the Valkyrie tossed the iron bar over the guardrail, down the side of the mountain.

"Thank you," Hawk told him.

"No problem sir," the pilot responded, fired up his engines, and flew back towards his hover truck. In the meantime, Hawk returned to his vehicle and climbed into the TC's seat again.

"All right, let's go," he instructed Sergeant Almazan. Almazan pulled the truck forward and passed the toll booth. He slowed down on the other side until the last vehicle in the convoy—about a mile behind them—radioed that they had driven past the open gate.

Soon, the road began to make sharp S-turns through the river basin of the Kanawha, forcing Almazan to brake at every corner or risk rolling over. The interstate meandered like this for another ten miles until they arrived at another toll plaza. This time the gates had been left open and everyone proceeded unhindered.

As they were slugging along, Angel made an insightful observation. "Hey, since we left the Winston-Salem area, has anyone noticed that there have been no other cars on the road? I mean, even destroyed ones?" Hawk thought about it for a moment and nodded in agreement.

"Yeah I've noticed that too. Road has been pretty clear since we left North Carolina," Amanda pitched in.

"Probably because once all this started happening everyone went to their homes or to a shelter. And everyone stayed off the highways," Almazan argued unconvincingly.

"Yeah probably," Amanda conceded, not altogether satisfied. She wondered what was lying ahead of them as they continued through the winding stretch of interstate and along the river into Charleston.

After an additional ten miles the trek reached the third and final toll plaza which had been partially destroyed. Almazan slowed down to observe the damage and scanned the surroundings for signs of danger and survivors. Convoy in tow, he bumped through the scattered rubble of a crumbling toll booth and then proceeded further north, passing a suspended railroad bridge.

It wasn't before long that the expedition came to a halt. Lieutenant General May ordered everyone to turn around and head back to the railroad bridge that spanned the Kanawha River on Charleston's south end. Their direct route into town—via the Charles Chuck Yeager Bridge—had been destroyed and was almost completely submerged in the river, along with the unfortunate vehicles that had happened to be crossing it when it collapsed. Therefore, May explained, the only way across the Kanawha was by means of the railroad bridge.

Unfortunately, that particular overpass was not wide enough to fit the large Armadillo Combat Robot, compelling all androids to brave the waters. Lead by the largest one called a Warhammer, the robots stepped into the river and slowly navigated to the other side.

In no time, the smaller, eleven-foot-tall machines vanished in the Kanawha. Even worse, something had latched onto one of them, dragging it far beneath the water's surface. One of the Sheppard robots following behind hurried to assist its "colleague." The Sheppard pilot swept the large arms of his own robot through the river, trying to locate his buddy.

Suddenly, a few meters downstream, the first robot came up from the deep with a giant serpent wrapped around its body. Everyone in the convoy heard the radio call for help as the reptile tore into the android's torso, slicing it with huge claws attached to its hind legs. As the two struggled, water sprayed around them. The attacker kicked and pierced ferociously, while its desperate victim attempted to free itself from the deathly grip.

A damage indicator screen showed that the reptile was causing serious injuries to the structural capacity of the robot. In response, a gunner fired a couple of laser blasts at the snake's body as it moved in and out of the weapon's sight. The gunner missed several times until he finally got lucky, hitting the serpent in the back. The superheated bolt of energy pierced the reptile's tail bone, and it jumped off the robot screeching in pain.

Taking advantage of the brief lull, the pilot hastened the robot to the opposite side of the river bank before the creature could attack them again. Save one, the rest of the war machines were arriving at the shore unscathed and waited for one final comrade to make it to safety as well. They all targeted the serpent with a barrage of laser fire and missiles as it continued to pursue its lone prey. Each shot hit the mark, and moments later the reptile floated on the surface like a dead fish. The bizarre carcass eventually drifted downstream. As the robot platoon regrouped, they spotted more serpents lurking in the water, thirsting for victims.

Soon after they moved on, with one android following another in a single line. They scurried through the streets of an abandoned Charleston neighborhood and passed through an old DuPont paint factory. In due course, the robots found themselves on a freeway leading to their I-77 route. A few miles down the interstate, they connected to the eastern side of the city, skirting around the collapsed bridge where the rest of the convoy awaited them.

After giving the general a quick update, robots and vehicles resumed their journey. The highway, like the turn-pike, was littered with fallen trees and thousands of destroyed vehicles. Burned-out cars still carried their skeletal occupants inside their destroyed carcasses. The state capitol had also taken damage; a gigantic hole gaped in the north side of the beautiful, golden dome. The football stadium near the freeway was in tatters as well. Its bleachers had plummeted into a large crevasse that opened up when the earth expanded. This end time scenario continued for miles and miles north of Charleston, with scenes of devastation as far as the eye could see. From that morning until mid-day, everyone shared in this never-ending nightmare of chaos and death.

Throughout, the children remained surprisingly quiet, almost as much in shock as the adults. In fact, the adults appeared more haunted; many of them had grown up with a curious fascination of what the end of the world might be like. This was it—just in more vivid, horrifying detail.

In the course of the last two days, Madison had gazed at everything from mountains to rivers, bridges, and smoke rising from the ruins of an old city. She was quiet now, actively observing the once beautiful world around them as it rolled by at forty-five miles per hour. An hour north of West Virginia's capital, she snapped to attention when a call came over the radio reporting engine trouble with one of the buses. Lieutenant General May ordered the entire convoy to halt in order to repair the damaged vehicle filled with civilians.

Hawk told Almazan to pull over to the right side of the road near a steep incline. "I'll be right back," he told his friend, "I'm gonna check it out." After her husband had left, Angel felt uneasy. She didn't like the idea of being stuck in the middle of nowhere, especially with such a very curvy bend right in front of them. Anything could sneak up from around the mountain, she worried, and attack her family.

Almazan seemed to have read Angel's mind, because he unfastened his safety harness and stepped out of the vehicle, taking his weapon with him. He closed the door and drew out a pack of cigarettes and a lighter from his vest pouch. Inhaling deeply, he then breathed out with a sigh. It had a calming effect on him, but upset his wife Amanda. She had joined her husband outside and now nagged him to quit smoking.

Almazan paid little attention to her as he inhaled another drag. "Do you mind if I at least try to calm my nerves?" he told her with a sigh.

And yet Amanda continued to wheedle, "You know, it's bad enough as it is. Anything can come out of those woods and kill us all, but your smoking doesn't need to be another reason to get you killed." She thought she had a valid point. "That takes years! One cigarette won't kill me when I'm done with it!" Almazan shot back.

Unnerved by the whole situation, Angel looked around the cabin and found a rack with five M22A3s behind the kid's seats. She looked at Emily, who was in her own world listening to music through a set of headphones and browsing through the Spanish text book. "Emily, reach behind you and hand me one of those weapons," Angel pointed.

Emily peered over her shoulder and saw the rack of weapons. At first she wrestled with the latches, but finally got hold of a rifle. She passed it to her mother, barely grazing her youngest brother's hair with the butt stock. Jonathan rubbed his head with a sour look, making faces at his big sister. She apologized and gave him a hug, practically smothering him. Like all boys, he didn't like that kind of attention and grumbled disapprovingly. Emily smiled and rubbed his mop of hair to add a little more insult to injury. Jonathan first swatted her hand away and then punched her in the leg. "Leave me alone!" he shouted.

"Stop fighting!" Angel yelled as she was giving the weapon a closer look. There had been one late night, she remembered, when her husband was only an enlisted specialist in the Army, working as an armorer. This was before he had finished college and earned his commission. He had taken her down into the arms room and shown her how to handle, take apart, clean, and re-assemble this specific rifle. But it had only been a quick lesson. She also recalled fondly that being alone for a change led to other things that night.

"Hey Mom, where are we going again?" Jacob finally spoke. He hadn't said much since they departed Raleigh, and once in a while he would glare at his father's replacement with disdain. He had mixed emotions about Shane Hawk, but he knew his mother loved him. Rather than confronting Shane directly, he quietly resented him.

"We're heading to Detroit; apparently it's safe up there," she told him, still trying to make sense of the weapon.

"Why couldn't we have brought dad with us? They didn't have to throw him in the back of a car. We could've taken him with us," Jake complained bitterly.

Angel stopped for a moment and looked at her boy, "I don't ever want you to mention *him* again, you understand me?" she said coldly. "Shane is the father you kids never had and he loves you all very much."

She turned around to concentrate on the rifle in her lap, but Bubba Earl was still on her mind. Quietly fuming, Angel wished that she could point the gun at her ex-husband. She would pull the trigger and end years of aggravation and strife with one lead ball.

Pushing homicidal thoughts away, Angel continued to inspect the weapon. There was no magazine; the ammo counter read two big, red zeroes. Frustrated, she walked around the truck to seek Almazan's help. Amanda was still bickering about his smoking. "Angel! What's up!?" he asked as he noticed her standing with an empty rifle in her hands. He was glad to have found a distraction from his wife's squabbling.

Meanwhile, with his mother out of earshot, Jacob kept mumbling, "He's not my dad."

Only Emily heard Jacob's gripes and responded firmly, "Shane is the dad we *don't* fear." But Jake merely rolled his eyes. While he rested his head against a door window, he heartily wished he was somewhere else.

"Where's Shane?" Amanda asked Almazan, looking down the length of the convoy. She could see a crowd of soldiers gathering around the defective bus about a hundred yards back.

"He went to go check on the bus," her husband replied. Reaching into one of the lower pouches on his utility belt, he removed the Velcro cover strap to retrieve two magazines. He handed one to Angel who slapped it into the magazine feed on the bottom side of the rifle. The sergeant was a bit surprised when he saw her handle it so adeptly.

"Know what you're doing with that?" he cocked an eyebrow and took another drag off his cigarette.

"Shane showed me a few things about weapons a while ago."

Almazan laughed. He knew what Hawk must have done to teach her. Actually, it had probably been illegal, since civilians were not allowed into an arms room without proper clearance. But that was a long time ago, the sergeant shrugged. No one cared anymore, and neither did he.

Meanwhile, Angel saw her husband walking up the road towards them. He smiled as he got closer and noticed the rifle in her hands, recalling happier times. Almazan wanted to know, "How long is it going to take?"

"Ah," Hawk sighed. "About an hour, I think. The engine is clogged with ash and dirt and they're going to check out all the vehicles just to be safe," he explained while Angel frowned. "If anyone has to use the bathroom, better use it now."

Amanda thought this a brilliant idea and volunteered, "I'll see if the kids need to go." She walked back to the vehicle. "Put that cigarette out!" she snapped at Almazan and then asked the children if any of them needed a "bathroom break." Glad to get out and about, they all piled out of the vehicle. The girls found a thatch of thick bushes; the boys stood behind a refrigerator-sized boulder near the shoulder of the road.

As the girls were returning to the truck, Emily noticed activity nearby. Alerting her mother who was helping her husband clean the engine, she pointed up the highway and shouted, "Mom look!" Angel, Amanda, Almazan, and Hawk all turned their heads in unison to see what it was. Around the bend, some hundred feet away from them, a motley gaggle of people were walking towards them. Within seconds, more individuals rounded the corner. They were obviously survivors, but something seemed out of place;

their movements were disturbingly slow and trance-like.

All of them dragged their feet and their posture was slouchy. Confused, the children did not know what to make of the creepy spectacle. As the ominous crowd advanced, Hawk's party observed sunken eyes with dark shadows around the sockets. In fact, some creatures had their eyes missing and merely sported hollow cavities. Others exhibited brutal wounds that were still bleeding profusely. One fellow was without an arm. Hawk could hear a faint moaning sound emanating from the swelling throng as they drew closer.

Alarmed, he ran to the truck, ordering the children to stay inside. Then he keyed the hand-mike with trembling hands, "Alpha One, this is Scout, over," he waited.

"Scout, this is Alpha One, go ahead over," the response came.

"Alpha One, we have a crowd of some really messed up folks approaching us from the north end of the highway. We're gonna need a medical team up here stat."

"Roger that Scout, dispatching a medical team to you now, Alpha One out."

Sweating, Hawk dropped the hand-mike as Emily opened the rear door. She looked at him with her hands in the front pockets of her hoodie, her face full of questions. "What's wrong with them?" she pointed at one particularly nasty creature, who was chewing on a piece of flesh. Upon closer inspection it turned out to be an arm—a human arm complete with a shirt sleeve. It was drenched in blood, and Hawk could tell that the guy had been gnawing on the exposed bone for some time.

Hawk ordered Emily, "Get in the truck, pronto, and lock the doors." Frightened, his step-daughter and Amanda obeyed while Hawk darted over to Almazan and Angel. "What the hell is wrong with these people?" he asked himself rhetorically.

Angel was unsure, "What do we do? They look like they could use some help." She held her weapon tightly in her hands.

Almazan also didn't know what to think. The crowd of strangers was merely seventy-five feet away from them now and approaching slowly. Many were bleeding from wounds not caused by accidents or weapons fire. Even more baffling, some injuries would have killed any man in his tracks. One individual's entire rib cage was split open with some vital organs visibly missing. "OK," Almazan finally broke the silence. "That's messed up right there." He raised his weapon at the crowd with Angel following suit, but Hawk was still hesitant.

Moments later, medical personnel arrived. It was a combat paramedic team trained to fight, and when they stopped next to Hawk, Almazan, and Angel they immediately dropped their aid kits to draw their side arms. The ranking paramedic launched a round at the nearest ghoul, blowing its head off with the M19A2 .45 Caliber Pistol. Hawk flinched at the gunshot and stared in disbelief at the staff sergeant holding the smoking barrel. The whole crowd of zombies was sprinting towards them now.

"What the hell are you doing?" Hawk yelled angrily.

"They're zombies sir! Don't let them touch you!" he shouted back as the other three paramedics began firing their weapons.

"Well!" Almazan roared and launched a single shot from his rifle, blowing off the shoulder of one of the approaching women. The round detached her arm from the socket and knocked her down. He quickly aimed his weapon at another menacing target, but was startled when the one he had just shot was sitting up again.

"Aim for the head!" the staff sergeant screamed over the weapons' noise.

Angel grabbed her rifle and squeezed the trigger. Unfortunately, nothing happened. In the meantime, Hawk fired a round into the forehead of the closest fiend, severing its head from its neck. Annoyed, Angel looked at her weapon, "What the heck?" She could not figure out what was wrong and tried switching the mechanism from semi to burst and then to full auto, pointed, and still nothing. Sweat pouring down her back,

Angel pulled the charging lever back and a round loaded from the magazine into the breach. Charging it again, the round locked into the chamber: it was ready to fire.

The paramedics annihilated a few more zombies, but retreated as the throng of bloodthirsty undead drew even nearer. Hawk and Almazan launched gun bursts, followed by full, automatic fire.

Prepared to defend her family, Angel squeezed the trigger once more and a round finally blasted out of the barrel. It screamed towards its intended mark, but just missed the head of a female zombie. The undead being felt the heat from the kinetic energy whizzing by as the round burned the skin off its cheek. Infuriated, the walking corpse turned its grotesque face and began sprinting towards Angel.

Hawk rushed to the right side of the truck and popped off a few more rounds, striking several targets in the undead crowd. Equally undeterred, Almazan took a grenade from his vest pouch, pulled the pin, and flung it into a crowd of zombies that had come as close as twenty-five feet. The grenade tumbled between their unsteady legs and then came to a rest. Seconds later, a monster stepped on it and stumbled. But before its body hit the ground, the grenade exploded, sending body parts flying in different directions.

Only about a dozen walking dead were still lunging towards them now. One zombie reached out and grabbed the barrel of a medic's M71 Light Assault Rifle. The soldier pulled the trigger and the ghoul's arm exploded in a mess of flesh and blood. The heat of the barrel also burned patches of skin.

Another medic fired with his M19A2 .45 Caliber Pistol, putting a round through the cranium of one attacker, while Hawk sprayed his bullets at head level, striking three of the creatures dead. Only five remained, and Angel exterminated a particularly nasty one with a single shot. Meanwhile, Almazan smashed the end of his butt stock into the forehead of another undead being. The impact killed the creature with a skull-shattering crack and a splatter of brain goo.

Next to the sergeant, Hawk fired and struck the zombie threatening his wife in the neck. The ghoul gasped, but marched on. A medic slayed an additional fiend, while Angel concentrated on the undead female. The zombie woman was still in hot pursuit of her and just about to touch her with her bloody hands, when Angel jammed the barrel of her rifle into the creature's mouth, pulling the trigger. Its entire head exploded with the upper cranium shooting up high into the air. Pieces of skull landed amongst hundreds of shell casings that cluttered the ash-covered highway below a "No Littering" sign.

When it was finally over, with the last zombie's head severed from its neck, the paramedics returned to their vehicles. Hawk noticed the petrified children sitting silently in the truck, deathly pale with big, frightened eyes.

Then he noticed something else. A large shadow was forming in a copse of trees to the right side of the road. Grabbing his rifle, Shane launched a long burst of bullets and watched alien legs kick up spasmodically. Apprehensive but curious, he walked up to the grove to confirm the kill and recognized the scorpion-like monster that had murdered the police officer in Fayetteville a few days ago. Climbing back into the truck, Shane told the gang what he had found and added half-jokingly, "I think we need another name for this kind of creature."

Thyrion was the leader; Havok his scout and second in command. There was also a mechanical alien named Shiva—the Destroyer—equipped with four arms: two of its own and a pair of artifical limbs. The largest in the group was Kumbakarna, or simply Karna— the Giant. There were also the warrior twins Phobos and Deimos, and a female known as Tiamat—the Executioner. All zoomed through the low cloud cover over Charleston and landed on the golden dome of the city's Capitol Building. They sat there, perched high above and scanning the city for any signs of life. There was none, except for the gaggles of undead walking the streets. But their numbers were low and they certainly did not present much of a challenge. Still, the beings from outer space hated these human undead. Annoyed, Thyrion finally ordered, "**Kill 'em all.**"

Together they leapt from the golden dome, which collapsed under the pressure of their massive combined weight. The debris landed on other rooftops of the capitol building a few stories below.

The alien group then zeroed in on a pair of zombies rushing towards them and moaning for food with outstretched arms. But the female extraterrestrial known as Tiamat immediately struck out with her long-bladed chain whip. Each link had a razor-sharp blade connected to the next, with a jagged point at the end. The deadly weapon wrapped around one of the zombies, cutting into its flesh as it struggled to extricate itself from the monster's iron grip. Seconds later, after a quick tug, it was almost instantly shredded into dozens of pieces.

The other zombie now rushed at Havok and came as close as fifty meters, but the alien scout aimed his particle beam cannon at its face and fired. The energy blast disintegrated the dead human's head and the body plopped onto the road with a thud.

Two more undead humans came darting out of a back alley. Shiva aimed the bulbous end of his cannon at the ghouls, releasing a blast of energy so wide and powerful that it immediately obliterated both zombies.

Meanwhile, Phobos and Deimos had taken off into the air above the streets. A pair of cannon barrels extended out from their forearms in round protrusions, and both carried a set on each arm. The twins fired, raining down particle energy bolts into a crowd of walking undead trapped in one of Charleston's gated parking lots. The twins laughed; they relished mowing down the zombie horde.

Meanwhile, Karna bounced a long chain in his massive hands. At its end hung an enormous demolition ball that had sharp blades poking from the round surface. When he swung the ball above his head, energy charged the deadly weapon with an unknown destructive force. A soon as the zombies began pouring out of the parking garage in front of him, Karna hurled the chain high into the air, and then yanked it, pulling it over them. The lethal ball landed in the center of the undead crowd and burst into a greenish-white globe of fiery plasma. The ensuing explosion annihilated all mutant humans, but also resulted in a massive debris cloud as well as a crater at the point of impact.

If Thyrion could grin, he would have done so now. He was quite enjoying the spectacle of his servants slaughtering the ghouls with relative ease. But then he felt something moving around his feet. A lone female zombie, no more than eight years of age, had started gnawing on his metal foot plate. "**How pathetic!**" the alien shouted and pointed his particle beam cannon at the undead girl's head. The blast that followed vaporized the little zombie's entire body.

"**Asterym, we cannot dwell here any longer, follow me!**" Thyrion bellowed moments later as the boosters on his back reignited. He shot off into the sky without any further ado, with the others following him promptly. Karna, however, turned around in mid-flight, and angled his two artillery cannons at the human city. Both cannons fired, and as a pair of energy balls impacted the West Virginia State Capitol shortly afterwards, they incinerated everything within a ten block radius in yet another greenish-white firestorm.

Two hours later, after the conventional vehicles had been refueled, May's convoy was rolling again and crossed the Vietnam Veterans Memorial Highway from West Virginia into Ohio. Hawk noticed with horror that the entire town of Marietta was completely gone, vanished. It had been replaced by a strange, alien forest full of large, contorted trees that reminded him of oaks. Although it was the heart of winter, these odd trees bloomed, sporting even odder, blue-colored leaves and grey bark that zigzagged in a spiral up the base of each tree. But what set the mysterious forest truly apart from anything he had ever seen before was the dim blue light that glowed about each plant like an aura.

Tree roots had already spread across the road like tentacles, forcing the convoy to reduce its pace by half. Wheeled vehicles experienced a rough time as they bumped over every large root in their path. The hover trucks didn't notice a thing, of course. By 2200 hours, everyone was worn out and tired, even Hawk and Almazan. The children had passed out in their seats, using each other as pillows. Angel was still awake but drowsy, and Amanda was reading one of Emily's textbooks that she had picked up at the high school in Virginia.

A call soon came in from Alpha One to find a place to park and set up a perimeter for the night. Hawk told Almazan to keep his eyes open for any clearings and they found one only moments later. As Almazan drove the truck into the small open space, he realized that it wasn't big enough for the whole convoy. However, as each vehicle entered the glade, the alien forest seemed to strangely retreat on itself, as if it was making room for them. In no time, the gun trucks formed a 360° perimeter a few meters from the edge of the forest. The hover buses, HMTVs, MHMMV-44s, and APCs parked in the middle, while the five combat robots formed a pentagon around them, between the Combat Gun Trucks and the woods. The Magnums and the Valkyrie Battle Suits arranged themselves in a smaller circle around the APCs.

Another call came over the radio, "All convoy elements exercise noise and light discipline. No fires." In response, vehicle engines started shutting down as did all the lights on trucks and robots. Lieutenant Hawk peered into the back of the truck and saw that the kids were still asleep.

"Almazan, let's set up the Fast-Tents for tonight." The sergeant nodded his weary head in approval and they both opened a cargo hatch behind the driver's side rear wheel well. Almazan promptly pulled out three light bags and handed them to Hawk one by one. Hawk had already found a nice spot away from the truck on the inside of the perimeter to set them up.

Pulling on two plastic handles, he let the supports fold out into the shape of a hexagon. This kind of bivouac was large enough to provide room for eight adults and convenient for its ease of setup. Furthermore, it was light enough to be carried by one person. The military called them Fast-Tents, and it only took a split second to set one up or take it down.

Almazan and Hawk opened the remaining two tents and arranged them in a triangle pattern with the weather-proof canvas entrances facing each other. Afterwards, they placed thermal blankets inside each one together with inflatable pillows. Lastly, Almazan tied red chemlights to the ceilings.

Hawk returned to the truck where Angel was waiting for him. She was stretching; her muscles were stiff from the long drive and bumpy roads. "Hey," he suggested. "Let's put all the kids in one of the tents. Almazan and Mandy will take the second, and you and I can share the last one."

Tired, Angel nodded without saying a word. She opened up the rear door on the driver's side, scooped up Madison into her arms, and carried her daughter to the designated children's tent. Hawk quietly roused the other kids who groggily joined their mother and youngest sister in their temporary shelter. Angel put one of the soft inflatable pillows under Maddy's head, and then kissed her and the other children goodnight. Emily and Jacob gave her a big hug, while Jonathan had already fallen asleep, butt sticking up in the air with one side of his face flat on the blanket. Each told their mother that they loved her—except for the snoozing Jon.

As flakes of ash continued to float from the sky, Hawk leaned against the truck's front bumper. Angel could tell that he was lost in thought. "What's the matter?" she asked him softly after popping out of the tent door.

After a brief pause Shane explained, "I've been up and down this road plenty of times. I know this highway like the back of my hand. I could almost make the trip in my sleep. Yet, I've never seen this place before." He pointed at the glowing alien forest, "And like everywhere else we've been today, it's covered in a foot of ash and snow."

"Yeah, but I bet you never encountered an alien on any of those trips," she tried to lighten the conversation. "Or faced a horde of zombies, or escaped a ghost town with the help of a monster bent on our destruction, or seen devastation of this kind?" Shane didn't reply, but his smile turned to a worried frown.

"We'll have to clean out the engine in the morning," he yawned.

Suddenly, they heard the motors of two Valkyrie Battle Suits winding up near the Command APC. Seconds later, the pair took off, vanishing into the dark night sky. Shane and Angel would have lost sight of them immediately had it not been for the faint glow of their engines. Leaving earth behind, the Valkyries then disappeared into the black clouds of volcanic ash.

Angel turned and put her arms around her husband's waist, hugging him tightly. She gave him a little squeeze and rested her cheek on his chest. Her dark brown hair was a mess and sprinkled with flakes of ash. Shane kissed her head, inhaling the lingering fragrance of shampoo. Amidst the pervasive odor of sulfur and ash, this scent was beautiful and pleasant—a memory of less dramatic times. He held her close. She was shorter by a whole head, and he loved her.

Shane put his right arm across Angel's back, and together they walked to their tent. Almazan and Amanda were all ready in theirs, presumably asleep. With her right hand, Angel held Shane's that caressed her right shoulder. She led him inside, still holding his hand, and then turned around to face him as he pulled the zipper down on the flap. They stared into each other's eyes underneath the dim, red chemlight and began to kiss passionately.

It was cold inside the tent, and they scurried beneath the thermal blanket. Angel and Shane didn't sleep for the next few hours, because they made love with the most fervent intensity. After all, the end of the world was probably near …

"Sierra Echo 1-1-7, this is Sierra Echo 1-1-9, you read me Jack?" a voice came over the Valkyrie pilot's helmet radio as they flitted through thick layers of ash and snowflakes.

"I hear you Greg, you still on my wing?" Jack looked over his shoulder and could barely make out his colleague, Sierra Echo 1-1-9.

"Yeah I'm still here, but I can't see a friggin' thing in this mess. I can barely see you," Greg complained about the zero visibility hampering their mission.

"I know it's horrible. I've never flown in conditions like these before," Jack responded.

"I'm sure the FAA would have someone's butt for this one," Greg laughed.

"Yeah, if there was an FAA left to regulate anything," Jack frowned beneath his helmet's visor. "My radar is showing there's a bend in the valley up ahead, stay close to my wing."

"Roger," Greg acknowledged.

The two Valkyries banked slightly to the right, following the length of the valley. Mountains flanked them on either side, and though they could not see them, they knew they were there. At four hundred miles per hour, one false move could splatter them against the rocks "Man, I've got absolutely nothing on my radar. How about you?" Greg asked Jack after a few miles.

"Ditto Greg," Jack shook his head. "My screen is blank too."

His vision restricted by opaque ash and snow clouds, Greg almost overlooked a glowing, red light to his left. "Hey Jack, I'm seeing a dim red light, eleven o'clock low, maybe eight hundred meters." Jack looked over, but just as he was about to acknowledge the tiny light source, the red glimmer erupted into a massive beam of energy that zoomed across their flight path. "Whoa!" Greg yelled out as both slowed down to a hover. "What the hell was that?!"

"I think someone's shooting at us!" Jack shouted while another energy flash cut the air between them.

"What do we do?" Greg screamed.

"Shoot back!" Jack leveled his VMG-30 Rail Gun on his shoulder. Greg did the same and the two Valkyries launched spewing rounds at blazing speeds. Tracers ripped through cloud layers into the mountainside, and for a good fifteen seconds both Jack and Greg fired into the void, praying for the projectiles to hit their unknown attackers. They paused to see if anything was still alive.

"Think we got 'em?" Greg finally broke the silence. That's when another beam of red energy tore through the clouds, indirectly answering his question.

Unfortunately, it also struck him squarely in the chest. "Ahhh!" Greg winced in pain.

"Greg! Greg!" Jack screamed and reached for his friend as the latter's battle suit lost altitude and then disappeared in the dense mist. "GREG!" Jack yelled again.

Seconds later, Jack's Valkyrie was hit too. The red energy ray struck his left wing and damaged the side engine mounted on his back. The unit lost power and Jack struggled to remain airborne. After a few panicked seconds he realized that the best he could hope for was a controlled crash at the bottom of what-ever loomed beneath the thick fog.

Hours passed until Jack finally came to again. Aching all over, he was also freezing and trembling with cold. His legs and left shoulder were submerged in water, while his head rested on an inch-thick sheet of ice. As his vision cleared, Jack espied a mountain stream that had frozen over. By crashing, he had broken through parts of the solid ice layer, and from what he could tell, this particular section of the river was at least a foot and a half deep. He wasn't sure if he had shattered any bones or punctured his suit. Despite the cold Jack broke into a cold sweat after realizing that he couldn't feel a thing below his neckline.

That worry soon became an afterthought as the Valkyrie pilot heard something heavy rustle through the woods on the other side of the river bank. "Greg?" Jack mumbled anxiously. "Greg, is that you?" When no reply was forthcoming, the downed airman attempted to move, but his body refused a response. He knew that something wasn't right and eventually stopped trying.

All of a sudden, a dark, shadowy figure appeared from behind the trees. It was a large, mechanical alien, and Jack realized with a sinking heart that he didn't stand a chance. The giant stepped onto the ice, shattering it beneath its massive feet. Jack caught a glimpse of some sort of weapon on one arm, and a massive shield on the other. As the monster trampled towards him, Jack could make out the eerie glow of Thyrion's gel layers underneath his heavy armor, which flickered like a fire in the night. The alien's featureless face was red, except for the angry white spots that flashed where his eyes should have been.

"Sierra Echo 1-1-7. This is the Artificial Defense Acquisition Mainframe," a child's voice came through on Jack's helmet radio.

"A.D.A.M.," Jack felt somewhat relieved. "I need help. I'm badly hurt and there's an extraterrestrial coming for me right now. Please send help."

"Captain, activate your unit's helmet camera and voice recorder," A.D.A.M. instructed.

Jack did so unquestioningly, but as the behemoth drew closer, he started to wonder, "A.D.A.M., I need help NOW."

"Thank you Captain, you've done your country a great service," A.D.A.M. mocked, and began to transmit images and sounds through the Valkyrie's sensors. A rush of fear, loneliness, and betrayal assailed Jack like a tidal wave.

Seconds later, Thyrion came upon the wounded human lying helplessly in the icy stream. He stopped a meter short of Jack who struggled, but was still unable to move. "**Puny human! I am…THYRION!**" the monster blurted out as it aimed its particle beam cannon at Jack's face. The injured pilot closed his eyes and cried. He did not want to die alone like this, and prayed that the treacherous A.D.A.M. would receive his comeuppance in the very near future.

Meanwhile, A.D.A.M.'s recorded video of Thyrion turned into static as the alien's arm cannon fired into the camera. Unfazed, A.D.A.M. played back the voice recording. "**Puny human! I am…THYRION!**" A.D.A.M. edited the footage and listened to it once more, "**THYRION!**"

The processor began searching through trillabytes of information referencing the name Thyrion and any image relating to Earth's history. Its ultra-fast mainframes buzzed and its hard drives tweeted until several documents of information were found. They described several mythological references concerning the so-called "Return of the Nine"—a stone inscription found at Monument 6 of the Mayan site Tortuguero in southern Mexico.

One remarked on the return of nine gods in the year 2012. However, A.D.A.M. discovered no event in 2012 to support this claim. There was only one connection between Thyrion and any of the divinities depicted in A.D.A.M.'s databases. It was the Aztec deity Tezcatlipoca who had been known to carry a safeguard known as the Mirror Shield. A.D.A.M. logically assumed that Thyrion had nothing in common with this particular god and had never been to Earth before.

A.D.A.M. then relayed all the information he collected to the String of Pearls satellites, which in turn beamed the information to every unit commanders computer for study and analysis. This information, woke General May from his sleep at the chair of his command console inside his APC. He looked the information over, studying it and committing every word to memory.

Lieutenant Hawk suddenly woke from his dreamless slumber. He didn't exactly know what was going on, but had a hunch that something was wrong. Angel was next to him, sound asleep. She was lying on her side, cuddled up against him under their thermal blanket. He pulled the cover off and sat up. It was still pretty cold outside.

Goosebumps rippled over Shane's body. He wrapped Angel's exposed shoulders and back with the coverlet and got dressed in the uniform with the black, grey, and white digital pattern. Then he pulled his lightweight armored vest over his head, tightening it around his torso. Afterwards, he strapped the holstered M19A2 pistol around his right thigh, and finally picked up his helmet. After turning on its functions, Shane grabbed his M22A3 rifle. Moments later, he stepped into the cold, ash-covered world outside. It was still nighttime.

Still shivering, he checked on the children. He unzipped the tent flap and counted them from left to right. There was Emily, Jake, and Jon, whose butt was still sticking up in the air. Shane first cocked an eyebrow; then he got nervous. He repeated the quick headcount, but there was no doubt: only three of his step-kids were inside the tent. Unsettled, he searched around outside, hoping to spot little, blonde-haired Madison.

Suddenly Shane froze in his tracks. Looking down, he noticed two small sets of shoe prints scattered amongst his nine and a half size footprints that had traveled around the back of the tent and out to the truck. "Maybe she just got cold and went to sleep in there?" he thought to himself. Hands trembling, he quickly opened the vehicle door and peered inside: it was empty. Growing ever more worried, Shane scanned the ash that had blanketed the area overnight and picked up the trail of the small footprints again—this time leading into the woods. His heart skipped a beat. Beneath the dark sky, Shane followed the tracks that led him outside the safety of the perimeter.

They led up and over a few hills and around some very huge trees. After twenty minutes Hawk stopped since Madison's footprints were becoming blurred. Strange gusts rattled the leaves in the trees, but as far as Hawk could tell, there was no wind at all. He activated the motion tracker on his helmet, and the electronic screen popped up on his Heads-Up-Display (HUD). A circle pulsated with his center icon. Every few seconds the small ring expanded away from the center. Suddenly, a small yellow dot appeared on the edge of Shane's motion tracker. It was moving away from him, but he picked up his pace, energized by the prospect of having located Maddy. He followed the blinking dot up the side of a steep hill. Hawk didn't care that he was braving the cold and running up sharp inclines; he loved his step-children and had vowed to protect them, even with his life. And so he ran on, even when his legs begged him to stop.

Minutes later, Shane was dashing at full speed. He was in excellent shape and could cross a mile of open terrain in just under seven minutes. The 82nd Airborne Corps still maintained the highest physical fitness standards, and was considered one of the best units in the entire US Military. Running was an everyday exercise and something he'd been doing for years. His move to the 71st Special Forces Group had resulted in even more strenuous workouts, both mentally and physically.

By keeping the fast pace, Shane was gaining on the small, yellow dot on his HUD. As he closed in, he found himself in a thick patch of forest with a spring bubbling out of the ground up ahead. The same distortion of energy that had torn entire cities apart now formed an orb around the fountain. Shane stopped at the edge of the cove and discovered Madison sitting inside the orb. Her head was tilted back and her eyes closed. Shane did not know if he was awake or dreaming when he saw the little girl floating a foot off the ground, arms extended out to her sides. He was scared now, because he didn't know what to make of it.

Taking a deep breath, Shane leaned his rifle against a tree and reached inside the force field. He was grabbing Madison with both arms when an image of a white city, embellished with a blend of Greek, Incan, and Persian architecture, flooded his mind. In its center stood a temple pyramid with a large obsidian globe on top, radiating energy. But just as Shane focused on this foreign metropolis, the vision disappeared. "What the hell?" he wondered.

With his mind back on Madison, Shane dragged her out of the energy sphere. She had an eerie, bluish-white glow about her—the same dim shade of the forest. He shook her gently. "Maddy... Maddy!" She moved her head forward and slowly opened her eyes. Shane let go of her and the bluish-white glimmer faded. But her skin was pale now; her lips dry and slightly purple in color. Shane realized that she was very cold, since her teeth were chattering.

By now, the child was also shaking badly. Shane held her tight, rubbing her back with his right hand. A little more alert, Maddy embraced her step-father and began to cry; she didn't know where she was or how she had gotten there. She also missed her mother tremendously. "Where's Mom?" she whined.

"She's back at the camp hunny," he told her soothingly. "Come on, let's go back to Mom." Madison nodded in agreement and wiped some frozen tears from her eyes. Shane picked up his helmet and pulled it over his head.

As he turned around to face the fountain, Shane was struck in the faceplate by something hard. Suddenly light-headed, he fell on his back, still holding on to Maddy so that she wouldn't hit the ground. Alarmed, Shane touched the crack in his faceplate. Cold air was leaking in, and he could feel it sting his nose and lips. He looked up and saw an armor-clad alien stepping out of the energy sphere.

It wasn't Thyrion. This one had something reminiscent of black dreadlocks protruding from the back of its head and sported a face plate with a sharp crown as well as two slanted, red eyes. The chest plate had been designed in the shape of a skull, but was stylized and angular. On the monster's forearms, twin blades—razor-sharp and four feet long—hung all the way to the ground. Though its legs were similar to Thyrion's, they did not have a shield or powerful cannon strapped to them.

Trembling with fear, Hawk staggered to his feet, while Maddy hid behind him. The creature glared at them with fiery eyes and Hawk noticed that they functioned without an iris or pupils. Then the giant spoke, "Gre'Zatu Gle Tah day." Hawk was puzzled; he had been all over the world, but had never heard such a language before. The monster pointed at Madison who by now was holding onto Shane's leg.

"Give me the girl or die, human," the extraterrestrial bellowed.

"Who the hell are you?" Hawk fired back at the alien.

"I am known in your language as Gilgamesh. I am Thyrion's best assassin. Now hand over the child or I will cut you down and take her from you by force," he threatened.

"Who is Thyrion?" Hawk tried to delay Gilgamesh's demand for Madison as long as possible.

"He is the leader of the Asterym, the Lord of All. And he will lead us to the Masters' world and destroy them too," Gilgamesh continued.

"You mean," Hawk paused, "Earth is not you're final stop?"

"You humans look exactly like the Masters, and therefore you will all die before we gather enough resources off this miserable rock to make the final jump to the Masters' home world," the behemoth explained.

Hoping to stall the alien a while longer, while simultaneously collecting intelligence, Hawk fired another question, "Who are the Masters?"

Gilgamesh divulged, "The Masters created the Asterym and exploited us as a slave labor force for millions of your Earth years—until Lord Thyrion rebelled and began the war. We armed ourselves and annihilated the Masters on our planet. Those that survived fled to their home world, one jump away from your planet." He might have been an assassin, Shane thought, but he wasn't that bright.

"What do you want with Earth?" Hawk inquired further.

"We will use all your water resources to produce enough energy to jump back to the Masters' planet. The extinction of your race is a secondary objective, seeing that you closely resemble the Masters," Gilgamesh was starting to grow impatient.

"What do you want with the girl?" Hawk knew this was the final question.

"Lord Thyrion has noticed something special about this human, female child, and wants to study her more closely. He will dissect her until he finds his answers."

That was it. "Ah hell no!" Hawk yelled. He spun around and scooped Madison up in his arms. Gilgamesh wasn't amused by his resistance and growled loudly. His mind racing, Hawk took half a step back while the creature flinched and snarled, grinding its sharp pointed blades together. Obviously, it wasn't just going to let them leave without a fight.

Carrying Madison with his left arm, Shane slyly unfastened the pistol strap inside his holster with the other. The creature was already marching towards him, he calculated, intending to rip Madison from his grip. In one swift motion, Hawk drew the .45 Caliber M19A3 pistol and squeezed the trigger. The round launched at a blazing speed and point-blank range, striking Gilgamesh directly in the chest. At such close distance, the extraterrestrial felt the impact of every pound of kinetic energy produced by the electromagnetic rails lining the barrel of the pistol. The mach one accelerated projectile blasted the creature off its feet and onto its back as the shot resounded through the forest.

Surprised and aching, Gilgamesh turned clumsily on his side. Meanwhile, Hawk re-holstered his pistol while keeping an eye on his adversary as he picked up his rifle. The extraterrestrial still laid there motionless, but the thick, red, oily blood that had gushed from its wound only moments earlier was now flowing back into it. The alien armor was sealing the gaping hole caused by the high-impact round.

Aware that he had no time to lose, Hawk raced through the forest as fast as he could, rifle in his right hand and Madison in his left arm. Behind him, the creature's wound was healing rapidly; its eyelids had already snapped open. Bursting with rage, red eyes glared in anger. Gilgamesh was thirsting for revenge and blood—plenty of blood.

Hawk had been able to get a few hundred meters away from the cove in the woods when his motion tracker detected a large red dot chasing after them. Hawk continued to run, but kept an eye on his tracker as the alien steadily closed in on its prey. Surprisingly, it suddenly dashed off to the right and disappeared over a small hill. Hawk only caught a glimpse of the giant fading away in the darkness. Darting further up a path, it eventually vanished from Shane's motion tracker.

When Gilgamesh stopped moving altogether, Hawk knew he was setting up an ambush. The monster could be hiding behind any tree, he thought nervously. He placed Madison on the forest floor, telling her, "Stay here Maddy, I'll be back in a second." Too scared to protest, Madison remained on the ash-covered ground and didn't say a word. But then she discovered that the ash felt like soft, powdery snow. In no time, the little girl laid down on her back, kicking and waving her arms. Giggling contently, she made little "ash angels."

It was clear to Shane Hawk that Madison was still confused, possibly in a daze, and without any idea where she was or what was going on around her. He carefully treaded with his assault rifle pointed ahead of him, looking through the sight. The red dot in his sight picture was very accurate, and he was a deadly shot even without it. Shane was about five meters away from Madison when he looked up and saw Gilgamesh leaping from a branch in the tree right next to him. In response, Hawk launched a burst of rounds but missed. The massive assassin landed directly in front of him, swinging his fist. In one motion it backhanded Hawk.

Hurling through the air, Shane dropped his rifle somewhere in the trees. Meanwhile, Madison shot up from the ash-covered earth, terrified to see her step-father staggering to his feet while wincing in pain. But there was no reprieve for Hawk. The alien was already stomping up to him to grab him by the vest.

Roaring loudly, it hurled the hapless earthling over its shoulder in Madison's direction. Hawk's back slammed against the tree trunk once more. The pain took his breath away for a few seconds, but there was the monster again, ready to storm over to him.

Hawk was still on his knees, struggling to get up, when Gilgamesh clutched him by his throat, lifting him off the ground. As his legs dangled in the cold air, the behemoth snarled and began to tighten its grip around the human's neck. Hawk couldn't breathe; he wiggled and tried to grasp the alien's large wrist. But then he heard Madison's voice. The little girl had run over to the gigantic assailant and kicked it in the shin, yelling, "You leave my Daddy alone!"

Immediately, the alien dropped Hawk who landed gingerly on his feet, but then stumbled backwards, bracing himself against the trunk of a tree. While he gasped for air, Gilgamesh reached for Madison. Beside herself with terror, she shut her eyes tightly and screamed, "Leave us alone, you big ugly meanie!" Constricted by its iron grip, Madison nevertheless managed to flail her arms around and yelled again at the top of her lungs.

Hawk could not believe his eyes, but the trees in the forest appeared to tremble in fear, causing ash to float from the canopy of leaves and branches. The forest clearly amplified the little girl's voice, and the sound wave made the red liquid beneath Gilgamesh's gel layers vibrate most violently. Madison's wailing not only drove the alien back, but hurt him so severely that the boosters on his back quickly sprang to life. Seconds later, he rocketed through the woods and into the early morning sky.

At first, Madison feared that the demon still held her in his clutches, but after a moment she peaked through one eye and saw that it had gone. At the same time, Hawk shook off his mental cobwebs and stared at his step-daughter with absolute astonishment. The extraterrestrial was no longer there; only a toad remained on the ground between two extremely large footprints. Madison had seen it too. She giggled, walked over to the animal, and poked it with a stick as it tried to hop away. Hawk just stood there baffled. He didn't know what to make of it all. It almost appeared as if the entire forest had granted Maddy her little wish, and turned the evil fiend into a toad.

Eventually, Hawk cleared his throat and readied to leave, "Come on Maddy. Let's get out of here." He held out his left hand. She dropped her stick and ran towards him, her arms reaching to be picked up by her step-father. Relieved, Shane swung her around, planting a big kiss on her forehead. Afterwards, Hawk grabbed his rifle and together they made their way back through the forest and towards the camp.

As Shane arrived at the perimeter, two NARC soldiers approached him and he set Maddy down. They snapped a salute and one of them said, "We've been expecting you sir."

"If you'll come with us sir? General May is waiting for you," the other soldier continued.

"Waiting for me?" Hawk asked somewhat puzzled as he followed them. "What does he want with me?"

"Your wife had reported you and the girl missing as of an hour ago. General May put everyone on alert, but wouldn't send anyone to look for you," the private responded as they passed some trucks and entered the bivouac.

"How long have I been gone?" Shane wondered aloud.

"About two hours sir," came the polite reply.

Hawk was baffled again, "Two hours? It seemed like thirty minutes."

"Does time move slower in the forest or when I had the vision of the ancient city?" he pondered, but came to no satisfactory conclusion.

"I don't know what to tell you sir; your wife came to us about an hour ago," the soldier shrugged as they approached the Command APC. There was a NARC sentry standing guard by the side entrance hatch and as they stopped in front of him, he punched a number combination into a keypad. The door hissed and opened with a thud. Hawk walked inside, Madison still in his arms, to face General May who had gotten up from his seat and glared at him stony-faced.

To Shane's great delight, Angel and Emily were present as well and both ran up to him, overjoyed to see him alive. Madison jumped into her mother's arms and the two exchanged hugs and lots of kisses. Even the stoic May broke into something of a smile during this emotional reunion. But then his expression hardened as Hawk approached him. "Report Lieutenant!" he snapped, clearly annoyed.

"Sir," Shane stood at attention. "I woke up during the night and went to check on the kids, when I noticed that Madison was missing. Of course, I went looking for her. I realized that she had left the perimeter and followed her tracks into the woods," he explained.

"Maddy! You know better than to run off like that," Angel scolded. Confused, Madison put her head on her mother's shoulders and quietly frowned. "God, I'm glad you two are safe!" Angel exclaimed and embraced Shane with Madison in her arms. His interview interrupted by this very public display of affection, May merely cleared his throat, obviously unsympathetic to the situation.

Flustered by the general's peculiar reaction, Hawk eventually took his helmet off and they all saw the dried-up blood on his nose. "Oh my God, what happened to you?" Emily shrieked.

"I encountered an alien out in the woods when I found her," he explained, rubbing his dirtied face. "It seemed very intent on fighting me in order to get to Maddy," Shane continued. "I shot it at point blank range with my .45 and escaped into the woods with Madison. But the monster set up an ambush and would have killed me, if Madison hadn't screamed. Then it disappeared," he trailed off, without mentioning what had happened to the alien afterward.

"It just … disappeared?" May asked dumbfounded, obviously questioning Shane's honesty. "How does that happen Lieutenant?"

"I don't know, sir. I can't explain it; it just disappeared as if Madison had wished it away."

"Wished it away, sure," the general sneered. By now, even his family gave Hawk puzzled looks, followed by a momentary silence. Finally May barked condescendingly, "Whatever Lieutenant, take your family and get some rest. We're rolling out in four hours." Hawk nodded and rendered a salute which the general returned. "And Lieutenant, get yourself cleaned up. That looks nasty."

Hawk and his loved ones quickly left the APC. Back at the tents, Almazan and Amanda were waiting for them. The sergeant had his weapon slung over his shoulder and donned his "snivel gear"—Army slang for winter wear like gloves and scarves. He was cold and said somewhat reproachfully, "You know I was about to go look for you."

Enervated and exhausted, Hawk merely mumbled, "Sorry, I had slightly more pressing concerns."

Almazan shrugged. He didn't blame his friend. If it had been his child, he would have done the same thing. However, what continued to astound Almazan was Shane's devotion to those kids. Madison and her siblings weren't even his, but Shane loved them as if they were his own. The sergeant had always admired this particular character trait of Hawk's, but never said so openly. Instead, he gave Shane lip about it.

"You shouldn't have gone out there alone, sir," he reprimanded him with a shrug.

"Yeah I know. But when it comes to my family," Hawk paused for a moment, "I'll always act first and ask questions later." Almazan shook his head in feigned disagreement, while he and Amanda returned to their tent.

Feeling scruffy, Lieutenant Hawk retrieved some baby wipes from the truck's back cargo hatch and started cleaning himself up as best he could. All the while his thoughts wandered back to the events in the forest, the alien he had fought, and General May's dismissive response after hearing of his step-daughter's rescue.

More importantly, why did the general blow the whole incident off so suddenly?

That's when Shane felt something else on his face as he wiped the blood off. He needed a shave, something he hadn't done in the last few days.

On The Sixth Day,

Ten miles south of Cleveland the convoy stopped to clean out the vehicle engines at a functioning fire department. They also sprayed down the clogged ash that had gotten stuck in the joints of the combat robots. It had taken the May expedition most of the morning and mid-afternoon to find an alternate route around the decimated city of Akron, since the freeway had become impassable due to blast craters and collapsed bridges.

While half of the trek was still going through a makeshift wash-rack, General May ordered the vehicles that had already completed their maintenance to scout out the city and stock up on supplies. They were also to rendezvous with smaller mobile regiments from Nashville, New York, Philadelphia, and Washington D.C. that had radiocd May's element a few hours prior. In fact, the Nashville contingent was only twenty minutes away, while the New York, Philadelphia, and Washington D.C. expeditions were a little more than an hour out. The general had instructed some of his men to wait in Akron until the other convoys arrived.

Lieutenant Hawk, his family, as well as Almazan and Amanda drove into the city. Shane had the sergeant pull into a parking garage and drive up to the roof. After parking the vehicle, they all dismounted. Hawk looked at his wife carrying the M22A3 in her hands.

"Let's go up that building there and get a birds-eye view of the city," Hawk told them and walked to the back of the truck. After moving aside some ammo boxes and the kids' bags of clothes, he came upon four parachute trays. He held one up and scrutinized it. After passing it to Almazan, he picked up another for inspection. Almazan placed the first one snuggly against the back of Hawk's armored vest.

"And what are we going to do with these sir?" the sergeant asked, not seeing the potential for their use. Hawk turned around and locked Almazan's parachute pack tray onto the vest's back.

"See that big, tall building in front of you?" Almazan duly took note of a three hundred story edifice attached to the much smaller parking garage. "We're going up to the roof to have a look-see. If this mess hits the fan, I want an escape option," Shane explained. The sergeant nodded with a bit of a shrug.

"I'm coming too," Angel interjected as she walked around the rear of the vehicle.

Hawk had almost secured Almazan's pack tray and replied, "It'll be dangerous sweetie."

"I know, but I'm going with you," she insisted.

The lieutenant knew better than to argue with her. He knew she was good at getting what she wanted when she wanted it. "All right," he sighed resignedly. He reached into the trunk and fished out another parachute pack. After inspecting his wife's jump gear, he helped her put it on, tightening the harness straps down to her thighs, around the waist line, and over her shoulders. Then he explained how to operate the device. "IF" they needed to use it, Shane told Angel gravely, she had to count to "four thousand" after her foot left the edge of the building.

"If it doesn't open automatically, like it should, by the time you reach six thousand, slap the release button," Shane impressed on her and pointed to a red knob on her left hip. "If we jump, drop the weapon. And also, make sure you keep your feet and knees together upon landing."

"Just let your body go limp as soon as your toes touch the ground," Almazan piped in.

"Wait," Angel paused. "I have to count to four thousand? What if I lose count around 3, 250?"

Shane and Almazan laughed, "No sweetie," Shane giggled, "Count one-thousand, two-thousand, three-thousand, four-thousand."

"Oh! I was was gonn'a say…" she gave her husband a goofy smirk.

"I'll stay back here with the kids," Amanda informed them. Almazan removed his M19A3 pistol from the hip holster, double-checked the magazine to ensure rounds were in it, and handed it to her.

She took the pistol and sighed, "Be careful baby."

"You know me," Almazan smiled at her.

"That's what I'm afraid of," she frowned.

Angel nodded and together with Hawk and Almazan set out for the entrance of the skyscraper adjacent to the parking garage. As they climbed up thousands of stairs, the small band was struck by the chaos surrounding them. The power was naturally out and loose papers lay scattered about everywhere, along with overturned desks, broken cubicles, and shattered windows. When the wind blew in through the glassless openings, paper wafted out the other side. And the higher they went up the stairwell, the colder it became.

Angel started to get tired mid-way up the staircase, "What floor are we on?"

"Somewhere around seventy-something." Almazan puffed.

"Good lord! Where do you guys find the energy to do this and keep going throughout the day?" she pondered.

"We get our energy from you." Shane smiled. Angel cocked an eye-brow at him. Sergeant Almazan shrugged in agreement.

"What you mean?"

"We push ourselves to get to the top and beyond because of you, our loved ones. You are what drives us to do better, to push ourselves. If we fail, it could spell disaster down the line. So getting tired, failing, giving up is not an option for us because at any moment, you may need us." Shane explained as they reached the hundredth floor.

Angel pondered what Shane must go through every day. She never quite understood why he would come home some nights late from work and not want to anything but sit on the couch and watch the television. But now, as the near the final steps to the top of the building, did she realize that was all she wanted to do. However, knowing her kids were down below inside the CGT with only Amanda there to protect them, did she muster the strength to carry herself to the top. That thought suddenly made her regret coming along.

On the roof, arctic air blasted, chilling them to the marrow. Hawk, with Angel in tow, dragged himself to the north side of the high-rise. Looking out over the city, it took him a moment to notice the commotion a few miles further east at street level.

An energy distortion bubble had sprung up on a corner, and thousands of armored aliens were pouring out of its sphere. "What's going on down there?" Angel asked.

"We got company," Hawk answered grimly.

"How many?"

"A good thousand, maybe more," he groaned as the tiny creatures spread out, flooding the streets.

"Alpha One this is Scout, over," Shane called over his radio.

"Go ahead Scout, over," a voice replied.

"I have thousands of aliens pouring into the city five clicks from your position, over," he reported.

"Roger that, wait one," the voice confirmed.

"Let's see how we're going to get out of this mess," Almazan deliberated.

"Oh my god," Angel stared at the extraterrestrials emerging from the event horizon of the energy sphere. "What are we gonna do?"

"Scout, this is Alpha One, over," a voice asked for Shane on the radio.

"Alpha One this is Scout, go ahead, over."

"Oscar Alpha 3-1-7 is online, window only available for 5 mikes, over," the voice informed him. Hawk smiled underneath his reflective visor.

"That's an outstanding copy Alpha One," Hawk sounded happy.

Angel leaned next to Almazan and whispered, "What's Oscar Alpha 3-1-7?"

Almazan shrugged as he had no idea, "I dunno."

Holding out his right arm in front of him, Shane pulled the Velcro flap on his forearm and flipped open the small, three inch LCD screen attached to his uniform. He read the grid coordinates on the electronic map, scanning the demon-infested area. Then he touched a button on the side of his helmet with his left index finger. A laser activated, displaying the targeting information on his LCD screen. "Alpha one, target grid coordinates are 44305-16090, how copy over?"

"Scout, Alpha One, I copy 44305-16090, over," the radio voice replied.

"Roger, that's a good copy Alpha One" Hawk declared.

"Shane, what's going on?" Angel inquired, clearly frightened.

"Watch this, you're gonna love it," he paused for a moment.

Sergeant Almazan was curious too, "What's going on sir?"

"Just watch," Hawk repeated.

"Scout, this is Alpha One, Oscar Alpha 3-1-7 indicates round out, over."

"Roger that Alpha One," Hawk smiled and waited.

High above the Earth, in a geosynchronous orbit overhead the North American continent, Orbital Artillery Station 317 came to life. The satellite reconfigured itself as a single, five thousand pound, uranium-tipped artillery round loaded into the satellites firing block. Shortly afterwards, the satellite's maneuvering thrusters adjusted with precision, aiming the cannon at the exact coordinates relayed by General May's Command APC. Then, in the dead of space and amid a flash of light, the five-thousand-pound bomb silently glided from the satellite, on a collision course with Earth.

As the explosive penetrated its atmosphere, a special heat shield broke from the tip of the warhead. In the thin air, sixteen miles above the state of Texas, a streak of condensation cut across the sky. It traveled at a speed of thirteen thousand kilometers per second, and approached its target impact area in the blink of an eye.

Hawk was listening patiently when Alpha One's voice suddenly came back over the radio. "Splash!" Hawk blinked, and just then the entire alien army exploded into millions of bits and fragments.

He cheered loudly, "Dead on Alpha One! Fire for effect!"

"Roger that Scout, rounds out," Alpha One replied.

Within a matter of moments, additional explosions obliterated the two city blocks, leveling buildings, cars, and disintegrating anything within the kill zone. Angel covered her ears as the noise from the incoming rounds screeched like nails on a chalkboard. More missiles cut through the sky with detonations rattling the entire city. Almazan applauded the deafening thunder, while Hawk just stood there, maintaining his composure and glaring down at the rain of destruction.

"Alpha One, this is Scout, hostile enemy forces have been neutralized," Hawk scoured the area for any surviving creatures that may have escaped the devastating orbital bombardment, but found none. "I say again, enemy forces have been neutralized, one hundred over hundred."

"Roger that Scout, good shooting, bring it on in," Alpha One ordered.

"Roger Alpha One, returning to you now," Hawk closed the LCD screen on his forearm and turned off the laser designator in his helmet.

After surveying the damage once more, he turned around and said, "Let's go."

Angel reached for his hand and together they walked back to the stairwell. But Almazan didn't follow; instead he darted to the southern edge of the rooftop. Clambering up the side of the high-rise were a dozen armored fiends with weapons strapped to their backs, snarling fangs and beady red eyes. "Oh no!" Almazan aimed his rifle at the closest one and opened fire. The creature hissed and leapt off the building as the rounds danced in place. Seconds later, boosters on its back ignited and it lunged upwards through the air towards Almazan.

After hearing the gun shots, Shane and Angel sped back to the rooftop terrace. They spotted the sergeant balancing on a ledge, just as a four-foot-tall, armored alien soldier was about to knock him on his back. Shane didn't hesitate; he raised his rifle and unleashed a barrage of fire on the extraterrestrial grunt. Red, oily blood sprayed about the wounded creature as each projectile punctured its armor. Still airborne, it screamed in pain, eventually crashing onto the very edge of the concrete roof. Mortally wounded, it then slid off the side, and fell three hundred stories to its death.

A relieved Almazan jumped to his feet, grabbed his weapon, and ran over to Shane and Angel who were still standing by the stairwell entrance. "Thanks sir!" he panted.

"How many are there?" Shane counted with his weapon at the low-ready.

"About a dozen." Almazan took comfort in standing next to them.

"We gotta get out of here," Angel remarked anxiously, "The kids are all alone down there."

"Right, let's move!" Shane yelled and was about to hurry down the steps when he heard snarling from the staircase. "They're inside the building now."

"Now what?" Almazan exclaimed tersely.

"We'll jump," Shane patted him on the shoulder, and even though neither the sergeant nor Angel could see him smiling through his visor, they knew he was. Shane noticed the look of fear overcome Angel's eyes.

"Just remember baby, drop the weapon, feet and knee's together, and let your body go limp when your feet touch the ground." He consoled her.

Moments later, Shane took off in a dead run and leapt off the building's eastern ledge, dropping his weapon over the side. Angel, of course, was extremely nervous, and so was Almazan.

"He's nuts!" he told her, shaking his head.

A sudden growl from the stairwell interrupted their conversation. Rather than face an alien, Angel decided to follow her husband. Jumping into the void, she too dropped her weapon as her feet left the ledge.

"You're both nuts!" Almazan shouted as she disappeared into the cold December morning.

The scraping of talons on metal stairs hurt the sergeant's ears. He was still not looking forward to parachuting, but as soon as he noticed a three-fingered hand grasping the door frame his mind was made up. "Ahhh, this is nuts!!!" Almazan yelled and took off after Shane and Angel. As he leapt off the rim, the wind rushed up and carried him away from the high-rise. Momentarily distracted, Almazan accidentally let go of his weapon. He cursed himself, but then spotted Angel and Shane's green silk parachutes a hundred feet below. With a sense of relief he felt the shock of the parachute opening, and grunted as his body was yanked against his armored vest. Approaching ground, his decent slowed considerably.

Shane was the first of the three to reach the top of the neighboring parking garage. He rolled as his feet touched the pavement. Shortly afterwards his parachute collapsed and he ejected the pack tray from his vest. Running over to the Combat Gun Truck, Shane saw that all the children and Amanda were still inside. "Everyone all right?" he asked with a grin as he pulled another M22A3 rifle from the rack and loaded a new magazine into its well.

"We're ok Shane!" Emily spun around, watching openmouthed as her mother landed on the pavement several meters behind her stepfather. Arching an eyebrow, she blurted out, "Mom?" She could not believe that her mother had just jumped from the top of a skyscraper.

While his stepdaughter pondered Angel's courage, Shane pulled back on the cocking lever, loading a round into the breach. He then pointed his rifle in Almazan's direction. His wife was unbuckling her parachute harness as Hawk carefully watched the sergeant descend. He was well aware that several aliens were poking their heads out of the building's broken windows, leering at the prey floating past them. One of them banged its head against a window frame, hissing in frustration.

With no time to lose, Shane squeezed off a single round. The tracer burned through the air so fast and close to Almazan that he could feel its heat rush by him. Due to Hawk's accuracy, however, it soared above the sergeant, striking one of the monsters between its beady, red eyes. Reddish brain matter splattered against the top of a ceiling, while its arms and empty gel sack—the alien version of a skull—slumped over the windowpane like a deflated balloon.

"Hey! Watch where you're shooting that thing!" Almazan scolded him from the air.

"If you were any slower, I would've hit you!" Shane shouted back.

Terrified that the aliens might get to her children, Angel picked up the last M22A3 rifle from the back of the truck, loaded a magazine, and took position next to her husband.

"Crap, here they come!" Shane noticed another beast leaping from the building's eighty-second floor. He began firing as Almazan landed a few meters away from him. Angel also shot into the air as aliens began to swarm around them. It was much harder to hit moving, let alone flying targets, but one of Angel's tracer rounds struck an extraterrestrial's boosters. It exploded into a fireball, splashing to the ground a dozen meters away from the vehicle.

Almazan hurriedly ejected the pack tray from his vest and then ran over to the Combat Gun Truck. He climbed into the turret, swiveled the .50 caliber rail gun around to the rear, and arched the weapon to its highest angle. As soon as the first alien soldier came into his sights, he opened fire, blowing it into tiny bits.

Of course, the exploding rounds scared the children who sat huddled up in the truck. Out of their wits with fear, they covered their ears. In fact, Jon and Maddy cried out after each devastating bang.

In the meantime, more aliens swooped and dived out of the high-rise. Approaching ground, they grew increasingly proficient at dodging bullets, fluttering past them by following the line of tracers. "Get in the truck!" Shane ordered his wife.

"There's only a few left!" she yelled back over the noise of the fifty cal."

"We gotta go! Now go!" he shouted and gave her a shove.

Stumbling backwards, Angel got angry and shot him a stern look of disapproval. "GO!" he yelled again.

"Fine!" she dashed back to the vehicle, closed the back hatch, and climbed into the driver's seat. Meanwhile, Shane launched a few more rounds at four creatures less than a hundred feet above them. After clambering into the TC's seat, he looked at his wife and pressed her, "Go! Go! Go!"

She threw the truck in reverse as Almazan continued to blast away with the rail gun. One of the monsters had landed behind them, and everyone heard a thud and crunch as the heavy tires squashed their attacker. Satisfaction left a smile on Angel's lips. The truck was hurtling down an exit ramp and several levels of parking garage to the street level when it suddenly screeched to a halt. A large fat alien stood there waiting, blocking their path. "Run him down!" Shane barked.

Angel pressed her foot on the gas pedal and the engine roared. At the same time, Almazan swiveled the gun to the front and released a barrage of gunfire at the fat fiend. Shane watched with grim pleasure as the rounds ripped the extraterrestrial apart and splattered guts and various limbs across the concrete. The body collapsed just as the truck's front bumper hit it head-on. Bouncing violently, its tires ran over the corpse, smearing the road with blood and flesh. Cold sweat ran down Angel's back as she turned south to reconnect with May's convoy at the firehouse.

There weren't out of danger yet. A pair of aliens was in hot pursuit of the fleeing vehicle, forcing Almazan to continually fire his rail gun. A lucky fifty caliber round vaporized one ugly head, turning it into a cloud of red, oily mist. The body then splattered on the street. Furious, the last surviving demon of the group bared its fangs, but then sped down an alleyway in between two large buildings. Rather than ending up dead, it gave up the chase and let the humans escape.

Almazan switched the weapon to safe mode, climbed down from the turret, and closed the hatch above him. He plunked himself down on Angel's seat and took a deep breath, leaning against the chair. Amanda reached across and placed her hand on his. He was trembling. "It's ok baby," she tried to reassure him.

"Are they gone?" Jon looked around, his eyes filled with terror.

No one said a word.

Angel continued to rush through Akron's abandoned streets.

"Right here," Shane told her as they approached an intersection. But she was lost in thought, missed the turn, and drove on.

"Angel!" Shane yelled. "Slow down! They're gone."

She looked at him with a strange glare in her eyes. Shane took off his helmet. "Turn us around hun. We're heading back to the firehouse," he repeated and placed his hand on her shoulder. She nodded absentmindedly, took her foot off the gas pedal, and made a U-turn. As they were heading back north Shane instructed, "Left here," pointing at the junction they had passed before. This time she made the turn, followed the road back to the freeway, and joined the southbound lanes.

They drove for a mile and a half and then continued on a maintenance road, passing by several MHMMV Combat Gun Trucks and one APC before pulling up alongside General May's Command APC on the north side of the firehouse. Exhausted, Angel slumped back in the seat, eyes closed. A few minutes later, she crossed her arms and buried her face in the steering wheel. Shane could see her tearing up. "This is why I didn't want you to fight with me," he thought to himself. After patting her on the back, Hawk climbed out of the truck to brief the general on their scouting mission.

Chapter Seven: Cowboy Diplomacy

Shane Hawk's family in Monroe, Michigan was gathered around a large, holographic plasma video screen, watching the String of Pearls Satellite System broadcast the unfolding cataclysm for the sixth day in a row. More and more television stations had stopped transmitting, and there were only a handful left to flip through now. All repeated the same horror stories of devastation and destruction across the globe. One channel aired news out of Detroit, some thirty miles north. A flustered reporter labored to explain a phenomenon happening just behind him, as police and NARC forces stood helplessly confused around an energy distortion bubble.

Then something stepped through the event horizon behind the correspondent. Gun and laser fire erupted only seconds later as energy plasma bolts and beam cannons began to pursue a large, armored alien creature attacking the bystanders. Chaos ensued, the reporter panicked, and a plasma projectile was hurled directly at the camera. The screen subsequently turned to static, forcing Marshal to look for another channel.

The next station was nothing but news again, but at least this anchor sat safely ensconced behind a desk. "Early this morning, Jackson Penitentiary saw the worst prison riot in the history of this state. It is unclear how many prisoners escaped the maximum security facility, but Michigan State Police report that infamous serial killer, Matthew Clark, also known as "Bear," is among the escapees and currently at large. Police urge viewers to report any sightings of the dangerous criminal."

He continued, "In other news, the North American Regional Command Weapons and Armory Depot in Plymouth, Michigan was raided by unknown individuals. Lieutenant Colonel Jimmy Westlake of the Selfridge Air National Guard has issued no comment at this time."

While the TV voice blared on, Harris tried to control Safyre, his five-year-old daughter. Meanwhile, his youngest brother Marshal and wife June were largely oblivious to the ruckus around them. They sat in two armchairs, intently watching the video screen as their one-year-old son Paulee chased the dog around the house. Eventually June offered Safyre a cheddar goldfish cracker and she came running over, mouth wide open. Relieved to see her distracted, Harris suddenly got up.

"Where are you going?" June asked.

"Gonna call John again. Just want to make sure he's ok," Harris replied.

Walking around a partition in the house, he then grabbed the phone off the desk set in the kitchen wall. He paused before dialing and looked out the large, sliding glass doors that led to the snow and ash-covered backyard. There was a pond back there, and he could see some Canadian geese swimming around peacefully. Staring at the tranquil scene, Harris hit the redial button. The numbers beeped and a connection was established.

"What's up Harris?" John asked while his hover bike hummed softly in the background.

"How far away are you man?" Harris inquired.

"About five minutes. Turning onto M-50 now," John informed him.

"Make it snappy. The whole world is falling apart. The reports on the TV are getting worse," his friend cautioned.

"Did you see the news on the Yellowstone Super Volcano eruption?" John wondered.

"Yeah, and it's been dropping ash and snow all over the country ever since. Just get here in one piece," Harris exclaimed nervously. He was gazing at the pond with its swimming geese again when something caught his attention. A large bird came diving out of the sky and into the water, clawed its prey with sharp talons, and took off into the clouds again. "Whoa! That was awesome!" Harris was excited.

"What?" came a question over the phone.

"A bald eagle just snagged a fish out of the pond out back. That was so awesome!" he explained to his best friend.

"Sweet! Hey, I'm pulling into the neighborhood now," John told him.

"Good," Harris hung up and walked to the front door, the image of the majestic eagle still fresh in his mind.

Safyre sidled up next to him.

"They are reporting some kind of powerful storm traveling in this direction from the west. Heavy lightning warning and possible tornadoes," Marshal informed him from the couch.

"Marshal, take June, Paulee, and Safyre downstairs," Harris called into the living room.

"OK!" his brother yelled back in annoyance, rolling his eyes and stomping his feet as he chased Safyre around the house.

"Can't catch me Uncle Marshal!" the little girl smiled and took off running.

Amused, he chased after her.

"What about Ambyr?" June wondered.

Harris furrowed his brow and thought hard. His younger daughter had gone to her Grandmother Lori's house for a few days while she was on winter vacation from pre-school. But Plymouth was a forty-five minute drive and he foresaw trouble. Scott—his ex-wife Kim's irritating brother and Safyre and Ambyr's uncle—would also be there. The man had a nasty disposition and, like his sister Kim, was a self-proclaimed know-it-all. Scott not only tried to tell Harris and even Kim what he and his nieces would be doing on any given holiday, but often acted in the most irresponsible manner. Without so much as asking their parents, he would take the girls out and fail to return them at the scheduled pick-up time. As a result, Harris and Scott had engaged in their fair share of altercations, although it had never come to blows.

His mind racing, Harris walked into the garage and had John park his hover cycle next to piles of boxes and junk stacked up alongside the wall.

"John, I need to borrow your bike," he pleaded when his longtime friend had taken his helmet off. Pulling his long hair away from of his face, John gave him a look of mock surprise.

"Harris, you know better than that. Nobody drives this baby but me," he frowned.

"John, I need you to stay here and help Marshal protect the house while I go get Ambyr. It's a forty-five minute drive in the truck. I can get there in half the time with the bike," Harris entreated him.

"If there's a problem with Scott, I want to be there too," John retorted, hoping for a chance to a get a crack at the hated brother-in-law. "You know I don't trust that fool."

"I can handle Scott. I was in the Marines, ya know," Harris grinned proudly.

"That was ten years ago bud. How many fights have you been in since then?" John badgered.

Harris looked at his friend. He was a couple of inches taller than John at 5'9", but far thinner. Still athletic in his own right, Harris possessed a wiry strength that had often surprised John when they roughhoused or wrestled.

"I can see you don't look all that convinced, John, but this is something I have to do," Harris appealed to him.

"Well...I'm worried that it won't be just Scott there. He may have his little peon lackeys with him," John reminded Harris of his former in-law's drug-addicted friends.

"Well, as soon as things start to go down, I'll yank this out to clean it," Harris pulled a semi-automatic .45 caliber hand pistol from his waistband. "Just in case," he added gravely.

"You know, I didn't see a single cop on the road. I think everybody's hiding at home, waiting to see what happens. You might have a clear run into Plymouth if you hurry," John made mention of his own mental notes and then threw Harris the keys. His friend snatched them and returned to the house,

"Let me say goodbye to Safyre."

John followed Harris and opened the door to the basement stairs. From below they could hear more awful stories coming in from the radio that Marshal had just turned on. As soon as they reached the bottom steps, Safyre ran over to John and wrapped her arms around him. Marshal gave Harris' friend a brotherly welcome with a one arm hand shake, a butting of the shoulder, and a pat on the back.

"Good to see you bud," John told him as he let go of his strong grip. Although Marshal towered over him at six feet six inches, he weighed as much as Harris. Being that tall and light made him skinny as a rail, but his true strength didn't come from his physical prowess or endurance. Marshal was smart and musically inclined. He enjoyed playing chess against Harris and John and had often humiliated them with a few simple moves. Cold and calculating in his game tactics, he could be equally devious with people he disliked. He owed much to his wife June and their son Paulee, who had managed to smooth Marshal's rough edges.

"I'm going by myself to pick up Ambyr. I'll be taking John's hover bike," Harris determined.

"No! We should all go together!" Safyre yelled. Marshal rolled his eyes, while June paid no attention to them. Instead, she carried Paulee to the fish tank in the back of the basement, which hadn't had a good cleaning in over a month.

Concerned, Harris hugged his frightened, shaking daughter. "I'm going with you!" Safyre sobbed as she buried her face in his shirt, clinging to him.

"I'll bring your sister back, darlin'," Harris whispered into her hair.

Safyre's head immediately jerked up, clocking Harris in the jaw and stung like hell. He bit his tongue and refrained from getting angry as his eyes teared up. Instead he shook off the pain, rubbed her head where his jaw hit her and kissed it. "Darlin" was a term of affection Harris didn't use very often, and it told her two things: first, that he was confident in his course of action which she needed to trust, and second, that he did love her.

Rubbing the pain on his chin with his hand, he remembered back to the last time he was hit so hard. He and Shane had gotten into an altercation the night before Shane left to join the Army. The altercation came to blows and Shane caught Harris with and uppercut which should've knocked his teeth out of his mouth. That memory made Harris wonder where his younger brother was, if he was still alive, and if he would ever see him again.

"I will be ok," Harris claimed, now addressing his family and friend. "I've got the .45 and there's no faster ride than with John's bike."

June set Paulee down and he waddled over to a stack of picture frames near the storm doors. He picked up the topmost photo in his tiny hands and carried the dusty frame across the basement floor, holding it up to his father. "Jay Jay!" he muttered happily.

Marshal took the portrait from his blonde-haired, blue-eyed son and commented, "Your uncle Shane isn't here Paulee, sorry."

The toddler didn't quite understand, but he missed his crazy uncle. He then made his way to a shelf in the corner, where an open plastic box of toys invited him to make a mess. Shane didn't see much of his family after marrying Angel, but Marshal and June brought Paulee down to North Carolina six months ago to introduce Paulee to his new aunt and uncle and cousins. Marshal thought the world of Paulee for recognizing his uncle Shane from an old photograph.

Meanwhile, Harris picked up Safyre again and covered her sweet little face with kisses. She giggled when he rubbed his unshaven face against her cheeks, tickling her. When he put her down, the others all looked away, "I hope Shane is ok," Harris thought aloud about his brother. Again, nobody said a word.

"I'll call you from the bike's phone when I get there," Harris continued after a moment's pause. Then he ran up the stairs and into the garage. John followed him to open and close the garage door. Harris straddled the hover bike and turned the powerful engine over. He was immediately lifted off the floor with a steady hum. Dust and dried up leaves that had blown into the small building flew around chaotically.

"Hey," John caught Harris before he was about to ignite the throttle, "See you when you get back." As the door slid open, the wind rushed inside. Grey clouds with thick, dark thunderheads were rolling in from the southwest. Harris hit the accelerator with a nod and sped out of the driveway while John just stood there, hoping that he hadn't seen his friend for the last time. Moments later, Harris exited the neighborhood.

He turned onto M-50, the divided highway that stretched from Monroe to the western side of the state of Michigan. The four lane highway ran east and west through the lower half of Michigan all the way to Jackson past Ann Arbor—the farthest he'd ever traveled on the road in that particular direction. This time, however, Harris drove east until he arrived at an intersection and then turned north onto Telegraph Road. He took care to follow the speed limit, watching for cops. But he hardly saw anyone. Monroe was a ghost town. There were a few people locking up their businesses, but they seemed in a hurry to reach home before the storm rolled in, which loomed like hell on the horizon.

Harris reached Interstate 275 after a ten minute drive and veered onto the freeway. Here he revved up the throttle, pushing the bike well over the permitted speed. Keeping a close watch on the radar detector, he didn't notice any other traffic, let alone police. The hover bike was racing along nicely as he reached speeds in excess of one hundred sixty miles an hour. Halfway to his destination, the radar detector began to blare a warning. Harris slowed down to the legal limit straightaway, and watched for a cop to pull him over.

Seconds later he spotted a BMW hover sports car. It was being chased by three policemen in hover vehicles on the other side of the interstate, heading south. Harris slowed down even further and merged into the right lane to give the chase plenty of room. After all, something stupid might happen, like the sports car jumping the median. He needn't have worried; everyone just darted past him. Soon the blaring sirens trailed off into the distance as he continued on his way.

Harris hit the throttle again and the hover bike lurched forward. In no time, it shot along the concrete until Harris reached the M-14—another freeway that ran east and west—where he turned on the exit ramp. With no traffic in sight, he raced down another interstate, took yet another exit, and then turned right. Suddenly, the eerie silence was shattered by sonic booms screaming above the tree line as well as the thunderous roar of engines. Confused, Harris didn't know what to make of the commotion; he couldn't locate the source of the noise above his head.

Paved roads soon ended and turned to dirt as he blew through a traffic light. A short curve and three minutes up the rolling country lane, Harris calculated, and he would hold Ambyr safely in his arms. All of a sudden, however, he was forced to slow down. A strange, airborne distortion was cutting him off from his destination. Bended light flitted across the dirt path as Harris hit the airbrakes. He was almost thrown off the hover cycle when the apparition's air foils opened like parachutes.

For several minutes Harris just stood there, awestruck by the shimmering energy source. Its line was about twenty feet tall and glowed intensely, even in the dim afternoon light. Harris resolved that this radiant force couldn't hurt him, and accelerated slowly through it. He was right. It didn't hurt. Instead, Harris felt energized…even physically stronger.

Utterly intrigued, he stopped the bike in the middle of the alien force field. He had studied metaphysics for years and knew that many ancient cultures believed in "ley lines" of magic energy that crisscrossed the planet. Of course, Harris never thought that he'd be able to see one. Many bygone societies had placed monuments where they suspected intersecting lines. Stonehenge, the Great Pyramids of Egypt, the Temple of Ur in Mesopotamia, and the Statues of Easter Island are prime examples among many others.

Harris decided to perform an experiment. He closed his eyes and concentrated on the aura, visualizing a thick energy shell surrounding his body. Immediately, he felt a powerful pulse surging through his veins. Shortly afterwards, Harris opened his eyes and cycled out of the energy distortion. The force field had become "stuck" to his inner being, and he now glowed softly as well. But his vision was suddenly blurry and Harris removed his prescription glasses, rubbing his eyes. Before putting them back on, he noticed something peculiar. His eyesight was sharp—so sharp that his pupils ached. Harris didn't know what to make of it. Perhaps it was a blessing.

After marveling at his restored vision, Harris picked up the phone on the bike's instrument panel and dialed his number home. Unfortunately, all he got in response was an out of service message. "Crap," he put the phone back. He was worried if his daughter, John, Marshal, Paulee, and June were still alright. Looking up, he noticed that the energy line had moved on and across the property where Ambyr was staying with her grandmother. Harris sped down the long driveway. Nobody was outside as he parked the bike, but he did see a few horses stick their heads out of the barn windows. Running up to the front door, he found it wide open.

Inside the farmhouse, Harris was alarmed by a cacophony of noise. Radios and TVs blared in several rooms at a very high volume. Wincing at the assault on his ears, Harris wondered if his hearing capabilities had been heightened as well. He quickly made his way through the kitchen to the guest bedroom. Ambyr was sitting on a couch, earphones on, playing a handheld video game. Harris wanted to remain unnoticed for the moment as he combed the house for additional occupants. He carefully closed the door and began a room by room search. The closet next to the side entrance was full of coats and other winter items, he noticed, indicating several visitors.

The second guest bedroom was empty as was Grandmother Lori's room. Harris knocked on the spare bathroom door which had been left slightly ajar. When it swung open, Harris drew his breath in. Lori was lying face down in a bathtub filled with her own blood. Shocked, Harris briefly touched the back of her neck and realized that she was ice-cold. She must've been dead for a while, he thought, his mind racing. While he had no love for the sixty-eight-year-old woman, it pained him to see her like this. In truth, she had been the only member of his ex-wife's family that he had grudgingly respected.

Suddenly, he sensed someone standing behind him. Out of the corner of his eye, Harris saw Ambyr, her eyes wide with terror. He rushed out the door and slammed it behind him, not wanting his daughter to bear witness to the gruesome spectacle.

"Is Gamma Lori ok?" Ambyr asked, her entire body shaking. Tears were running down her face, and all Harris could do was swoop her up and wrap her in his arms.

"She's sleeping," he lied. Sensing that this was untrue, Ambyr began to sob. Harris quickly carried her into the kitchen. Setting her on the counter, he looked his daughter in the eye, "Ambyr, do you know where your uncle is?"

"He was in his room earlier," she replied.

"Ambyr, I want you to stay in your room and keep playing that video game," her father ordered.

"I'm on the forth level!!!" the little girl yelped excitedly.

"Shh. Ok, just be quiet for a few minutes and then I'll take you home," Harris promised.

"Ok daddy," Ambyr jumped from the counter and ran back to the guestroom. Harris heard the door close as he looked out the windows into the pasture.

Moments later, as he hurried towards Scott's room, a shadow appeared in the hallway, halfway across the living room. It was Harris's former brother-in-law, with a razor-sharp blade of jagged steel taped around his right hand. "I knew you were coming Harris," Scott grinned menacingly, "I've been waiting for this moment for a long time."

Before he could duck, Scott lunged forward, aiming the tip of his homemade weapon at his chest. Unable to draw his firearm, Harris threw up his arms…and the point of the blade skipped off his softly glowing protective shield. Unbeknownst to himself, he was still enveloped in the aural armor that he had acquired on the road. Both men looked at each other in surprise. Harris smirked, overjoyed that the shield was working. He held out his hand and concentrated.

Years of dealing with this impossible in-law had left reserves of pent-up anger in Harris that he couldn't measure. Suddenly, all of that anger erupted. Arches of lightning shot out of Harris's fingers and struck Scott in the chest. Astonished, he examined his hand while Scott was catapulted five feet backwards, crashing against the wall. Twitching from the residual electricity coursing through his body, the demented man could not keep his fingers on the blade. It fell to the floor, sticking tip first into the carpet. Dazed, Scott slowly rose to his feet, his eyes glinting with fury. In fact, he was driven to the point of derangement by the unexpected powers Harris had just displayed. When his former brother-in-law took a menacing step forward, Scott bolted towards the front door. Harris let him go. Ambyr was more important.

Turning back into the house, he walked up to the spare bedroom where his daughter was playing the handheld game. She was still wearing her headphones, and Harris realized with relief that she hadn't overheard his recent altercation with her uncle. She looked up as Harris appeared in the doorway.

"Ambyr, time to go," he urged.

"But I need to get my clothes."

"No time for that. Put the game in your pocket and let's get out of here," Harris said firmly.

"Alright daddy," Ambyr looked confused. Together they dashed out of a side entrance. Hurrying to the front, Harris discovered that the hover bike was no longer there. Long scrape marks indicated that it had been dragged away, towards the pasture.

"That son of a...." He paused and then told his daughter, "Alright Ambyr, you stay here on the porch and wait for me to come back."

"But I want to stay with you!" she implored him.

"Sorry sweetie, this is something that I need to take care of myself."

"OK daddy. But please hurry, it's scary out here," Ambyr pleaded as the wind ruffled her clothes. Flashes of lightning pierced the sky and thunder crackled all around them.

"I will. If you see someone, hide under the bed in the guest room ok?" Ambyr's chin quivered, but she nodded reluctantly. Feeling very uneasy, Harris left his daughter behind to follow the scrape marks. He had only walked for about a minute when he spotted Lori's white, dually pick-up truck rocking back and forth in the field. Harris let out a yell when he realized that Scott was repeatedly running and backing up over John's beloved hover bike.

Letting out a long stream of expletives, he jumped over the fence into the meadow and ran to the driver's door. Harris yanked it open, but swiftly ducked as Scott fired both barrels of a side-by-side shotgun at him. The majority of the buckshot missed, but a few pellets pinged off Harris's shield. Furious, he grabbed the barrel with his hand and pulled hard. The move caught Scott off guard and he lost his balance, tumbling out of the seat and into a pile of horse manure. Tossing the empty shotgun aside, Harris kicked him in the face. Scott let out a bloodcurdling scream as his nose shattered and blood stained the ash-laden snow with red.

Meanwhile, the big farm truck was still in gear and began to roll forward. Harris stepped on Scott's head, burying his broken nose in the manure, and jumped into the vehicle. While he slammed the shifter into park, Scott reached forward to grab the shotgun again. He labored to fumble new rounds from his pocket into the breach, but Harris interrupted him. Stepping calmly away from the truck, he sneered, "Lower the weapon Scott."

"Screw you! You and Kim always wanted this property, and now that I've seen to it that my Mom is dead and Kim is in jail, you probably think you deserve it! Well you got that wrong! No no no no no no no!!! This place is mine, and nobody can take it away from me! And by the way, Ambyr is mine too!"

Scott had finished loading the shotgun and began to wave it in Harris's direction. But Harris had decided that enough was enough. He concentrated until his hands began to glow, enveloping the deranged man with a wave of mystic energy. Harris could hardly believe his new powers, but Scott visibly shrank right in front of him. Furthermore, his skin morphed into fur. A moment later and Scott had turned into a Chihuahua. The little dog yelped in surprise and fear, and then turned to run away. But Harris rushed forward and grabbed it by the neck. In turn, Scott, tried to bitc him, but could only struggle in vain against his adversary's firm grip.

Picking the snarling canine off the ground, Harris pulled a length of bailing twine out of the pickup truck, looped one end around the dog's neck, and the other around the vehicle's back bumper. The tiny pooch struggled, but Harris had secured it tightly. He then picked up the shotgun and returned to the house. Ambyr was still waiting on the porch.

"What happened to Uncle Scott?" she asked.

Harris grinned happily, "Don't worry about him. He won't be hurting anyone else."

His daughter climbed into the passenger seat and pulled her seatbelt on. "Puppy poocher," she mumbled to herself. Harris laughed; Scott was so…different now.

"Stay here for a second Ambyr," he was still smiling at the truth of his daughter's comment. "I'm gonna go grab those heavy winter coats and a few other things. We're going to need them later."

"OK," she responded. "Oh! Can we bring my PlayBox 720?" Together with John, they had spent many hours, days and nights, playing with the most sophisticated gaming system in the world. Ambyr especially loved the graphics; they were so realistic that many games— especially the sports games—could be mistaken for real television.

"Sure hun, give me a few minutes," Harris agreed. He went back inside, gathered up a few things, and then unplugged the PlayBox from the television. He also collected the controllers, wires, and extra equipment needed to play the games. Soon after, Harris threw an armful of cold weather gear and the PlayBox into the backseat of the truck.

"Let's go home," he sighed as he pulled out of the driveway and crossed the distortion line again. Passing through the force field, Ambyr stared at the mysterious blended light with wide eyes. "What is that?" she asked, clearly confused.

"That is what is turning the whole world upside down Ambyr," her father explained.

While she silently contemplated the distorted energy source, Harris sped up. Immediately, yelping could be heard from the back of the truck.

"What is that?" his daughter wondered.

"Oh, just some garbage that got stuck to the rear out in the pasture. Ignore it, it'll fall off eventually," Harris grinned a little maliciously while Ambyr nodded. She was certain the noise came from a dog and turned about in her seat trying to locate the animal.

Back on the main road, the father-daughter duo drove past a large passenger plane that had crashed onto the eastbound freeway. Jet fuel was burning ferociously and there was destruction all around them. Forced to turn in the opposite direction, Harris cursed under his breath. Taking US-23 south would take much longer now.

He pushed the big truck as fast as he dared while winds were howling and lightning danced across the sky. After swerving around many abandoned and destroyed vehicles, Harris found a good open stretch that allowed him to push the gas pedal to the floor. Suddenly, three alien creatures clad in armor raced across the road in front of him. They looked much like the ones he had seen on the news, terrorizing downtown Detroit. As Harris slammed on the brakes, the wheels locked up and the heavy vehicle skidded to a stop. Seconds later, the extraterrestrials swiveled their necks towards the sound of the squealing tires.

Shorter than the truck's hood, the monsters from space glared at the humans. Harris eyed them just as warily until the tallest of the fiendish trio leapt onto the hood, its clawed feet dancing on the waxed, shiny surface. But Harris wasn't willing to allow it a toe hold. He bore down so hard on the gas pedal that the four back tires left a trail of rubber on the pavement. The alien was first thrown against the windshield and then rolled off the side of the truck. Visibly afraid, the remaining two monsters gave the big, white vehicle plenty of room as it sped past them.

"Ambyr, you ok baby?" Harris asked.

"Yeah!" she replied with a laugh. "That was funny daddy!"

Harris grinned at his three-year-old daughter. He was glad to have rescued her from the clutches of her psychotic uncle and relieved that they had withstood their first extraterrestrial encounter so successfully. His grin widened after he heard another yelp from the rear.

The pair continued on in silence. Harris watched out for new dangers, while Ambyr fiddled with the radio. All she got was static. Her father eventually turned onto US-23 and headed south. Farm fields and storage businesses that commanded large tracts of land began to drift in and out of view. The little girl glanced out of the passenger window.

"Daddy, look!" Ambyr called out excitedly.

Harris slowed down and peered out the window as his expression switched from mild interest to complete terror. An alien—known to his younger brother's family as "The Reamer"— was stomping into view. Its massive eye balanced on a long neck, and it gleefully danced through the open field on three legs, squashing panicked cattle. Twenty feet tall and rippled with sinews and muscles, the creature also sported curled horns which extended from its temples. A large, prehensile tail lashed around its back. There was also a dark shadow or smoke that clung to its form. Harris noticed it even in the fading light that was slowly being swallowed up by the incoming storm clouds.

He revved up the engine again and the truck barreled down the freeway. The monster, realizing that the truck was the only moving thing in sight, hurled itself into the sky and disappeared behind a bank of low clouds. "Ambyr, can you still see it?" Harris asked calmly.

"No, it flew into the sky," the little girl reported excitedly. "Like whoosh!" She gestured with her hands above her head.

"Keep an eye out, it could come back from anywhere," Harris warned. In response, Ambyr leaned as close to the passenger side window as she could, diligently scanning the horizon.

Harris turned a knob to open the sunroof. He might not be able to stop the attacker from outer space, but he would do his best to see it coming. Unfortunately, neither father nor daughter noticed the alien zooming in from out of the blue. It just dropped into the truck bed, causing the vehicle to swerve violently due to the extraterrestrial's enormous weight. Fortunately, the sturdy pick-up held together. The weight of the creature grinded the axle down on the supports, but the big dually was a Ford, and built tough.

But then the monster reared up, banging its massive fists on the truck's cab. Ambyr screamed and Harris slammed on the brakes. The creature, caught off-guard, went flying over the vehicle's roof and landed in front of the grill with a dull thud. Seemingly unfazed it jumped back on its feet, drawing itself up to full height.

The bailing twine tying the Chihuahua to the back bumper of the truck broke free, and the human turned dog fell to the concrete highway. Dazed, the pint-sized little dog bolted underneath the truck, but was scooped up by the massive hand of the Reamer. The dog yipped in fear, snarled and bit at the Reamers hand, but fell to its doom inside the massive mouth of the Reamer. The Reamer bit down on the little snack, but cringed at the taste, and spat the crushed carcass of the dog out onto the hood of the truck.

"Hell, even an alien beast didn't even like the taste of him!" Harris laughed to himself.

In response, Harris threw the truck in reverse, hitting the gas pedal. He backed up about fifty feet, tires squealing, and then stopped. Pulling the .45 from its holster, Harris forced his body through the sunroof and emptied the clip into the monster just as it was bearing down on them. The Reamer flinched, rounds bouncing off its ash-encrusted skin. In fact, it just stood there laughing, amused by the human's puny weapon. Seconds later, it hurtled toward its victims.

Ambyr screamed—but not at the monster. Harris turned as he heard the sound of jet engines and then spotted two F-37 stealth fighter jets buzzing over the farm field. A volley of missiles shot out from the undercarriages of the fighters until the sleek aircraft banked away. Long trails of smoke arched in the sky as the warheads homed in on the Reamer's colossal body.

The alien momentarily disappeared in a fiery ball of white, incandescent plasma. The exploding rockets had created a shockwave and slammed Harris into the back edge of the sunroof. His lower back screamed in pain; his legs failed him. Dropping the .45 caliber pistol into the bed of the truck, he crumpled into the driver seat. Ambyr whimpered, terrified by the earthshattering noise and vibrations around her.

Minutes later, Harris peeped through the space between the dashboard and the curve of the steering wheel as the monster strolled out of the smoke cloud, apparently unharmed. Frustrated, he gritted his teeth, jerked the transmission into drive, and pounded on the gas pedal. But the alien ignored the truck and its occupants, clearly more interested in the fighter jets. Racing after them, it almost bowled over the pick-up, and then jumped into the sky in pursuit of its new prey.

The ensuing reverberations, triggered by the beast's trampling gait, made the truck rock from side to side for several moments. Then, at last, it seemed that the creature had gone for good. A smell of sulfur was all that was left and it wafted into the cabin through the open sunroof.

"You ok Ambyr?" Harris looked at the frightened little girl. She was crying with her face tucked between her knees, and feet propped up against the dashboard.

"I want my Mommy," she whimpered softly.

Harris paused for a moment, but continued to race down the freeway. He wanted to be home with the rest of his family just as much as his daughter. "I'm scared too," Harris eventually remarked with a frown. He could not let his children know that he would never allow their mother back into his life, or theirs.

Twenty minutes later they turned on the exit ramp at Dundee. A large Cabela's hunting store was just off to the right as were a number of other buildings lining the road to the factory outlet mall. As Harris headed east on M-50, he looked in his rear-view mirror and noticed several vehicles leaving a sports bar on the corner of the intersection and the highway.

To his surprise, the cars gave chase and Harris accelerated. "Now what?" he cursed and raced the truck through the old village center.

"What is it Daddy?" Ambyr looked at the passing buildings. They sped across the Raisin River Bridge and several railroad crossings.

"We're being followed," Harris kept an eye on the mirror as the vehicles behind them grew larger.

Ambyr repeated his curse.

Harris was shocked at the word that came out of Ambyr's mouth. He tried to contain himself from laughing, but instead scolded her, "Ambyr, do not repeat what I say!"

"Daddy, do not repeat what I say!" she laughed at him, thinking it was a game.

Suddenly, muzzle flashes lit up the twilight. "Get down!" he pushed Ambyr's head into the bench as bullets shattered the back windshield. More rounds punctured the tailgate and the pick-up skidded across the road.

"Who the hell are these guys!?" Harris shouted to himself.

"Yeah, who the hell are these guys!?" Ambyr continued to repeat her father in her game.

"Ambyr! Knock it off!" Harris yelled at her. Ambyr, sensing the anger in his voice, curled up into a ball and tears began to form in eyes.

Darting down the highway, Harris realized that they still had fifteen miles to go. How far could they get, he wondered, before these jokers disabled his vehicle, or worse. Moments later, one of the cars pulled up to him. Harris looked over and counted two individuals in the light pick-up truck. The driver wore a set of tinted goggles and a black vest, and sported a spiky, green mohawk. As they sped past a raging house fire on the north side of the road, Harris noticed that the man's right arm was cybernetic. Its metal gleamed in the pale light.

His passenger was a more heavyset man with a slightly graying black beard and matching full head of short, curly hair. A furry unibrow gave him a sinister, grizzly appearance, which was further heightened by the Jackson State Penitentiary tattoo on the back of his neck. He seemed angrily surprised to see Harris staring back at him.

"No way...," Harris murmured.

"Bear?" The rugged ex-convict rolled down the window while Harris did the same. "Pull over Harris!" he shouted.

"Who let your sorry carcass out of prison?!" Shane's brother yelled back.

"It's amazing what happens when the world goes to hell! Now pull it over!" he barked impatiently.

Harris looked ahead and then at his old friend from high school. "Leave us alone dude! We're not looking for trouble!" he screamed over the noise of the wind rushing by at ninety miles an hour. While his left hand controlled the steering wheel, Harris picked up the shotgun with the other, but kept it low and out of sight.

"Last warning dipstick! Pull over!" Bear roared. In response, Harris raised his rifle and aimed it out the window. The driver slammed on the brakes as he pulled the trigger. The dual barrels immediately demolished the smaller car's engine and smoke rose through pellet holes left in the hood. The pick-up eventually slowed to a halt as the larger white truck raced away. The remaining pursuers stopped as well, with "Mohawk" and Bear diving into another vehicle. Harris was about two miles away when they gave chase again.

The big, dually farm pick-up slowed down as they approached their neighborhood. Entering the family driveway, Harris bypassed his usual parking spot by pulling off into the grass, in between his and a neighbor's home.

"Hurry Ambyr! Get inside the house!" Harris tried to remain calm, but he knew that it was just a matter of time before Bear and his thugs would be flying around the corner. He shut the engine and lights off and looked across the farm field, over the pond, and down the road to see if they were still being pursued..

"Maybe the bad men didn't see us?" Ambyr opened the door and climbed out.

"I can only hope," Harris muttered and reached into the back seat, grabbing the stack of winter coats as well as the game system. While his daughter dashed towards the house, Harris—arms full—kicked the driver's door closed. The little girl opened the front door and led her father inside. Suddenly, they heard someone running up the basement stairs. John jumped out of the doorway, fists clenched, and ready for a fight. "Who goes there!" he yelled.

"Wow!" Ambyr laughed, clearly impressed. "You're funny John!"

"Easy buddy, it's just us," Harris smiled. His friend immediately let his guard down, "Thank God, took you longer than I expected."

Harris looked embarrassed, "Yeah about that … Scott destroyed your bike, I had to take Lori's truck."

"WHAT!?" John snapped. "Where is he?! I'll kill him!"

"Ambyr, please take this stuff into the basement," Harris handed his daughter the coats and game system. She tried to balance the stack which almost equaled her own height and wobbled down the wooden steps.

When she was out of earshot, Harris confided in John who was still wondering about Scott's whereabouts. "He got ate by an alien behemoth." Harris divulged with a shrug.

"What?" his friend tried to stifle a laugh, although he was still angry.

"But we have another problem," Harris changed the subject as they walked towards the front door. "Now what?" John wondered.

"Remember my old buddy Bear? The one who went to prison for killing 130 people in Detroit on Devil's Night ten years ago?" Harris cringed at the thought.

"Yeah?" John raised an eyebrow, his attitude not forgiving.

"Yeah, we ran into him on the way back here and I'm pretty sure he's on his way with a gang of thugs." John paused at the door and wondered.

"How do you know?"

"Well, I think I pissed him off by shooting out the engine of his truck," Harris snickered.

"Yeah, that would do it," John nodded in agreement as he peered outside, "It's getting dark."

Harris had noticed it too. "Strange, it's only three in the afternoon," he remarked as he checked his watch.

"Your Dad still keeps the shotgun in his closet?" John pointed a thumb upstairs.

"Yeah, I think so," Harris replied.

With no time to lose, John rushed up the flight of steps and into the master bedroom. Harris soon trailed him into the large walk-in closet where his friend had already started sorting through piles of miscellaneous items. Eventually, he came upon three large rifle cases and pulled them out one at a time, handing a box to Harris.

Together they opened all of them. One was a relatively new pump-action shotgun, while the other two were hunting rifles: a lever-action and a bolt-action .270. "What I wouldn't give for my Classic Desert Eagle right now," John muttered.

In the meantime, Harris pulled out the lever action 30-30 from the case, inspected the clean chamber, and levered the bolt forward. Setting the rifle down, he vanished in the closet for a moment, returning with four boxes of ammunition. There was enough for each rifle and the .45 pistol he had dropped into the bed of the truck.

After tossing a box of shotgun shells to John, both loaded the weapons. Harris first filled the 30-30 with bullets and then continued with the .270 bolt-action rifle which carried five rounds. When they were finished, the men stuffed their pockets with the remaining ammo and took the rifles down the stairs into the living room.

"Marshal! We need you up here!" John yelled as he switched off all the lights on the ground floor.

Marshal came stomping up the stairs and closed the door to the basement. "What's up?" he asked as Harris handed his little brother the .270 rifle.

"Remember Bear?" Harris looked at him and loaded a round in the chamber.

"Yeah? What about that idiot?" his brother pulled up and back on the bolt action lever and then pushed it forward, loading a round into the chamber.

"He escaped. We passed him on the way here and he's pissed off. I think he's coming here," Harris informed him briefly.

"Good, I've been meaning to kick his butt for a long time now," Marshal grinned. "I hate that guy."

Moments later, faint popping sounds could be heard in the distance. John peeked out the living room window and saw vehicle headlights snaking around a bend in the street.

"Here they come!" he announced.

"What's going on up there!?" June's voice rang out from the basement.

"Stay where you are with the kids! We've got company!" Harris yelled back.

"Who?!" she shouted.

Harris didn't respond, because two pickup trucks were speeding around the corner. One skidded to a halt on the front lawn, while the other parked on the opposite side of the street. Six men jumped out of the vehicles and immediately began shooting at the house. John ducked and rolled behind a lazy-boy chair as the first shotgun blast blew out the large living room window.

In the meantime, Marshal ran up the flight of steps and into the guest room. The elevated position of the second floor provided him with a much better view of the attackers, since he could peek through the sizeable window above the front door unnoticed.

While Bear and his gang continued to pelt the house with bullets. John crouched behind the chair. Leaning to one side, he aimed the shotgun at an individual standing in front of his pick-up on the lawn. He squeezed the trigger and buckshot ripped the man's chest open, exposing his sternum and spilling guts into the snow and ash. His body crumbled to the ground as the others scrambled for cover.

"You're all gonna die!" Bear's hoarse voice thundered over the gunfire.

Undeterred, Marshal darted to a bedroom at the end of the hall, cracked the window, and stealthily placed the stock of his rifle on a windowsill. He opened the scope's lens caps and positioned the cross-hairs between the eyes of the first individual that came into his sight. Marshal carefully pulled the trigger and the rifle thumped into his shoulder. He rejoiced when he observed the top of the attacker's cranium explode with a slight pop. The lifeless body then fell backwards, behind the hood of the pick-up.

Enraged to the point of insanity, another thug aimed his 9mm Uzi up at the double windows, spraying them with rounds. But Marshal had expected as much. He had already sought shelter behind a thick wall while 9mm bullets smashed the glass panes.

At the same time, Harris pointed the iron sights of his 30-30 through the main window. He pulled the trigger and the bullet shattered the glass. Unfortunately, it deflected just enough to miss the man with the mohawk and the cybernetic arm. Instead, the round punched a hole through the pick-up's windshield, forcing the brute to dive for safety.

While his colleague flung himself into some bushes, Bear pulled a sleek pistol from his hip holster, carelessly aimed it at the house, and fired. A laser dart shot out of the barrel and burned a scorch mark into the brick wall.

Next to him, the hoodlum with the Uzi targeted the main window and showered the back wall and part of the dining room with 9mm rounds, knocking the chandelier off its chain. It crashed onto the living room table with an earsplitting bang.

John waited until the Uzi stopped firing, jumped up, and blasted a hole into the rear quarter panel of the truck as the ruffian dropped the submachine gun's empty magazine and reloaded. Seconds later, John flung himself on the carpet covered with glass shards as another shotgun blast obliterated the holographic plasma video screen on the credenza. "Crap! That was a nice TV!" he yelled as the destroyed device fell forward and smashed into the floor.

Meanwhile, Harris aimed his rifle at the front bumper of the rear truck, waiting for Bear to pop up again. Instead, a different criminal sprang up and made a mad dash for the house. The man with the Uzi covered his comrade with suppressing fire. John was pinned, and Harris's rifle jammed as he tried to pull the trigger.

"It's jammed!" he yelled.

Lying on his belly, John slid his shotgun over to Harris's feet who then dropped the malfunctioning 30-30 and picked up the substitute.

Upstairs, Marshal inched to the window once more, taking quick aim at the man firing away with the Uzi. He pulled the trigger and the rifle kicked his shoulder again. A quick glance assured him that he had successfully neutralized his assailant: his target's brains were splattered across the street.

Heartened by his brother's kill, Harris pumped a round into his shotgun while John jumped to his feet, scrambling to the front door with a large buck knife. The manic thug was already rushing towards the house, and then leapt towards the entrance. Harris calmly pulled the trigger. The buckshot blew out the gangster's belly, spewing guts all over, and sending his body flying through the air. It eventually slammed into the sidewalk and slid to a bloody halt against the family's snow-covered rock garden.

Alarmed, Bear looked at his last remaining associate and barked, "Get in the truck!"

The hoodlum with the mohawk clambered inside as Marshal blasted a hole through the rear windshield. In return, Bear fired his laser pistol at the house, pinning John and Harris against the walls as he jumped into the passenger seat. The vehicle's tires first swerved in the snow, but then gripped a patch of road and accelerated, departing the neighborhood at breakneck speed.

"I'll be back!!!" he threatened.

"Crap!" Harris bellowed. "It's not over until Bear is dead!"

"Jerks!" John shouted out the door. "Why the TV?!"

Moments later Marshal came down the steps without the rifle. He rushed past Harris and John and disappeared into the basement. Exhausted, he fell into a vacant easy chair, but was granted little rest. Safyre, Ambyr, and June immediately bombarded him with a barrage of questions. Ignoring them all, he pulled out a pack of cigarettes from his pocket, lit one, and inhaled deeply after closing his eyes.

Relieved, Harris and John also joined him for a smoke, while Safyre and Ambyr gave their daddy a hug and a kiss. John gazed at June and she smiled. "Don't look at me! I got a man," she laughed, her eyes on Marshal.

Chapter Eight: Be All My Sins Remember'd

By late afternoon more than 190 vehicles had joined General May's convoy: a mix of MHMMV-44s, APCs, robots, Battle Suits, and civilian trucks. An approximate head-count estimated the surviving refugees at seven-hundred-fifty.

Lieutenant Hawk still led the expedition as they continued to press north. Surprisingly, it didn't take them long to reach the Ohio Turnpike. Heading west towards Toledo, Hawk thought wistfully that he wasn't but two or three hours from his home in Monroe, Michigan.

"Have any of my friends or family survived the chaos?" he thought anxiously. General May ordered the trek to stop at an abandoned service plaza outside Sandusky; one of his staff officers wanted to see if any of her family or friends had survived the cataclysm.

It took about an hour to assemble a recon team, and Hawk and Almazan volunteered to lead it. In the meantime, Angel, the children, and Amanda stayed behind at the plaza.

Hawk did a quick, informal headcount: eight men were to scout out the town. He would have preferred a whole army, but volunteering to help were Staff Sergeant McMeen, Corporal Lock, Private McCracken, Private Bruzinski, and

Private Downes. They wanted to assist Second Lieutenant Sheehan, a NARC Intelligence Analyst, with finding her family. All volunteers were 82nd soldiers with the exception of Lieutenant Hawk, who was with 71st Group. He had long taken note that NARC soldiers refrained from volunteering for any dangerous or hazardous duty, and figured that this would spell trouble someday.

The recon unit climbed into Hawk's vehicle and then proceeded across a farm field to a maintenance lane which led directly into town via the main road. Twenty minutes later, they arrived at Sandusky's southern edge. Lieutenant Sheehan halted and gave everyone directions to her parents' home on the eastern side.

She had gone quite pale, and it was clear to Shane that she was horribly saddened by the sorry state of her hometown. Most of the shops had been looted, and there was significant damage to the overall infrastructure. A wild dog dashed across the thoroughfare as their Combat Gun Truck rumbled through deserted streets. Not a single telephone pole was still standing, and all the power lines and fibernet cables lay scattered about the concrete. Someone had thrown a stop sign through a shop window and looted the store afterwards. Several homes were nothing but blackened cavities, burned to the foundation, with only their skeletal frames still upright. Stains of blood—days old—discolored the snow-swept streets.

"Someone must still be alive here," Lieutenant Sheehan blurted out, "There must be bodies! Unless someone removed them."

No one said a word in response.

They drove past a cement plant. One silo had toppled over, and gravel had spilt out around a second one. The plant was damaged beyond repair as machinery and parts littered the factory yard.

"We'll see, but from the looks of it, they could have gotten killed or fled days ago," Almazan felt compelled to give the lieutenant a brutal dose of reality. Blanching, Sheehan just glared back at him.

"I mean, I hope someone made it out of the chaos, I'm not *that* insensitive," he added ruefully.

By now the truck had pulled up to a farmhouse on the outskirts of town. The dwelling had certainly seen better days and looked deserted as Almazan ungraciously pointed out.

"This is it, we're here," the lieutenant whispered dejectedly. Almazan steered the truck into the snow and ash-covered driveway and parked a few meters away from the front porch. Lieutenant Sheehan hurriedly dismounted and rushed to the main entrance.

Still talkative, Almazan peered at the house and remarked uncouthly, "This is like Little House on the Prairie meets House on Haunted Hill in a post nuclear winter wonderland."

"At ease, Sergeant," Hawk wanted him to shut up. It was bad enough that people had to suffer such losses, but to provoke and hurt them further with insensitive wisecracks was completely uncalled for. It reminded Hawk of Bubba Earl.

"Just sayin', it's creepy," Almazan mumbled.

"Then keep your goddamn voice down," Shane snapped back as he signaled his men to take their positions. McCracken and Bruzinski were to pull security around the truck while Downes climbed into the gunner's turret. Almazan left the engine running in case they had to make a quick escape. Meanwhile, McMeen and Lock walked to the back of the house, with Almazan and Hawk joining Sheehan at the front door.

Visibly nervous, she fumbled through a set of keys until she found the right one and inserted it in the lock. She turned the key, but it was stuck. Giving it a little more effort, the key suddenly snapped off. "Crap!" she cursed, "It's frozen shut." She stepped to the side, peered through a window, but could barely make out anything inside.

Tired of dithering, Almazan simply kicked the door in. Part of the frame splintered and Hawk was about to reprimand him when Sheehan wordlessly entered the foyer. The sergeant moved to follow, but Hawk held him back, pointing a finger in his face. He wanted to say something, but Almazan just looked at him, confused, "What?" he shrugged, and continued into the house.

"Mom? Pa? Hello?" Sheehan called, checking the kitchen, the study, and the living room. She peered up the stairs to the second floor, "Lacy? Hello? Anyone?" Unsettled, she eventually climbed up the staircase, each step creaking loudly.

"Dude, not to be a jerk, but I got a bad feeling about this place," Almazan blathered on. The windows had been left open, allowing dust, ash, and snow to blow in and cover the floor. By now, Hawk's frustration with Almazan was reaching its boiling point.

"If he won't shut his mouth," he thought angrily, "the sergeant was going to get his tail kicked."

While Almazan and Shane bickered, McMeen and Lock scanned the backyard. They soon spotted an old barn about thirty meters away. Its main door stood slightly ajar, just enough to fit a man through. Like the main house, the barn looked like it had seen better days. The pair walked up cautiously to the wooden structure, weapons at the low ready. As they came within a meter of the entrance, both sensed that something was terribly wrong.

McMeen knelt down in the snow. Pressing his large fingers into one of several overlapping footprints that had entered and exited the barn several times, he exclaimed.

"Oiy, check this out." His Scottish accent was ever so thick, but Lock had understood him this time and inspected the tracks as well. "There's at least a dozen footprints leading to and from inside 'ere," McMeen told his colleague.

"Yikes, some of the packed down snow is covered in blood, look at that," Lock shivered as he pointed to an imprint behind the burly sergeant. Filled with dread, McMeen got up and noticed the tracks leading back towards the house.

"I gots a bad feelin 'bout what's behind door number one," McMeen gestured towards the dark barn. Lock just nodded in silent agreement.

Meanwhile, McCracken and Bruzinski were leaning against the parked truck, thoroughly bored. "Man, we already know the world has been destroyed, but why do we have to keep searching for people's relatives along the way?" Bruzinski griped sourly.

"Because dipstick, wouldn't you want to find out if your family was still alive?" McCracken shot back.

"Well… yeah. But they're probably dead already," Bruzinski retorted defiantly. McCracken could hear in his voice that his team mate didn't care one way or the other.

"Nice to see you give up so easily Bee. Remind me to find someone else to watch my back when the shooting starts."

Irritated, McCracken pulled out a cheap, filtered cigar and took his helmet off. The cold air nipped at his cheeks, turning it red almost instantaneously. In fact, he could feel the hairs in his nostrils freeze. "The things I do for a good smoke…" McCracken jittered through his teeth as he lit up the cigar.

"You're a crazy guy. No way would I be lighting one up in this weather," Bruzinski chimed in again, even though he didn't smoke. It was much colder than usual, and the wind was blowing sub-freezing air about. There was a lack of sunlight, because its rays could barely penetrate the thick layers of ash and clouds, rcsulting in super cooled air below. Nights were even worse, as temperatures often dropped far below zero.

Inside the farmhouse, Lieutenant Sheehan searched all the rooms. She checked her parents' bedroom and her little sister's, but found no one. Horror-stricken, she realized that some sort of nasty struggle had taken place in her sisters' room by the way the desk lamp had been knocked over, the scattered books, and the messed up bed. It was the same in her parents' bedroom. Trembling, she took off her helmet, and set it on the bed as the cold bit her cheeks. "Why is it so chilly in here?" she wondered.

Suddenly, a terrible smell stung her nose. The muscles in Sheehan's face froze as her gaze shifted towards the closet door. She approached it slowly, not sure if she wanted to see what was behind it, and yet the door seemed to stare back at her.

After wrenching it open, she jumped back and let out a tortured yelp. Immediately, Hawk and Almazan came running up the stairs. Weapons drawn, they approached the closet door. Shane lowered his weapon as Sheehan turned away from the horrible sight. He put a comforting arm around the woman's shoulders while she held her hands up to her face and wept.

Almazan couldn't believe what he saw. The entire closet was bathed in the family dog's blood. Red-stained, white fur stuck to the walls, floor, and ceiling. Frozen, charred flesh clung to bones that were scattered around the closet's bottom. The upper half of the poor canine's snout was still attached to the skull, but the eyes were missing. Shaking uncontrollably, Sheehan staggered out of the room, while Hawk motioned Almazan, "Let's go."

But the sergeant's focus was still on the horrendous scene. "It looks like the dog exploded from the inside out. Look, there's no damage to the inside of the closet," he explained matter-of-factly, pointing at the walls and examining the door.

"Forget it, let's go," Hawk rushed out of the room, trailed by a hesitant Almazan. It was a gruesome way to die, but for some sick reason the sergeant remained morbidly fascinated by it. Of course, he didn't mention this fascination to anyone else.

He silently concluded that a disturbed individual had force-fed the dog a grenade or some other explosive.

The men followed Sheehan down the stairs. Exhausted, she eventually sat down at the kitchen table, crying and sniffling. A few minutes later, she looked out a window towards the backyard and noticed Corporal Lock stumbling out of the barn. Pulling his helmet off, he threw up violently in the snow. Alarmed, Sheehan rushed out the back door and ran towards him. By this time, McMeen was also teetering out of the wooden structure. He was gasping for air, but managed to control his unsettled stomach.

Hawk and Almazan followed her outside as McMeen held out his hand and warned, "Ma'am, don' go in th're." But she pushed past him and stormed inside the barn; nothing was going to prevent her from finding out what had made them sick to their stomachs.

By now, Shane and the sergeant had reached McMeen while Lock was still trying to stand up straight. "You don' wanna go in there sir," McMeen cautioned, his face green with nausea.

"What's in there, Sergeant?" Hawk demanded to know why he shouldn't go inside.

"It's her Ma' and Pappy, and a little lass strung up by their necks, gutted, and skinned alive sir. And it would also seem the rest of the townsfolk are in there too. Gutted, burned, splattered all over the horse stalls." The thought of it made McMeen want to throw up again.

Seconds later a gunshot went off in the barn. Hawk rushed inside and found Lieutenant Sheehan's body on the ground beneath her slaughtered family. The lieutenant's pistol was still in her hand, while her brain had splattered all over a gruesome horse stable.

Feeling faint, Hawk closed his eyes, shook his head, and walked out of the farm building. He shut the big door behind him while his men were curious to find out what had just happened. "Ah hell!" he snapped and started punching and kicking the giant, wooden entrance. After a brief pause, Hawk hurried back to the house, his men in tow. He looked over his shoulder and barked, "Almazan, burn it. Now!" Then he looked straight ahead.

The sergeant stopped in his tracks and carried out the order. After cracking a few inches of the barn door open, he took an incendiary grenade from his utility belt, pulled the pin, and tossed it into a random hay stack. Running back towards the front of the house where his team was already assembling inside the vehicle, he wiped the sweat off his brow. Moments later, everyone heard a faint popping sound as Almazan climbed into the driver's seat.

McCracken looked puzzled, "Where's Lieutenant Sheehan?"

"She not coming, lad," McMeen told him firmly.

"What? Why Sergeant?" Bruzinski wondered aloud.

"She shot herself, end of story." he responded curtly.

No one said a word.

They drove off in silence, down the ash and snow-mixed driveway, and soon arrived at the main road. The barn was completely ablaze as they rounded a right turn and headed into town. The rest of their expedition was uneventful, and Shane and his men followed their vehicle tracks back to the service plaza where the rest of the convoy was still resting.

Together, Hawk, Almazan, McMeen, Lock, McCracken, Bruzinski, and Downes walked towards the large gas station. Soldiers and civilians alike had gathered around its entrance, smoking in the cold. The group went inside, and found the place extremely crowded. The only light available came through the glass doors and a few windows as the power was out. Shane located Angel, Amanda, and the children sitting at a corner booth in the food court area.

Still grim-faced, Hawk ordered his enlisted troops to find something to eat and rest up while he reported to the general. He then glanced at the table where his family had gathered and frowned. Angel immediately knew that something bad had happened.

Pulling himself together, Hawk approached Lieutenant General May and stood at attention in front of his table. The general paused his conversation with a Colonel Smith, looking at Shane, "How'd it go Lieutenant?"

"Not good sir. There were no signs of survivors in the town. We then made it to Lieutenant Sheehan's home on Sandusky's outskirts and found her family had been butchered and hung in the barn behind the house along with the rest of the towns people murdered inside. Lieutenant Sheehan was so overcome with grief that she pulled her service revolver from her hip holster and shot herself in the head. We had no time to intervene," he concluded despondently.

One could have heard a pin drop. Everyone within earshot suddenly paused to take note of

Hawk's report. He continued, "There was nothing we could have done to stop her, sir, as she had gone into the barn alone. Since the crime scene defied description, I ordered my men to burn down the building."

"Crap," General May muttered, pounding his hand on the table. "All right Lieutenant, go relax, we leave in thirty minutes," he sighed. Hawk did an about-face and walked towards his family's table, shoulders sagging. Relieved to see their step-father alive and well, the children quickly scooted over to allow him to sit. As Shane leaned back with a groan, the power and lights crackled back to life. Sighs of relief could be heard as the generators kicked on and heaters began pumping out warm air.

"What happened baby?" Angel asked him and reached for his hand. He swiftly grasped hers, holding it tight.

"We lost someone today. Her family was murdered in the most atrocious fashion and she turned her weapon on herself as a result." It pained Shane to have such words leave his mouth.

"I'm so sorry punkin," his wife tried to comfort him, but she couldn't muster a smile. Instead she found herself worrying with Shane, deathly afraid of what fate might hold in store for them.

Half an hour later, the entire convoy departed the plaza, heading west towards Toledo. For the next ninety miles, Hawk sat with his right arm propped up against the passenger window and rested his head in the palm of his hand, unable to speak. He blankly stared at the rolling, dark thunderclouds on the horizon from which lightning spat out of every possible angle.

Almazan finally broke the silence. "Check it out," he pointed southwest.

Everyone looked up and followed his finger to a large, cylindrical cloud spinning vertically into the sky. It was a massive tornado.

"That thing has got to be at least ten miles wide. Just look at it," he remarked with fearless awe.

"Wow," Angel murmured. "Do me a favor Ignacio, don't go near it."

"Yeah no problem," he chuckled.

"Mommy, what's this?" Emily pointed at the base of the massive twister. Three miles in circumference and swirling around the base of the tornado, the ground churned. It was as if the windstorm sat in the center of a giant turntable. The Earth was shaking, but Hawk and his family didn't notice, mesmerized by the rumble of this mind-boggling, natural engine.

Nothing man-made could withstand the force of the rapidly revolving soil. Spinning in the opposite direction of the tornado, it caused flying debris to strike anything within its zone at nearly five hundred miles per hour. Everyone was frightened.

"Thankfully that thing is at least fifteen miles away from us," Hawk finally spoke.

"Look how high it goes!" Amanda pointed out. Shane and the others looked skywards as a break in the clouds showed them just how massive the tornado really was.

"Holy crap," Hawk mumbled, sounding amazed.

"That thing has to be at least 40,000 feet tall," Almazan guessed. He was close; it had actually spun up to almost 50,000 feet.

"Unbelievable," Angel stared. At the same time she was worried about her husband. She had observed him lost in thought, painfully aware of how much the suicide of his fellow officer had upset him.

Occasionally, she would gaze out the window while the open farmlands of Ohio were whizzing by. If things had been different, she mused, they could have owned their own farm up here. Not that it would have mattered with weather phenomena like that. Nothing could survive such a calamity. The land behind the super twister had been scraped clean, leaving a river valley in its wake that was thirty feet deep.

It was 1800 hours by now, and the survivors finally approached the city of Toledo, leaving the powerful "Finger of God" miles behind. There was smoke billowing up from the city center, and Hawk barely recognized the landscape as he led the trek down the 80/90 freeway. They passed the north-bound I-280 exit ramp, because Hawk determined that the bridge over the Ohio River had most likely been destroyed. Turning the convoy around at the bridge entrance would be a complicated and lengthy affair, he calculated. The city had long been building a new, raised skyway system over the river, but it had not been completed before the cataclysm.

Instead the trek traveled further down the turnpike, crossed another bridge, and eventually turned onto the I-75 freeway. Unfortunately, the freeway into the city was a mess, with destroyed vehicles and ash-covered corpses littering their route. Angel noticed that the skyscrapers in the downtown area were covered with eerie, giant webs that spread from one monolith to another. She also observed a large, black spot in the spidery netting and clammed up. Angel hated spiders, and the thought of an enormous species of the kind gave her goose bumps.

Jonathan felt equally unsettled. He looked at Shane, then at his mother, and felt something stirring in his stomach. Too embarrassed to say anything, he prayed for another break at a rest stop.

Although he was not afraid of spiders, Hawk didn't like what he was seeing so close to his home and ordered Almazan to pick up the pace. The entire convoy snaked around the destruction and within half an hour they crossed the border into Michigan. On the way, they drove by a freeway rest area familiar to Hawk that was nothing but a smoking crater now. A fuel truck had caught fire and wiped out the entire station, while debris littered the three lane freeway. Hawk and his family also passed some burnt up and mangled state police hover cruisers between the road and the station. The concrete barrier that had once divided the highway was also destroyed and vehicle pileups cluttered the southbound highway for miles.

With a heavy heart, Hawk realized that most of the exits leading into his hometown of Monroe were blocked by demolished cars. Eventually, he led the convoy to the Exit 15 off-ramp which appeared passable. Everyone veered to the right and crossed an overpass. On the other side, buildings and twenty-four hour service stations stood in ruins, a tangle of crumbling concrete. The local diner, once very popular with teenage kids, had been completely vandalized and partially collapsed.

Wild dogs dashed across the road as the convoy trailed Hawk's vehicle around a bend and past the local ice rink. Some vehicles sat still intact in the parking lot, but the building was in shambles as sections of the roof and the entrance had crumbled completely. Up the road, at the corner of Monroe Street, Almazan stopped the truck and everyone took a moment to silently look at the old bronze statue of General George Armstrong Custer. It had also been desecrated by vandals.

Disheartened by the devastation, Hawk told Almazan to hang a left and soon they traversed a bridge over the Raisin River. An even bleaker picture unfolded there. The old historic town to the south was no more as most of its structures had been shattered. Bricks covered the streets and sidewalks on both sides. Slowly, May's expedition headed west, past the remains of the old newspaper building as well as bombed-out neighborhoods leading to Telegraph Road.

They were now on M-50 and crawled towards Dundee. At a four lane highway, on the eastbound side of the road, they discovered the wreckage of a small civilian airplane from the airport across the river. Past it, Hawk looked to the south and saw that his old high school—a quarter mile behind the old bank and the health commission building—was still intact. As far as he could tell, there was little damage to the structure. "Well, everything else in this town is practically destroyed, but for some reason, no one bothered to knock the school down," he laughed to himself.

Emily looked over her shoulder at the large building her step-father was eyeing, "Can we stop there and see if there are any more school books we can pick up?"

Shane thought for a moment, but remembering their last visit to a school he decided against it. "Um, not after what happened in Virgina, sorry dear."

Emily frowned and sat back in her seat.

Jon leaned forward and tapped his mother on the shoulder. "Mom," he whispered, "I gotta go poop."

"Can you hold it sweetie? We're almost there," she asked him, although her tone of voice indicated that she did not mean to give him a choice.

Jon understood and sat back in his seat, the muscles in his abdomen tightening.

Another mile down the road, they passed an entrance to one of Monroe's many golf courses. It was close to Hawk's neighborhood, and he received a call over the radio.

General May ordered Shane to proceed while the convoy waited on the highway. Hawk gave directions and Almazan turned left. Moments later they arrived at a T-shaped intersection and took a right down another street. Even in the dark Shane could see that many of the homes had been vandalized and a few burnt down.

Feeling uneasy, he ordered the sergeant to stop in front of one particular house on their right. A shot up, small pickup truck was parked on the lawn and three bodies lay beside it. Shane inspected the corpses and took comfort in knowing that he didn't recognize any of them.

Angel and the kids had visited his hometown in previous years. Hawk had taken them on vacation to Michigan after his last tour of duty to the Korean Peninsula. None of them had been back since, but they remembered it well.

"Is this your house?" Almazan asked him and looked out the passenger side. The home's front window had been smashed while the walls were covered with burn marks caused by laser fire. Bullet holes riddled the front and garage door as well as the siding. There were no vehicles in the driveway, but a large, banged up pickup truck sat to the left of the house.

"It looks like it used to be a nice neighborhood," Almazan commented and looked at the no longer elegant, two story homes on the street. Each one had been shot up, destroyed, or burned to the ground.

His heart pounding rapidly, Hawk unfastened his safety harness and opened the car door. A flash of lightning and explosion of thunder startled him. He grabbed his rifle and darted through the ash-covered snow to the front porch. On the way, he almost tripped over the lifeless body of a thug in his mother's rock garden. The storm door had been smashed, but he realized with relief that someone had swept the glass off the veranda. Trembling, he tried the door handle, but found it locked. "Maybe someone is still alive?" he thought, becoming more hopeful.

Pulling a set of keys from his right pocket, he unlocked the door. As it swung open, Shane found himself pushing the barrel of a shotgun away from his face. The gun went off and shattered the large window above the door. Most of the glass shards blew outward, but some landed in the front foyer and Shane heard the chandelier rattle. Luckily he was still wearing his helmet which muffled the sound. The shooter of the gun was a man four years older than Hawk. They were roughly the same height, but the "assailant" was much skinnier. It was his older brother Harris who had anger and stress written all over his face.

After taking a deep breath, Shane slung his weapon over his shoulder and removed his helmet. By now, Harris had finally realized that he was dealing with his brother whom he had thought lost in the chaos. He eased his grip on the shotgun which Shane grabbed by the barrel and set down on the landing. Harris then took a step forward and gave his brother a well-deserved hug.

"Thanks for the welcome home Harris. I missed you too," Shane said sarcastically.

"Took you long enough! Was starting to think that ARMY training had finally caught up with you," Harris released his brother from his firm grip.

"Sorry to disappoint you."

"Angel and the kids ok?" Harris asked as he looked over his brother's shoulder and out at the gun truck parked in front of the house.

"Yeah, we're all fine. Kids are safe and she's doing well," Shane told him. Smiling,

Harris turned around and opened the door to the basement. He yelled, "Hey guys! Shane's here! I can't believe he's still alive!" Immediately, several voices called out.

One female exclaimed happily, "Shane's here!?" and another said, "Holy cow!" There was also a third, deep baritone which boomed, "No way!?"

"Come on up here! It's ok!" Harris shouted again. Seconds later, the brothers could hear several people scrambling up the wooden steps. Harris retreated into the foyer and one by one, Safyre, Ambyr, their younger brother Marshal and his wife June with Paulee in her arms poured into the hallway. They all crowded around Shane and closed in on him with a group hug. Marshal was near tears.

Eventually, they let go of him as Shane turned to check on the truck. Excited, he waved for his family to come join the happy reunion. Angel and the children climbed out of the vehicle and quickly made their way across the front yard and into the house. Harris and

Marshal received hugs from all of Angel's children. Then, another set of footsteps approached from the basement. Long-haired John raced around the corner to embrace his friend. "Shane!" he jubilated.

Like her husband, Angel was glad to see everyone alive and well, but wondered, "Hey, where's your folks?" Harris and Marshal exchanged meaningful looks, while John just turned away. Soon it became clear that Angel had asked one of those questions that nobody wanted to answer. Of course, Shane asked anyway.

"Yeah, where's Mom and Dad?" he gestured to the upstairs bedrooms. Angel gently closed the front door.

"They took a road trip to St. Louis, Missouri," Harris told them. "They left the day before all this happened."

Shane scowled. "Have you heard from them?" he asked softly.

"No," June shook her head.

"But, you're not gonna believe what happened around here!" she quickly changed the subject.

"Your nieces are doing well. Can you tell they've missed you?" Harris interjected.

"Uncle Jay Jay!" Ambyr smiled.

"Yeah, we've missed you!" Safyre grinned and gave him another squeeze.

"Good, I'm glad everyone made it. But, have you heard from anyone else?" Shane inquired. Again, no one said anything. "What about Mom and Dad?" he insisted, this time more sternly. They shook their heads.

Sighing, Harris looked at the broken living room window to his left. "You remember that old friend of ours when we were growing up?"

Shane stopped to think for a moment, "Which one?"

"The one that went to jail for killing some 130 people?"

Angel's expression turned to one of disgust as did the children's who were paying attention to the conversation.

"Yeah, we used to call him Bear or something, didn't we? That was before he got sent to jail," Shane recalled with a shudder.

"That's the one. He escaped prison when all this happened. Then he came here with a gang of thugs and started shooting up the place. His henchmen are just as crazy; one of them ran straight up to the door during the raid, even when I had the shotgun pointed at him. I ended up killing him before the last two drove off," Harris informed them.

"Oh really?" Shane wasn't happy about the news. "I see you haven't cleaned up the bodies, but managed to sweep the glass off the front porch."

"We've had very little to defend ourselves with. When I went up to rescue Ambyr, I took what little was left, but all we found was this shotgun, two of Dad's hunting rifles, a couple boxes of ammo, and some winter clothes," Harris explained and pointed at the weapon on the landing.

"We managed to get the generator that your father had bought a while ago up and running in the basement. That means that we have hot water and electricity, but it won't last long. We're almost out of gas, unless you got some to spare?" June told them.

"Hot water!" Angel yelled excitedly. She hadn't had a shower in a couple of days, let alone a change of clothes. The kids needed baths too. Angel looked pleadingly at her sister-in-law, "Do you mind if we all grab a quick shower?"

June pointed upstairs, "Sure go ahead. Generator should have enough gas to last a little while. Harris filled it up this morning."

Soon afterwards, John fired up the generator and the lights came on in the house. Shane looked around. The living room was thrashed. The big television had been blown to smithereens while the walls were peppered with bullet holes. The couch was now blocking the broken window and someone had nailed protective boards into its frame.

Meanwhile, Angel told the children to get cleaned up. Tired after days of travel, they obediently filed upstairs and one after the other took a shower in either of the two bathrooms.

Angel then turned to her husband, "You wouldn't happen to have another set of those uniforms, would you? I don't have anything else to change into."

Shane thought for a moment and smiled, which resulted in a playful hit on the arm by his wife and a wink to pull his mind out of the gutter, "Ah, as a matter of fact I do. I remember leaving a set here last time we visited, because they were too small for me. They might fit you," he grinned.

June told Angel, "I know where they are. I saw them in the basement yesterday when we were digging through boxes. I'll get 'em for ya." After thanking her sister-in-law, Angel went upstairs to check on the kids. Jon had already commandeered the master bathroom. He had found a toilet and locked the door for a well-deserved, undisturbed restroom break.

Shane and the rest of the family congregated in the kitchen.

Safyre took a soda can from the refrigerator, while Harris was eager to find out more details from Shane, "How many survivors did you pick up on the way up here?"

"A few from New York, Philadelphia, and Nashville. We joined Lieutenant General May's convoy from Atlanta," Shane informed everyone.

"We've had our fair share of excitement here too." Harris told his brother about his encounters while picking up Ambyr, the alien creatures, the Reamer monster, and his fight with Scott. He neglected to mention the strange energy power that he had tapped into and used against his former brother-in-law.

Shane nodded, not surprised by Harris's tales. "Man, we came across ghosts, zombies, Reamers, Squiddies, extraterrestrial soldiers, and the leader of the alien invasion on the way up here. His name is Thyrion," Shane revealed.

"Thyrion?" Harris was interested.

"Yeah, I think so; it was the one thing that didn't attack us, so..." Shane paused.

"Wow, no kidding," Marshal seemed surprised.

"Listen, it's not safe here. The convoy is heading west towards Dundee and then up into Detroit, I want you guys to come with us," Shane urged them.

His brothers looked at each other.

"You don't want to go to Detroit, man," Harris advised him.

"But we think it might be the one place that hasn't completely succumbed to all the devastation. So we're heading there," Shane explained.

"There's been a lot of alien activity in Detroit," Harris warned. "For example, on TV they showed some sort of gigantic alien building downtown."

"Is there?" Shane frowned.

"Well, they seem to be everywhere else. It wouldn't surprise me at all if they were setting up a Command Headquarters in the city. Nevertheless, NARC has a large military base there, and I'm sure they're holding their own. We're leaving in the next half hour or so. So bring only what you can carry," Shane instructed.

"All right," Harris conceded. He looked at Marshal and shrugged, "There's nothing left for us here, and it's probably a lot safer to travel with a large group of armed soldiers than to go on our own."

"Yeah, I suppose," Marshal responded unenthusiastically.

"Anyway, I need a shower too. I'll be right back," Shane got up.

He climbed up the stairs and found Angel who had just finished bathing Madison. "I told them about Detroit," Shane informed her.

"They're going to come or stay here?" she asked.

"Probably come with us," he paused.

June came into the bathroom and handed Angel a folded set of fatigues. It was the same color pattern as her husband's.

"Madison, go find Emily and see if they have anything to eat for you." The little girl smiled and ran off, cautiously walking down the stairs. June followed, urging her niece to be careful as she took one step at a time.

Finally alone, Angel smiled at Shane, cocked an eyebrow, and snatched a towel from the basket above the washer. "Well?" she asked flirtatiously. "Are you going to close the door?" He did so with a big grin and walked towards her.

The children had all gathered in the kitchen and were busy telling Harris, Marshal, June, and John about the exciting and scary events of the last few days. Emily and Jacob described the Reamers, the zombies, and how boring the drive was. Angel's oldest daughter also told them about the night Madison had disappeared and wandered off into the alien forest, and how Shane had gone out to rescue her by himself. Jon stayed quiet, while Safyre and Ambyr played with some toys left in the study.

Sometime later, Shane and Angel came out of the shower. They seemed to glow, even in their rather drab fatigues. A smile crept across Angel's lips as they entered the kitchen.

As they walked in, they were greeted by Almazan and Amanda who had joined the party and were sharing stories of their adventures with Shane's family. "You two ready to get going?" Almazan asked Shane, who had wrapped his arms around his wife.

"Yeah, we're ready," Angel answered with a sigh, leaning into him.

"The convoy is waiting. They found a few more survivors in the neighborhood and around the area. They're sending buses to extract them," Almazan reported.

"Cool, are you guys all packed up?" Shane looked at Harris and Marshal.

"Yeah, we're all set to go," his older brother nodded.

Shane kissed Angel on the cheek, slid his right hand down her back, and ushered her towards the front door with a gentleman's grace. "Shall we?" he smiled broadly.

June looked at her husband with a surprised look on her face. "Gee, I wonder what they were doing in the shower?" she laughed.

Chapter Nine: Love Your Friends and Bring a Gun

On The Seventh Day,

Along with Lieutenant Hawk's relatives, twenty-two civilians from the neighborhood had gathered at the front lawn of his family's home. Almazan called back to General May to send a bus into the suburb, and within a few minutes the refugees were shoving into the hover vehicle. Captain Dyson and his 43rd Group Special Forces soldiers acted as their escorts. It took nearly an hour to load up all the survivors, which thoroughly irritated Dyson.

In the meantime, Harris backed the white farm truck into the street. The large pick-up with its extended crew cab and eight foot bed seated everyone in the household, minus Angel, Shane, and the children who continued on in the gun truck.

The white dually was coming in very handy, but it wasn't in Harris's name. It still belonged to his ex-wife's mother Lori, who had died at the hands of her own son Scott. In turn, Harris had killed his former brother-in-law by turning him into a Chihuahua, who was subsequently eaten by an alien Reamer.

Harris occasionally checked to see if any wild animals like the bald eagle he had noticed earlier in the day and wondered if he should have fed Scott to the birds. While his oldest brother wallowed in thoughts of revenge, Marshal and his wife June were hauling up three bags of clothes from the basement. John was sharing a cigarette with Shane outside, and Angel and the kids had taken some blankets to set up their MHMMV for a more comfortable ride. Shane and John were talking about weapons, particularly the M22A3 assault rifle. The latter was boasting just how good of a marksman he had been back in Arizona.

Shane led him to the back of the Combat Gun Truck, opened up the rear door, and unlatched the locking mechanisms on the weapons' racks. He pulled a rifle from the frame and opened an adjacent ammo box which contained the magazines. Carefully, he handed his buddy John the weapon as well as seven magazines which he stuffed into his cargo pockets. Always responsible, Shane kept a mental note on how much ammunition they had left. Even though the three NARC and one 82nd HMTVs were still full of assorted munitions, Shane wanted to keep track of his surplus.

Excited, John slapped a magazine into the well and pulled back the charging lever. A round immediately loaded into the chamber and he started looking through the sight at objects in the street. But the rifle wasn't zeroed to his sight-picture, which prohibited him from making perfect shots until he could either get to a range or find an Army helmet that would automatically align his aim. However, John couldn't use someone else's helmet, because each Advanced Readout Helmet was custom fit for each individual. Ultimately, all he could hope for is to shoot some rounds downrange and perhaps hit something in the process, provide covering fire, or at least scare off any future enemy that dared to threaten them.

Meanwhile, Harris pulled the white pick-up into the street and lined up behind Shane's Combat Gun Truck. Angel was in the front and told Shane, "We're all set here," after she had tightened Madison's safety harness.

Shane looked at his wife and smiled. All the children were inside and he could see them talking amongst themselves. Out of nowhere, Captain Dyson approached and barked, "Convoy is ready to SP. Let's get a move on Lieutenant." Shane nodded, closed the Combat Gun Truck's rear door, and signaled Harris with a thumbs up that they were about to depart. He then walked around to the right side of the vehicle and climbed into his seat.

Eager to leave, Harris handed his shotgun to Marshal who put it in the pick-up's backseat, cocked it, and put it on safe. Seconds later, John clambered into the front passenger seat and closed the door. June had already put Paulee into his car seat, while Safyre and Ambyr waited in theirs. Harris put the truck in first gear and held down the clutch with his left foot. Shane's gun truck began rolling forward and they followed him out the neighborhood and golf course entrance to M-50. They soon met up with the rest of the convoy and headed westward towards Dundee.

Ten minutes down the road they passed large farm fields dotted by woods as well as a disabled pickup truck that was well known to Harris. With night approaching, it was pitch black now as they approached the small, historic town of Dundee. The scene there wasn't much different than that of Monroe. Most buildings had been destroyed while others had toppled into neighboring structures or collapsed, filling the streets with debris. Homes had burnt to the ground, small businesses and shops vandalized, while frozen bodies lay buried in the snow. The signs of battle were everywhere.

"We need to go north on I-23," Hawk told Almazan tersely.

"Check it out, there are fresh tracks in the snow," the sergeant interjected and pointed out the windshield while steering with his other hand. Shane noted with interest that the tracks were leading to the biggest edifice in the town. Some of the buildings on the other side of the I-23 overpass were still intact and a few pickup trucks stood parked in front of a bar across the street. One of them sported a heavy, unmanned machine gun.

The lights inside the bar were on, offering refuge to criminals, convicts, and murderers who were busy drinking, hooting, and hollering. With the end of the world approaching, the mob had trashed the place. One of them sported a green mohawk hairdo, a metallic, cybernetic right arm, and wore goggles over his eyes. He looked out the window after slamming a mug of beer on the counter and noticed the military convoy approaching from under the overpass. White hot rage gripped him when he recognized the white pickup that had eluded him earlier.

"Oh yeah! Fresh meat!" he yelled out. Without deliberating any further, "Mohawk" grabbed his axe and shotgun and stormed outside. The rest of the men followed, armed with a wide array of weapons. "Mohawk" immediately aimed his shotgun at Shane's lead Combat Gun Truck and fired a blast of pellets just as it began to turn onto the northbound entrance ramp. Within seconds, a detonation rocked the heavy vehicle since the thugs had previously planted explosives with an attached sensor in the snow.

The pellets bounced off the truck's armor plating and the windshield, but the explosion rocked it heavily. Scared to death, the children panicked. They were screaming and crying as Almazan steered the vehicle to a halt. Although in shock, Hawk quickly unfastened his seat belt and jumped out of the truck. He aimed his rifle at a thug coming out of the bar and fired a burst of three rounds, two of which struck the man in the chest and neck. The impact of the Mach two rounds tore giant chunks of flesh off the man's torso, nearly decapitating him an instant. As soon as the body hit the ground, the other criminals scavenged his corpse for equipment like vultures.

Felons and military personnel were now squaring off with three hundred meters between them, turning this once quiet town into a battlefield. Harris stopped the pick-up and John rolled down the window. He aimed his rifle and fired a burst into the crowd of criminals. Several of the men took hits and fell to the ground. The man with the mohawk fired his shotgun again, but missed Hawk. A real idiot, the thug hadn't realized that he was out of range. Instead of killing Shane, the pellets disappeared in the ash-mixed snow blanket.

Two of the criminals now hopped onto the truck with the heavy machine gun, while the driver fired up the engine. As they backed up, rounds from John's rifle punched holes through the truck bed.

At the same time, Harris jumped out of the driver's door and aimed his shotgun at the individual manning the machine gun. He fired a buck-shot round at the thug, but missed and blew out the rear cab window. The glass pane shattered into thousands of tiny fragments, littering the backseat. Always an excellent shot, Hawk released a burst into another attacker, killing him in an instant. By now, the crowd of criminals began to scatter as they realized that they were severely outgunned and outnumbered. Other convoy elements had arrived to assist Shane and Almazan and started blasting away. Clearly frightened, "Mohawk" jumped into the truck with the machine gun and sped off.

Unwilling to let his adversary escape, Hawk took aim and fired a single round at the man, but the vehicle swerved and the round hit the other criminal loading the machine gun. It struck him in the back and he collapsed onto the truck bed. Full of rage, "Mohawk" let off another blast of pellets, but completely missed again.

Frustrated, the remaining criminals raced away, taking the road westward. They turned right on a street leading to a large, still undamaged building. A giant, iron statue of a bear was calmly standing vigil in front of the main entrance of the Super Outdoors and Hunting Center.

Determined to snuff out the gangsters, General May commanded every combat robot vehicle to post security for the civilian transports and ordered all military and NARC units to surround the building. The convoy immediately circled the large structure as bullets flew out of the windows. Hawk told Almazan to halt the gun truck near the front doors and man the turret. Meanwhile, May's APC parked next to Hawk's vehicle and opened fire with its big M500 HPRC, or High-Powered Rail Cannon, mounted on top. The turret swung around and aimed the cannon at the front entrance.

After a volley of fire, the doors exploded into thousands of tiny glass shards and wooden splinters. Several NARC troops came running out of the APC's side hatch and set up defensive positions around it. Seconds later, three men darted up to the large brick columns near the front entrance and began firing rounds from their NARC GRL-30 Grenade Rifles. Enemy bullets continued to rain from the building, striking the columns. One of the NARC troops took a bullet to his shoulder, but his reinforced armor was so strong that the projectile eventually bounced off.

Hawk used the protection of a brick pillar to scout out the criminals' hiding place. He peaked around its right side and noticed a group of about a hundred men barricaded behind large items of furniture, museum pieces, and stuffed animals. They had actually parked the truck with the heavy machine gun inside the outdoor center, with "Mohawk" still manning the weapon. As soon as he noticed the approaching soldiers, he opened fire. The NARC troops quickly took cover, but one man was hit in the chest. The round didn't puncture his armor, but it cracked the chest plate and left a small crater. He fell backwards and one of his buddies pulled him to safety behind the brick pillars.

John came running up to Hawk and also took cover behind the column. Peaking around its left, he was quickly forced to duck as machine gun fire started blowing apart the bricks on the other side of the pillar. "Friends of yours?!" Hawk yelled over the deafening sound of the salvos.

"That's one of the crazies that tried to kill us a few hours ago!" John yelled back.

"What is he? Like the second in command or something?!" Shane tightened up as more rounds struck the pillar.

"Bear is sure to be around somewhere!" John told him. Seconds later, a grenade exploded between the doors and the pillars in the middle of the service road.

A super-heated plasma projectile flew out the barrel of a NARC PL-5 Plasma Rifle and into the building. It struck one of the large, over-turned desks that some of the criminals were using for cover and exploded. The men behind the bureau were sprayed with boiling plasma which burned through their clothes and skin. They screamed in agony as the splinters from the table also caught fire around them.

Firing into the outdoor center, Almazan then released a long burst of .50 caliber rounds and tore up most of the men's covers. Some realized the magnitude of the wave of destruction raining down on them and ran off to the back of the store, while others weren't so fortunate or smart. They met their fate as a pair of Mach five velocity, .50 caliber aggression blew through their hiding places and bodies, sending chunks of flesh flying through the air. Smoke and burning debris now filled the entrance and billowed out the front doors as something detonated behind a counter inside the building.

Shane emerged from behind the pillar and dashed with John into the outdoors center. As they jumped over a customer service desk, bullets pursued them and tore up parts of the counter. The projectiles spewed forth from the top of a mock mountain in the middle of the store as two of the crazies were still holding their positions. Shots also rained down from a second floor balcony in the back of the shop as more thugs had spotted Shane and John hiding behind the wooden boards.

All of a sudden, a familiar face jumped behind the desk and rolled over to Shane's side: his wife Angel. Hawk looked at her and laughed despite the gravity of the situation. "Ok, you can come too!" he yelled as bullets continued to fly over their heads and blew apart the plaster wall.

Seemingly unafraid, she returned his surprised gaze and cocked an eyebrow with a grin. John assumed a kneeling stance, aimed his weapon at the first target he could locate, and fired a round from his M22A3 rifle. Unfortunately, the round missed and he dove for cover. Touching the left arrow on the right side of his sight, he adjusted the red dot in his scope. He popped up and shot again, and this time he was closer to hitting the mark. John crouched below after failing on his second try to adjust his sight once more.

Angel now popped up, firing a round that struck one of the men on the second floor balcony. The thug tottered forward and fell over the rail. His lifeless body slammed into the ground floor, behind a maze of clothing racks. Shane's wife took cover as more rounds from the balcony and the mock mountain chewed up the counter yet again.

Moments later, Shane peaked over the desk with his rifle and fired a burst of rounds at the two men on top of the fake hill. His rounds cut straight through the wooden structure, but he missed the pair he had hoped to hit. Dodging more bullets, he yelled at both Angel and John, "We're gonna get stuck here!"

Suddenly, a large section of the rear wall burst as one of the eleven-foot-tall Magnums stormed through the rubble. The hoodlums stood aghast at first and then, out of fear, focused their efforts on the massive Battle Suit stomping towards them through the outdoor camping section. Four men from the balcony, however, swiftly took flight, aware that they stood no chance against a Battle Suit—especially a Magnum.

Just as the rest were about to fire on the NARC Suit, three more sections of the building collapsed and four additional Magnums stormed through the gaping holes in the wall. By now the thugs were panicking and started running down the stairs. Frantic, the duo on the mock-up mountain jumped from ledge to ledge as one of the Magnums fired a five pound glass slug at the structure's peak, obliterating it completely. The bullet traversed its target at lightning speed and then shot out the vaulted, three story ceiling. Seconds later, the sonic boom from the gun shook everything in the store, and everyone without a helmet or hearing protection like John and Angel were deafened by the blast. One of the crazies leaping off the ledge was struck by a round fired from the front of the store by a NARC soldier and tumbled to his death.

By now, a dozen NARC and 82nd troops had filled the front entrance and more soldiers entered the building from the escape exits. A leftover group of thugs still fired rounds at everyone wearing a uniform or body armor. Of course, the continued sounds of gun fire and missiles being launched could be heard outside as well.

A haphazard assault force of criminals with a repainted Armadillo robot suddenly closed in on the convoy from the north. In response, troops launched several missiles from May's Command APC and destroyed a few pick-up trucks loaded with felons. Two Valkyrie pilots took off from the civilian convoy perimeter and charged the new threat approaching from I-23. As they flew towards the hostile gang, they opened fire with their Rail Guns. The rounds tore more pickup trucks to shreds and blew one of the vehicles completely apart.

The stolen Armadillo—re-painted by the thugs in black and red—sported an identifying logo of a bear on its left chest plate. Lasers, bullets, and missiles crisscrossed on an open field on the north side of the shopping complex and the Interstate. Two missiles from the pilfered Armadillo struck the side of May's Command APC. Seconds later, the HPRC turret rotated and fired a round at the enemy robot stomping through the pasture. The heavy round struck the android's chest and detonated the remaining missiles. Explosions tore the front of the robot apart, but it continued to march towards the outdoor center.

Meanwhile, in the civilian convoy, Jacob's father was growing restless in the back of an MP Police Cruiser. He wanted to join the battle and pleaded with the military policemen to let him out.

"Let me out of here! I want to help!" he shouted as a rocket exploded nearby.

"Leave it to the professionals to handle it, scum," the MP driver barked back.

"I have training, I can help!" Bubba Earl begged, but the MPs ignored him. Frustrated, he stared at the action taking place over five hundred meters away.

Suddenly, six captured NARC Reaper Battle Suits crossed the freeway and ran towards the outdoor store, firing the same type of handheld weapons, but using different ordinance. Some shot slugs, others plasma blasts and laser beams, while only one released heavy, sub-machine gun rounds, which did little to stop one of the Magnums from exiting the building. As always, it left a sonic boom of destruction in its wake.

Back inside the large store, Shane looked over the counter and saw some of the 82nd troops still engaged in close combat with the thugs. "John, go left and take out that last guy on the balcony. Angel, go right and finish off the guy coming down the mountain. I'll cover both of you," he urged. They nodded and carried out his orders. John ran towards the main entrance and fired a long burst of rounds at the individual on the balcony. He hit his target and the man keeled over and died.

Angel was just as lucky. She had jumped over the customer service desk, taken to her knee, and aimed carefully at the criminal coming down the "mountain." Calmly, she placed the red dot in her scope on the man's forehead and squeezed the trigger. Filled with grim satisfaction, Angel watched his head disintegrate into pink mist.

Ever alert, Shane jumped up from behind the counter and rolled onto the floor as an axe came slamming down on the countertop. He got on his feet and dodged his attacker again as the crazed man with the Mohawk tried to swing his axe across Shane's belly but missed. Infuriated, "Mohawk" raised the heavy blade over Shane's head, gripping it with two hands. But his intended victim jumped to the left and one-handedly fired a round at point-blank range. He missed, prompting "Mohawk" to smash the axe against Hawk's rifle, knocking it out of his hands and onto the floor.

With his primary weapon out of reach, Shane pulled a long knife from the sheath on his shoulder. The large, curved K-Bar blade was almost a foot long from hilt to tip. In fact, even "Mohawk" seemed momentarily impressed by it. Seconds later, however, he brandished his axe in another botched attempt.

Eager to neutralize his stubborn opponent, Shane punched the thug across the face. The latter then spit out blood and a tooth. As red fluid was dripping from the criminal's mouth, Shane caught him with a high knee to the sternum. The man lost his breath and Shane leapt behind him, grabbing a fist full of shirt while pulling him backwards. As the thug gasped for air with his back arched, Shane swung his knife hand and jammed the blade through the man's neck, severing the vertebrae between the spine and head. His attacker's body went limp as Shane removed the knife and let the carcass fall to the floor.

Panting, Shane stood over the body as Angel and John approached him. The only sound of gunfire was now coming from outside as the rest of the NARC and 82nd troops had rushed there to assist in the still ongoing clashes. The Magnums were also joining them. A few minutes later the building shook as an explosion rocked the battlefield.

Shane darted out the front doors with Angel and John in tow. He ran over to the twenty-foot-tall statue of the bear to take cover behind the concrete foundation. Angel and John followed suit as bullets and lasers zipped past them. One after the other, they popped up from their positions and fired rounds across the field at anything coming towards them from the north. After every expended round, John made corrections to his sight. After the fifth try, he had the rifle properly calibrated as he killed a criminal running across the wide open parking lot with a perfect head shot.

Almost simultaneously, Angel released a round that finished off a man next to the one John had neutralized. Meanwhile, Shane shot five rounds of single fire, slowly moving from right to left. Each struck different targets as he aimed his sight on the center mass of each of individual running towards them. All five men dropped in their tracks. Shane hid behind the statue again as heavy machine gun fire from the back of a pickup truck sprayed the bear sculpture with bullets.

Angel and John looked at Shane in awe. His aim was perfect and the quickness of each accurate shot amazing. "Remind me not to piss you off!" John shouted over the gunfire and grenade explosions.

But Shane just smiled, "You should see me suited up!"

Nearby, Almazan opened up the .50 caliber rail gun on the gun truck and ripped apart one of the three remaining vehicles rushing towards them. It exploded and all of the occupants inside were either killed or ejected from the back of the truck.

The enemy Armadillo robot also took a beating from the guns of the Valkyries who were swooping down on the battlefield and assisted the Magnums' MARG-3 cannons. Another blast from the HPRC on May's Command APC and a volley of four missiles eventually destroyed the right arm of the renegade robot. In response, the rebel Armadillo launched a volley of rockets into the dug-in positions of a dozen NARC troops. The ensuing explosions resulted in a smoke and snow cloud that concealed any signs of survivors.

Determined to liquidate the murdering robot, Shane aimed his rifle at the Armadillo's sensor eye, targeting it with a long burst. Meanwhile, John and Angel fired their weapons at more crazies running across the field. Four of the men fell down; six more made it to a trench position and engaged in hand-to-hand combat with some of the NARC troops there. The two Valkyries swooped out of the sky again and strafed the Reaper Battle Suits with hundreds of rounds from their rail guns.

Plasma blasts from heavily armed troops picked the enemy Reapers apart; a sonic discharge from the Magnums' tremendous five pound slugs destroyed what was left of them.

By now, the black and red robot was not only blind, but a smoldering mess. It staggered forward and Hawk could see the pilot jumping out of its metal frame. He hastened towards one of the remaining, machine gun-equipped trucks. A pair of laser blasts from May's APC then struck the disabled Armadillo, and after a slight twitch it exploded, scattering armor plating and robot parts all over the farm field.

Without pausing, Shane put the fat pilot in his crosshairs. A round struck the man and knocked him to the ground. From the distance, Shane wasn't quite sure where he had hit him, and he fired another round into the body just to make sure he was dead. Demoralized, the few remaining criminals finally turned tail and ran. The six that had assaulted the NARC troops surrendered when they heard and felt their Armadillo robot explode as a concussive shock wave swept over the pasture. Angry, the NARC soldiers grabbed their weapons and lined up the criminal group in the snow. Binding their hands behind their backs, they made them kneel.

One NARC sergeant approached Captain Dyson, "What do we do with the prisoners sir?"

"We don't have any room for jailbirds, just kill them," he bellowed. Moments later, the NARC sergeant and four subordinates did just as the captain had ordered.

Eager to annihilate all thugs, the Valkyries gave chase to the remaining trucks and the sound of rail guns soon reverberated in the distance. Angel and Shane witnessed two explosions during their pursuit, and from behind a hill three plumes of smoke soon rose into the ash-laden sky.

Afterwards, NARC and 82nd forces began searching the outdoor store for lone thugs, while others checked the bodies outside. They executed all enemy survivors.

Shane strolled into the middle of the field and checked on the Armadillo pilot he had neutralized. He noticed the damage inflicted by the first round, which had struck the criminal in the leg. He knew that it hadn't been a fatal shot.

Shane kicked him over and stared at Bear who was holding a laser pistol in his right hand. Catching Hawk off guard, he fired.

With the air being knocked out of him, Hawk twisted his torso to the left as a laser dart burned a hole into the armored vest. It wasn't a direct or threatening hit, but it did startle him and he dropped his rifle. Hawk used his momentum to spin around and found that Bear was on his feet now. The latter had dropped his pistol and charged at him. Shane avoided the first punch by ducking and counter-attacked with an uppercut that caught Bear by surprise and right in the mouth. Stumbling back from the blow, he wiped the blood away with a curse and spit a broken tooth onto the ground.

Suddenly, Bear paused after noticing the name tag on Hawk's vest, "So, you joined the military, good for you." With his helmet on, Hawk knew his adversary couldn't have seen his face, but had read his name tag.

"Been a long time, Bear."

"Do you have any idea what fourteen years of prison will do to a man?" Bear glared at him.

"Gonorrhea?"

The burly man's face became even more twisted in anger, and he immediately swung at Hawk again. Hawk dodged the blow, jamming his fist into Bear's abdomen. He lost his breath as Hawk came back up and across with his left fist, catching his enemy with a left hook that knocked him to the ground.

With a little bit of air left in his lungs, Bear searched the ground in front of him and recovered the pistol he had dropped. He picked it up and brought the business end to bear on his target. Hawk had already placed one hand on his .45 Caliber, but not before Bear fired a laser dart into his lower left gut. The ceramic padding absorbed most of the blast's energy, but some rays penetrated his abdomen and Hawk gritted his teeth in pain.

Emboldened, Bear sat up and fired twice more. The first shot caught Hawk's armored vest below his left collar, while the second impacted him high on the right shoulder. The consecutive blasts also knocked Shane backwards to the ground.

Grinning triumphantly, Bear drew himself up to his full height. "Now you die," he smirked, blood dripping from the corner of his mouth and eyes pressed together to focus on his aim.

Hawk gazed up at Bear, while desperately trying to get on his knees. He cupped his hands together and with all of his might he swung. His fists plowed into Bear's chest and he screamed, "Not by you!" Bear's rib cage cracked and sent him flying off his feet. He landed on his back, dropping the pistol. Again, Hawk struggled to stand upright, but his wounded side surged with such pain that he collapsed onto a knee.

Clutching his injury, Shane was nevertheless able to pick up the laser pistol, and he eventually stumbled over to him lying on the ground. Bear's breathing had quickened because of a punctured lung—no doubt the result of a cracked rib.

"Do it," Bear told Hawk as the lieutenant pointed the laser pistol at his head.

"You're such a piece of dung, what was so wrong with life that you had to turn against the rest of the world?" Hawk asked him.

Bear chuckled. Blood covered his teeth and still dripped out of the corner of his mouth into his beard as he recounted, "I got tired of people. I got tired of not getting what I wanted."

"And this is what you wanted?"

"No! I wanted redemption for all my misery!" Bear shouted.

"So you thought ruining the lives of all those people you murdered would somehow fix your miserable existence? You're pathetic!"

"Do it little brother, kill me."

"I'm not your brother."

"DO IT!!!" Bear pleaded in anger and desperation.

Hawk, feeling nothing but scorn for his old friend, pulled the trigger and then fell on his knees, still holding his side.

Moments later, Angel and John caught up with him. John put his head underneath Hawk's left arm and helped him get on his feet. "You're gonna be ok buddy." Tears welled up in Angel' eyes.

"Shane...," she cried.

Shane turned around shaking his head. He was disappointed that this family friend of so many years had turned into such an evil monster. He never thought for a second that he would ultimately be the one to put him out of his misery.

As John helped Hawk across the field, Angel leaned over to look at Bear. He was still breathing, even with a laser burn singeing the center of his forehead. Determined to finish off the person who had hurt her husband, she took aim with her rifle and fired a single shot into his temple. The powerful round exploded while exiting out the back of Bear's skull, causing his brain to fall out in chunks.

After an hour of taking care of the wounded and dead, Lieutenant General May received a so-called After Action Report (AAR). Along with a listing of the names and ranks of the deceased and injured, the AAR read as follows: "Thirteen men dead and ten wounded. One individual killed in action was a civilian who had joined the battle in Dundee, but lost his life inside the blast radius of one of the Armadillo missiles that had struck the Command APC." The report also noted Lieutenant Hawk's stellar performance as well as the contributions of his wife and friend. It annotated their number of kills and involvement in battle, both inside the building and outside.

Mention was also made of another civilian, John Breier – Lieutenant Shane Hawk's family friend - who sworn an oath to NARC and had been given the rank of private by a lieutenant in General May's command right after the battle concluded. He had received a SR-25 Sniper rifle, NARC body armor, and standard equipment from some of the fallen troops. He had also signed a contract that promised $250 dollars in monthly wages, although there was no need for money anymore. Payment before the cataclysm for a private had been $2,400, but since then NARC could only afford to pay new soldiers about a tenth of that. After all, the economy was non-existent now and money almost worthless. Still, it amazed General May that his men were able to enlist anyone after such a vicious encounter and during such hard times. And yet the man's selflessness put a smile on his face.

In the meantime, Shane received much-needed medical attention. The nanobots worked quickly to repair the damage caused by the laser pistol. He needed a new, armored vest, but unfortunately there were none.

After reloading ammunition and supplies, Shane and Angel returned to their Combat Gun Truck and waited for the order to resume their expedition to Detroit. Almazan took the driver's seat again, while Angel sat in the back with the kids. Shane opened one of the side compartments of the CGT and retrieved a series of black bags. They seemed heavy to him in his weakened state, but he managed.

He unzipped each sack—eight altogether—and pulled out pieces of equipment one could only guess how to assemble. John and Harris watched him as he sat back against the rear fender. "What is all that?" Harris inquired about the jigsaw puzzle of equipment at his brother's feet.

Shane unzipped the largest bag and pulled out a heavy, armored chest plate. "You guys mind helping me with this?" he asked them.

"Sure, what is it?"

Shane took off his boots and slid his feet inside another pair of heavy boots that came up to his knees. Each featured two long cylinders on the sides with thruster nozzles at the ankles.

As he began tightening down the straps and tucked them away, Shane pointed out to John which pieces to connect. After fastening the armored thigh plates, he explained, "This is the Firehawk Battle Suit. It's a suit of armor for all environments that adds robotic strength and endurance to the wearer's natural abilities. It allows me to run faster, jump higher, and lift heavier objects than I normally could. It is also equipped with an Artificial Intelligence Combat Computer, or AICC, which assists me during battle and other operations. It's highly advanced as far as Battle Suits go, but not quite the work horse that the Valkyries and Magnums are. This Power Armor is more like a scout's wet dream. It's the fastest PA ever made, and was specifically designed for Special Forces Operations."

"Wow, does NARC have any of these?" John asked.

"Nope, these were made for the Special Forces of the United States Army only," Shane told him. "We use these when there isn't enough firepower to handle overwhelming odds."

"Seeing what we just went through, how come you haven't used one before?" Harris wondered.

"Because it's technically classified," Shane paused to attach the chest and back plates. In the meantime, John put the shoulder and upper arm plates together. "But right now, I don't give a damn about classified anymore."

Shane slid his hands into the forearm pieces as well as the attached gloves with carbon fiber knuckles. He then proceeded to connect the parts beneath the armor plating. Opening the last bag, he pulled out a brand-new helmet still wrapped in plastic. After removing the plastic and visor film, Shane donned the helmet and instructed John where to hook up the adaptors. Afterwards, Shane reached behind his helmet, underneath the base of his neck, and flipped a switch.

In an instant, the visor buzzed to life as did the rest of the armor. Then the ceramic, black matting beneath the reinforced layers conformed to his body, securing his limbs and chest. Joined with the helmet, the matting automatically sent signals from the wearer's head through his entire body, transmitting messages about the person's intentions. Sensors detected how the wearer wanted to move, prompting the armor to react with a lightning fast response. In fact, the helmet's "feelers" could recognize thought patterns to activate certain functions, like the leg thrusters or the weapon systems.

The Battle Suit was truly a marvel of the new technological Golden Age. Other Battle Suits worked in much the same way, but the Firehawk was without a doubt the pinnacle of human genius.

The helmet's HUD now displayed the boot up process for the Artificial Intelligence. Hawk waited patiently for the system to load, and once it did all special features activated. The standard suit came with a motion tracker, short-range radio, radar, voice recognition system, loudspeaker, targeting, and acquisition capability as well as, of course, the Combat AICC.

"Good Afternoon Lieutenant Hawk," Shane heard a voice inside his helmet. Shane replied, but neither John nor Harris could hear him talking. "Firehawk exoskeleton is online and operational," the A.I. chimed up again. Shane waited another second.

"Would you like to name me, Lieutenant Hawk?" the A.I. asked politely.

"Your new name is "Angel"," he instructed. "Confirm."

"Name change complete, now designated "Angel"," it replied. "Would you like to set a voice pattern sir?"

"Yes," Shane motioned his wife to assist him and she spoke into the A.I. computer which digitally recorded the pitch and sound of her voice. "Voice pattern recorded, processing...," it affirmed. Shane waited another moment and then heard the A.I. announce, "Voice pattern completed, would you like to save?"

Shane loved how the voice had been transformed by the computer to sound like his wife. In addition to being enamored with Angel's sound of speech, he felt more comfortable with a familiar voice than the standard, computerized version. "Yes, save," he answered happily. The A.I. computed and completed the modification.

During this process, Harris and John had just looked at Shane's futuristic armor in wonder. They couldn't see through the one-way, mirrored visor, but they could tell Hawk was talking. When Shane eventually got up, he appeared eight feet taller than his original, five foot eleven frame. Harris and John now had to look up to talk to him.

"So what kind of weapon systems does that thing have?" John wondered in awe.

"Vibroblades," Shane responded as two, forty-inch-long blades sprang out of the forearms above his wrists. He retracted them just as quickly. "Triple, high-powered blaster cannons," Hawk explained further as he showed off the three side by side barrels on each forearm.

"You can only fire those one at a time, right?" Harris asked about the cannons.

"No, I can fire one at a time, three at a time, or all six together," Shane clarified, "but they'll do a fair amount of damage to any target."

"…," John liked it. "How do I get one?"

Shane laughed, "Unfortunately you can't. These suits were issued to Special Forces only, and I doubt there are any left." Shane lied, he knew of exactly three more he had snuck away in the MHMMV full of ammo the night before they left Fort Bragg.

"That sucks, I really want one," John smiled.

"Yeah, me too," Harris said to his best friend.

"There's one more piece to it underneath the cargo floor, but it makes it impossible to sit in a vehicle, and I don't need it right now," Shane told them.

"What is it?" Harris looked at the seams concealing the compartment. "It's the jet pack. Two small jet engines and folded wings capable of speeds up to four hundred miles per hour."

"Dude, that is so awesome," John drooled.

Harris thought for a moment, "Yeah, well, if you die, can I have it?" he chuckled.

Suddenly, the call to depart came over the radio. "All elements, mount up, we're rolling out."

Shane looked at his brother and his best friend, "Time to go guys, just stay behind my truck."

"No problem," Harris promised as John and he returned to the white pickup together, discussing what they would do with such an incredible contraption.

Shane took his helmet off and climbed into the Combat Gun Truck. By now Almazan had noticed his shiny new armor. "Whoa, where'd you get that?"

But Shane didn't want to explain again and joked, "I got it at Wal-Mart, it was on sale." The sergeant just shook his head as Shane fastened the long K-Bar knife he used to kill the "Mohawk" man with to his upper left shoulder plate.

The radio crackled again, "All right, let's get moving people." Almazan shifted the vehicle into drive and immediately pulled onto the main road which led them to the northbound interstate. Other vehicles and robots followed, while Harris's white pickup trailed closely behind Shane's Combat Gun Truck.

Chapter Ten: Karna's Ambush

The convoy rolled north onto the I-23, completely unaware of the Asterym flying above it in the shadows of the clouds. Twenty minutes outside of Dundee, Hawk and his family found themselves traveling eastward towards the Detroit Metro Airport. And after another uneventful half hour, they crossed the airport's perimeter.

"Finally, we're almost here," Shane announced to everyone in the truck, although most were already asleep.

"Thank God," Almazan relaxed a bit.

"Yeah no kidding," Amanda chimed in. "We've been stuck in this truck forever!" she stretched her arms out with a yawn. Angel looked at her in approval and then out the window. "I'm really hoping we don't run into anything else for the rest of the trip," Amanda continued and leaned back in her seat, closing her eyes.

"Shoot!" Emily broke the moment of silence.

Concerned, her mother wondered, "What's wrong?"

"My music player has run out of batteries," Emily sighed and pouted, removing the earphones from her ears. She wrapped the wires around the small digital music player and then stuffed it into her pocket—a birthday gift from Shane earlier in the year.

Unfazed by the teenage battery dilemma, Angel stared out the front windshield and noted that the snow and ash were falling even heavier now. The strange lightning coursing through the clouds had become less rampant after the storm had passed, but it had left a thick blanket of white and grey matter that covered everything in its wake. Whisks of wind blew flurries and flakes across the road, making it very difficult to see. Almazan was forced to slow the vehicle down to a mere twenty miles per hour, and Angel knew that it would take them much longer than expected to arrive at the airport terminal.

"What time is it?" she asked.

Shane touched the display map on his console, "Almost midnight."

"Thanks," she whispered, leaned against the headrest, and closed her eyes. But Angel couldn't sleep. Looking at each of her children, she watched Madison in dreamland, a spot of drool dripping from the corner of her mouth. Jon was snoring away, his head resting against Emily's shoulder. Only Jacob was fighting to stay awake. He was intent on seeing the city lights of Detroit and wanted to be up when they appeared on the horizon. And yet he was so tired that he could barely focus and had already nodded off several times. Minutes later, after reclining in his seat, he was out like a light.

Jacob didn't much care for his mom's new husband Shane, especially since he had often heard his real father curse the lieutenant for the failure of his marriage to Angel. Jake didn't know that Bubba Earl was solely to blame for his parents' divorce, but the made-up lies his father had been spitting out only strengthened Jake's distrust of Hawk. He was also miffed at Shane for marrying his mother. Of course, he had never brought up the subject, because he respected and loved Angel. But, Jacob always saved that little nugget of resentment in the back of his head—just in case he got into an argument with his step-father.

Behind them was the big, white pickup truck. Harris was driving, John sat in the middle, with Marshal in the right passenger seat. Meanwhile, June, Safyre, Paulee, and Ambyr were crammed in the back. Ambyr felt uncomfortably squeezed as she tried to play her handheld video game. After hitting a high score, she became really excited, "Daddy, guess what?"

"What's that Ambyr?" Harris looked into the rear-view mirror at his daughter.

"I just scored fifty-thousand points on level five!" she gushed happily.

"Sshhh!" Harris shushed her. "Keep your voice down Ambyr, your sister is sleeping."

"Oh," Ambyr looked at something stirring in the other car seat. "Sorry," she whispered directly into Safyre's ear. It was too little too late though, since the little girl had already woken up.

"You need to be quiet," her father scolded her.

Ambyr felt sorry for being so excited, but quickly went back to playing her game. Somewhat bored, John looked down at the floor and kept his opinion on how to reprimand children to himself. With one hand on the SR-25 Sniper rifle which the NARC soldiers had issued him, he thought that he would have handled the situation with Ambyr differently. But he wasn't about to steal Harris's thunder. He turned around in his seat and tapped his friend's daughter on the knee, "Ambyr, your sister is trying to sleep. You just can't be yelling, especially when your Dad is driving and everyone else is trying to get some rest too. Ok?" John tried to soothe her in an understanding tone of voice.

Despite feigning disinterest, Ambyr had tears in her eyes. "I'm sorry," she mumbled sheepishly.

"It's ok hun," John assured her and turned back around. Meanwhile, Marshal stirred, propping himself further up against his seat and grunting, "God, shut up."

The friends sighed and looked at the tall man who had his eyes closed, a look of frustration on his face. Similarly irritated, John whispered, "Harris, do they make pacifiers big enough for adults?" The two chuckled and stifled a laugh. Marshal cursed them under his breath, leaving the friends in no doubt that he was in a hostile mood. Too exhausted to start an argument, however, they left him alone.

Gazing out into the dark, Harris noticed that Shane's truck had started to slow down as snow and ash began to bury the road. Gusty winds were whipping at the vehicle which made Harris grip the steering wheel even tighter.

Staring blankly at the taillights of the military truck in front of him, Harris kept a distance of about fifty meters between them. He was glad that John was wide awake, taking register of the flashes of lightning streaking across the sky. The latter's eyes were fixed on the dark rear of the Combat Gun Truck. His expression grew concerned when another lightning flash pierced the clouds above them. Suddenly, John sat up startled. He couldn't quite make out what was happening, but he had seen something ominous in the reflection of the Gun Truck's back windshield. For a few seconds he waited with bated breath, and then, as another bolt of lightning arched across the dark horizon, his eyes confirmed what his instincts had already feared.

Without hesitation, John hit the button on the sunroof and the panel opened. A rush of cold air instantly stung everyone inside the cab.

"John!!!" June scolded as he leaned outside, "What the hell are you doing?!"

Harris also looked at him confused, while trying to remain on the road. Marshal briefly opened his eyes and snorted; he didn't care and tried to fall asleep again.

Ambyr watched her father's friend with interest, but shivered as the icy blast nipped at her flush, rosy cheeks. By now, her sister Safyre had also woken up. She was crying again and June quickly placed a flannel winter coat over her small, trembling frame. "John, get back in here!" June yelled in exasperation.

But John continued to stand on the bench seat and only reached down for a moment to pull up his rifle. The biting winter wind whipped his body and snared his heavy coat. His long hair blew wildly about as he faced the rear of Shane's truck. Others in the five-mile-long convoy stared at John in disbelief, and he could see the wonderment written in the face of the big Scottish staff sergeant. Sitting in the passenger seat of the Combat Gun Truck behind them, John could almost read the big sergeant's lips cursing him in confusion. "What the hell is that fool doing?" McMeen seemed to ask aloud.

"John! John!!" June continued to shout his name, urging him to close the sunroof. But he ignored her and raised the sniper rifle to his shoulder. Peering through the scope, he aimed it skyward. The scope's digital display was pitch-black with the exception of the illuminated crosshairs in the center and triple dashes at the top indicating an undetermined distance to the target. Two small LED lights were also visible; one was blue and glowed brighter than the green one below it. Steadying his aim, John pressed the button next to the two LEDs, prompting the blue display to dim while brightening the green one. Seconds later, the black screen switched to night vision mode and different shades of green. Unfortunately, John couldn't make out any details of what was going on in the clouds above.

A few freezing minutes later, he still hadn't discovered anything when a sudden flash of lightning flared the scope's lens, blinding John for a second. After regaining his sight, he peered through the scope once more and watched a flight of armored aliens breaking through the haze high above the convoy.

Filled with horror, John now took serious aim and placed the crosshairs directly on the extraterrestrial leader's head, beneath the jaw and behind his chin. Pressing the trigger, a laser beam instantly cut through the sky.

In midflight, Thyrion suddenly felt a sharp, heated sting sear his throat. He flinched in pain and glared searchingly at the convoy. Scanning each of the human vehicles, he noticed a lone man poking halfway out of the second vehicle's cab, aiming a weapon at him. Only seconds later, another beam of light cut through the sky, released from the human's tiny rifle. Thyrion cringed when the charge impacted his forehead and honed in further on the puny earthling.

Deciding not to draw the attention of the humans' combined firepower by attacking, Thyrion opted to seek his revenge another time. With a mighty boost from his engines he climbed back up into the clouds and disappeared from John's sight. Nevertheless, he was almost literally boiling over with anger. With his gel-like layers throbbing furiously, he barked at his most powerful Asterym, "**Karna! Attack! Destroy all the humans!**"

This subordinate nodded obediently, "As you wish, my Lord…" Moments later, Thyrion and his entourage turned north towards Detroit.

In the middle of the metropolis, on the opposite side of the river, loomed the most massive alien spire in the northern hemisphere. It was easily twenty miles wide at the base and reached 1,600 meters into the sky, but the low cloud cover concealed three quarters of the spire's top.

"**Come my Asterym, to our base! We have work to do,**" Thyrion growled. Ever at his master's beck and call, Karna broke formation and dove at the convoy approaching the Detroit Metro Airport which was surrounded by snow and ash-covered fields. Following the massive Asterym alien, hundreds, if not a thousand subservient aliens at his command dropped out of the clouds.

"John! What in the hell are you doing!?" June still screamed in frustration. Harris's friend finally lowered himself back into the truck, setting his rifle down next to Marshal. Exhausted, he slumped in his seat after shutting the sunroof. Almost immediately, the cab began to warm up again.

"Just what on earth were you doing up there?" Harris was angry, along with everyone else. But John needed to collect his thoughts for a moment, while his frozen cheeks and hands were thawing. Mute, despite the angry glares, he decided to wait before telling the others what he had seen.

As Safyre cried herself back to sleep, John was finally feeling warmer, "I saw Shane's alien following the convoy in the clouds," he muttered, teeth still chattering.

"What?" June exclaimed, deathly pale.

"You serious?" Harris nervously peeked into the pitch-black, midnight sky.

"I took a couple of shots at it and then it disappeared." Grateful to John and a little ashamed, nobody said anything in return, but continued to scan the sky for the great menace. They could now see the city lights several miles to the northeast as they rolled into the passenger pickup area of the airport terminal.

"Thank God we're here," Almazan finally broke the silence and parked the truck at the main entrance. Shane looked at his display monitor in front of him. The clock on the readout indicated that it was almost 12:30 in the morning. Then, just as they prepared to dismount, a giant steel ball with protruding blades attached to a long chain smashed down on the hood of their truck.

"Whoa! What the hell?" Almazan put his helmet on, grabbed his M450C Machine Gun from the floor, and opened the door.

Shane keyed the convoy radio, "Alpha One this Scout, we're under attack!"

"Scout, this is Alpha One, why have we stopped, over?" the general's voice replied impatiently.

Adrenalin pumping, Shane flung the microphone on the dash, ignoring any further conversation. He donned his helmet, and removed his weapon from the door brackets. Looking back at his family, he urged, "Stay inside! It's not safe out here." Shane opened the door and the cold air rushed in. As he positioned himself in front of the vehicle, he heard Almazan switch the transmission into neutral. A mechanical thud also told him that the parking brake was on.

Shane carefully scanned the rooftops, but failed to locate the attacker. His heart was beating even more rapidly, when he noticed the bladed wrecking ball being dragged over the top of the terminal by the giant chain, although he couldn't determine who or what pulled it.

Meanwhile, Angel had opened the truck door and waited for her husband to give her the thumbs up to usher everyone into the terminal. Hawk looked over the rooftops a second time, but detecting nothing he signaled his wife and waved her on.

Angel jumped out of the vehicle, spun on her heels, and unfastened Madison's safety restraints. She scooped the girl into her arms, leaving the weapon in the truck. In the meantime, Amanda leapt out on the other side, while Jacob and Emily hastily followed. Jon, on the other hand, took his time and slowly climbed off the rear. "Hurry up Jon," his mother beckoned him anxiously.

But Jon was still groggy. He didn't know why he was being told to rush and confused as to what was going on. "Where are we Mom?" he mumbled, rubbing his eyes.

Irritated, Angel carried Madison in one arm, grabbed Jon by the wrist, and made a mad dash for the terminal entrance. Amanda, Emily, and Jacob hurried behind her while Almazan exited the driver's door.

When Angel reached the building's front doors, she found them locked. Even after rattling them, they wouldn't budge. "They're locked!" she yelled in exasperation.

"Move aside!" Shane hollered and pointed his right arm at the glass doors. An energy blast fired from one of the cylinders on his forearm and melted a giant hole into the glass.

Relieved, Angel ran through the opening with the two smaller children as well as Amanda, Jake, and Emily. They had just made it to the inside when an explosion rocked the ground at Shane's feet. He was knocked down, and by the time he recovered his bearings, he could see the massive alien known as Karna standing atop the terminal roof.

"What the hell is that?!" Almazan shouted at his friend.

"No idea!" Shane jumped to his feet and darted behind the cover of the gun truck next to the sergeant.

"Dude, that thing's massive!" Almazan remarked, momentarily impressed.

"No kidding, I hadn't noticed that!" Just then, the top of the vehicle caved in, crushing the M3A9 .50 caliber rail gun turret beyond repair. At the same time, Shane and Almazan were thrown forward by the impact.

Almazan cursed.

Witnessing the monster's attack with horror, Harris and John rushed the other children and

June through the hole in the glass door. Seemingly unafraid, Marshal fired away with his shotgun, but the pellets had no effect on Karna's seemingly impenetrable armor.

Just then, aliens of a similar sort appeared on the roof of the terminal and on different levels of the adjacent parking garage. Some leapt off the parking garage down on to the pavement across from Shane and his crew.

Amused, the extraterrestrial threw the spiked wrecking ball high over the center of the road. Marshal watched intently, but ran as the gigantic morning star began to glow. Karna yanked the chain and the alien globe almost crashed down on Harris's brother. Fortunately, he escaped being squashed by jumping aside at the last second. Seconds later the explosive matter inside the ball erupted, vaporizing the entire concrete roadway around it. The ensuing detonation sent Marshal tumbling through the air.

Shane was kneeling behind the gun truck's front tire, positioned his weapon over what was left of the engine, and fired a burst of rounds from his M22A3 assault rifle at Karna. The rounds impacted, but only pockmarked his thick, heavy armor.

Almazan leaned over top of the vehicle's smashed roof, which had been flattened by the wrecking ball and was now the same height as the hood. He aimed at the alien, pulled and held the trigger, firing dozens of rounds at the fiend. The rounds hit, some ricocheting off his armor, others leaving craters that appeared to affect their attacker not in the least.

After seeing June and the kids to safety, Harris and John stepped outside the terminal as well. John aimed his SR-25 Sniper Rifle straight up and fired a laser beam into Karna's chest. The alien flinched as sparks flew off his torso, while Harris fired a round from his father's 30-06 hunting rifle. Again, the round impacted Karna's armor, but did no damage. "I need a bigger gun!" Harris shouted as he and John ducked underneath a balcony.

Suddenly, the energy stream that had engrossed Harris when he rescued Ambyr from Judy's farm house seemed to surge in his veins again. In fact, the strange force was growing stronger in the presence of the alien. He could feel its powers coursing through his body. John immediately noticed that there was something going on with his best friend, but thought he might be coming down with a cold, "Are you ok?"

Confused, Harris merely mumbled, "Yeah I'm fine...I just feel different with that big guy up there."

"What do you mean?" John was curious.

Meanwhile, Karna hoisted the wrecking ball and began spinning it over his head in slow circles, scanning the ground below for the earthlings that dared to take aim at him.

The alien legion began attacking the convoy spread out far behind Shane's lead vehicle. Gun fire, explosions and tracers lit up the night sky. The entire area was now a war zone, and NARC and Military forces struggled desperately to fight off the alien horde and get the civilians to safety.

"I don't know," Harris didn't want to mention his newfound powers. "It's just weird."

"All right, whatever, let's kill this thing!" John determined as he emerged from the protective cover of the balcony.

His last words were still hanging in the air, when he vaporized into a cloud of pink mist and concrete dust—the unfortunate victim of Karna's spiked ball. Harris froze in sheer horror, and Shane, who was about to fire, hesitated after watching his friend being bludgeoned to death by the alien's massive morning star. Equally horrified, Almazan's jaw dropped.

"Noooo!" Harris shouted as the wrecking ball was hoisted back up, and then fired another round from his weapon. The projectile struck Karna between the eyes, but only made him flinch. Seeing that he had distracted the fiend, Harris ran out into the open road, fired another round at a smaller alien on the road taking aim at him, and put the miniscule .30-06 round through the eye of the alien, which fell over dead.

He found Marshal unconscious, lying in the middle of the thoroughfare, not four meters from the cover of the vehicle. Dropping his useless rifle, Harris grabbed his brother by the wrists and dragged him to the relative safety of the gun truck. Lowering him gently, he yelled at Shane, "Shane! Kill that thing!"

Having recovered his composure, Almazan fired a burst from his rail gun. This time, the rain of bullets actually forced Karna to raise his arms in attempt to shield himself from the gunfire. While the demon was momentarily distracted, Shane made a run for the gun truck. He grabbed the damaged door and ripped off the top hinges with the aid of the Battle Suit. Raising the door above his head, he threw it at Karna with all his might. Since Almazan had stopped firing, the alien lowered his arms, but couldn't react fast enough when the door struck him squarely in the head. The monster tumbled over backwards, and a frightened Angel and her children could see and hear the terminal ceiling crack above them.

Determined to slaughter the murderous fiend, Shane now ripped the gun truck's flooring open. He wrenched the jet pack from its compartment, set it up, and eased his back onto it. With a click, the jetpack's latches automatically snapped into place on top of his armor.

Ready for battle, Shane then joined his brothers and Almazan who were hiding beside the smashed vehicle. He pushed Harris aside and ripped open another hidden compartment below the driver's door. Reaching inside, Hawk hastily grabbed a soft weapon's case. He unzipped it and pulled out a specially made M71A2 Assault Rail Rifle. It was of bullpup design, with the magazine loaded into the butt stock. The barrel measured half an arm's length, while its diameter was .45 caliber.

Shane cocked the rifle, pressing a round into the chamber, and then set the rate of fire to single shot with the flick of his thumb. Surrounded by his friends, he got up.

"What are you going to do with that?" Almazan asked. Shane grimly pointed to the top of the building, although he could not see the alien, "I'm going to rip him a new one."

Moments later, the fold-up wings on the back of the jetpack flipped open and locked into place. The twin engines mounted on both of Shane's shoulders fired to life. Two flame columns spewed forth from the engines, propelling him into the black winter void. "Go get him little brother…," Harris mumbled to himself as Shane took to the skies.

Soaring high above the terminal, he almost immediately detected Karna, who was slowly getting back on his feet. However, his heavy armor and enormous size made it difficult for the monster to roll to one side. As Shane gained a little more altitude, he hovered, aiming the M71A2 at Karna's head. He fired the weapon and the round blasted out of the barrel with blazing mach two speed. The projectile instantaneously struck the alien between the eyes and exploded.

It blew most of Karna's face plate apart, exposing mechanical components beneath and splattering red, oily alien liquid all over his body as shrapnel cut open the gel like sack that contained the aliens natural liquid form. Shane took a moment to observe the exposed extraterrestrial's face and was shocked to merely see a pool of red beneath the mask. There were no muscles or organs to speak of. In fact, Karna's non-existent features reminded him of strawberry jam.

"What the hell?" he wondered as Karna covered his exposed visage and finally rolled over. Shane aimed again. Shortly afterwards, the alien jumped to his feet as his adversary fired another round. The charge exploded on the roof behind Karna as he made a run for the other side of the building, dragging the wrecking ball behind him.

Hell-bent not to let John's murderer get away alive, Shane flew after him, pointing his rifle carefully and taking his time as he hated to waste a shot. When he was close enough, Shane fired and the high-explosive round burst against Karna's back. The blast sent him reeling off the edge of the airport, crashing through a terminal gate, and ninety feet down to the tarmac below.

With grim satisfaction, Shane flew over the rim of the rooftop and landed ten meters away from Karna's crash site. While the extraterrestrial slowly recovered from the shock of the blast and fall, Shane fired four consecutive rounds at the humongous, walking artillery battery. Each charge ripped pieces out of Karna's chest plate, sending shards of armor and alien goo flying through the air. The monster roared in agony, but Shane barely got a glimpse of more reddish matter moving beneath the exposed exoskeleton frame.

Severely weakened, Karna lowered the large artillery cannons on his shoulders and fired a few half-charged energy plasma balls at his human attacker. But in his Battle Suit Shane was too quick for the fiend and leapt past the artillery rounds as they sailed three hundred meters away into a nearby field. They exploded without doing any harm.

Sensing victory, Shane took careful aim, releasing a single round that struck Karna in his exposed exoskeleton. The projectile punctured the membrane enclosing the pool of red fluid, got caught in the armored rear plate behind it, and burst.

A shower of red goop, sparks, smoke, and mechanical parts detonated in Karna's chest wound. He fell to his knees first, then his face, but before Shane could relish the triumph of fatally wounding the alien, Karna was already dead.

Or so Shane thought. The red alien strawberry jam poured out of the gel sack, and the small blotches scattered about in the snow and ash moved towards the main glop. Shane was both terrified and curious at the same time, "What the hell are these things?"

The mass of alien fluid gathered back up into a single pool, and then rippled from the center. From the rippling effect came a monstrous shout of anger. Shane fired another round from his rifle, which exploded and splattered the alien fluid in every direction. But after a brief recollection, the alien gathered itself into another pool of itself. Shane watched in horror as the red slim did so. What Shane didn't notice though, was that on the far end of the alien fluid was a sewage drain. Karna's fluidic body escaped Shane's wrath through the sewer. Shane was stunned, he couldn't believe his eyes. "Is it still alive?" Shane wondered.

On the other side of the large terminal, Harris and Almazan fought desperately against the smaller alien army that attacked the convoy.

They too, noticed that every dead alien leaked out a red strawberry soup that recollected themselves and escaped through every nook and cranny and sewer. The smaller aliens weren't tough to defeat, but NARC and military forces took their licks and their losses. One thing was for certain on everyone's mind, "Did they kill them?"

Chapter Eleven: New Frontier

It's A New Day,

Most of Detroit's skyscrapers and skyways that they could have seen from the terminal only ten days ago had collapsed. Hundreds of feet below, rubble and debris were now clogging the streets between the ruins. There wasn't a single high-rise that had not taken damage from either a firefight or the natural disasters of the previous week.

Feeling somber, the remaining troops and their vehicles passed by numerous NARC-controlled checkpoints as they made their way into the Detroit Metro Airport's multi-tiered parking structure. Detroit Metro had become the staging ground for all NARC forces and remnant US military units.

First Lieutenant Hawk even noticed two very large C-33 Cargo/Troop transport aircraft parked in a large hangar on the south end of the airfield's perimeter. One aircraft's tail wings had been inscribed with the insignia of Pope Air Force Base, right outside Fayetteville, North Carolina. The other hailed from McCord Air Force Base south of Seattle, Washington. Thinking of happier and less complicated times, Hawk thought it possible that both Almazan and he had once jumped out of the Pope aircraft during training missions. Both smiled at the familiar sight.

Inside the terminal the lights were on as the building was packed with soldiers, their families, and civilian refugees. Ash was still falling from sickeningly grey skies, along with snow flurries. In fact, it was getting hard to distinguish between snow and ash. It was also cold and ice blanketed the city like a thick winter coat. The low cloud cover enveloped the skies above, practically turning day into night. Most people found it disorienting and checked their watches time and again. It was earlier than everyone believed.

From his temporary headquarters, Lieutenant General May had ordered all convoy elements to form up in a makeshift motor pool on the lowest level of the parking garage. All 82nd MHMMV-44 Combat Gun Trucks and HMTVs gathered in one area while NARC units assembled in another section. Civilian cars and vans grouped together in a designated zone a level above the military vehicles.

The combat robots and Battle Suits had already departed the terminal, marching to the large hangar across two runways where the two C-33 Cargo/Troop aircraft stood parked. A pair of large bay doors slid open and closed behind them as the robots and Battle Suits went inside. A bus arrived a few minutes later; it had been designated to ferry the pilots from the hangar to the terminal.

Meanwhile, survivors and newly arrived military personnel made their way from the parking garage into departure and arrival lounges. Angel followed Shane and the children up a flight of stairs into a seated waiting area near now deserted gates. Temperatures were gradually rising in the building and the smell of freshly cooked food—even if it was greasy fast-food fare—pleasantly filled the hallways. The meals were prepared by civilian women who had nothing better to do. Many just wanted to honor their fellow refugees by serving them something hearty to eat.

Harris—with Ambyr in his arms—sat next to Safyre who was asleep. He watched as Marshal and June—her arms wrapped around Paulee— made their way through the throngs of soldiers and civilians. Marshal's arms, along with his forehead and right leg, were heavily bandaged.

He was carrying their bags of clothes and other items that they had thought necessary for survival. At this point, no one batted an eyelash about Marshal carrying a shotgun through the terminal as most civilians were also armed with some sort of weapon or another, not to mention the troops with their guns.

Feeling wretched, Harris could not stop thinking about John. He particularly couldn't shake the image of his best friend being pulverized by a half-ton, alien wrecking ball. He wanted revenge, but was too tired to act on his impulses, especially with his daughters in his care.

By now, Angel, June, Amanda, and the children had lined up to get some food while Shane, Marshal, and Almazan went outside to retrieve more gear from Harris's pickup truck. Within an hour and a half they were all sitting down enjoying their first hot meal in days. Afterwards, they set up their fast-tents near a deserted frequent flyer lounge and bedded down for the night.

Throughout the early morning hours and daybreak, more people trickled into the airport as convoy after convoy of military vehicles, robots, and Battle Suit engaged in disaster relief. Almost all the Valkyrie pilots had been tasked to scout and search the area for survivors. At any given hour, there were dozens of people up and about in the terminal, helping newly arriving refugees or assisting the weak and wounded.

General May had stayed up all night in his make-shift control center established by NARC. From there he evaluated the sparse reports that had filtered in from all over the country, telling of the massive devastation. Most of the dispatches were days old, but there was some current intelligence about a series of morning explosions in Gary, Indiana and a giant splash just offshore that impacted Lake Michigan. The general even learned that the President of the United States was alive and well at NORAD's base in the Cheyenne Mountain Complex. However, the vice-president, joint chiefs, senators, and congressmen hadn't been so fortunate. Rumors spread throughout the airport and Detroit that Michigan's largest city was the last one standing in North America.

And yet if Detroit truly were Earth's only surviving metropolis, Hawk thought, then it was on its knees. On its north side, fires were burning out of control in suburban neighborhoods. Only fifteen percent of downtown and outlying areas had any power, of which ten percent relied on generators. Shops, stores, banks, and markets had long been looted and robbed.

Detroit City Police hadn't been seen since day three of the Cataclysm, and one Lieutenant Colonel Jimmy Westlake of the NARC station outside of Selfridge Air National Guard Base (about forty minutes north) had been keeping the peace until yesterday. Unfortunately, he had been killed during an attempt to liberate the city of Windsor from an alien Asterym base. Its giant spire still loomed in the distance over the river like a towering monolith of evil. And no one felt safe or secure with the extraterrestrials so close to them.

A seasoned leader, Lieutenant General May immediately assumed command of all remaining NARC forces in the area. But when a few captains briefed him on the situation in the city, he was appalled to learn that originally most civilians had found shelter at the old Joe Louis sports arena. There, over fifty thousand had breathed their last when an attack—led by the alien known to everyone now as Thyrion—razed the stadium to its foundation and set the ruins ablaze. NARC troops at the scene had also been killed during the raid, and back up forces arrived too late.

One thing was clear to the general: if they were to survive, they would have one bloody fight ahead of them.

Shane rose from his seat after finishing his meal, although Angel grabbed his arm. "I gotta use the bathroom," he told her. She nodded, letting go as he walked away.

Seconds later there was a giant crash, like flesh breaking through metal grates. People screamed and shouted. A huge, cat-like monster had smashed through a large vent into the open terminal. Its skin was rugged and bleeding profusely. It sported a single eye in the center of its head and large, swept-back ears. Like other alien fiends, it had talons for paws and a razor-sharp, prehensile tail. Opening its mouth to a sea of frightened stares, the extraterrestrial revealed dozens of jagged, razor-sharp teeth and two twelve-inch-long fangs. Its hissing, four-foot-long tongue lashed out from its mouth, dangling along as it darted towards the center of the terminal.

Women and children screamed in terror as the large, tiger-sized demon cat bounded through the airport complex. It ran fast and then leapt—fangs protruding and talons extended—at a pair of humans in its path.

The two petrified earthlings jumped to the side and out of its way, but a meter behind them was First Lieutenant Shane Hawk, reaching back with his right forearm vibroblade extended. The demon cat flew at him and Shane Hawk executed his strike.

To be Continued…

Join The Firehawk Chronicles Facebook Page
for updates, discussions and more!

www.Facebook.com/TheFirehawkChronicles